Only AN AUTHOR LIKE TAY-
LOR CALDWELL COULD CAPTURE
THE TUMULTUOUS PASSIONS AND
DOOMED RULE OF THE MOST
GLAMOROUS QUEEN EVER TO
HAVE REIGNED. *THE ROMANCE
OF ATLANTIS* IS A UNIQUE WON-
DER, REMARKABLE IN CONCEP-
TION. IT BRINGS TO LIFE AN
ADVANCED AND DECADENT CIV-
ILIZATION ALL TOO SIMILAR TO
WHAT OUR OWN MAY BECOME. . . .

"QUITE REMARKABLE."
                    —*Publishers Weekly*

"A HIGHLY ENJOYABLE STORY
. . . FIRST-RATE . . . ANOTHER
BESTSELLER."
                    —*Library Journal*

The Romance of Atlantis

Taylor Caldwell

with Jess Stearn

A FAWCETT CREST BOOK

Fawcett Publications, Inc., Greenwich, Connecticut

THE ROMANCE OF ATLANTIS

THIS BOOK CONTAINS THE COMPLETE TEXT
OF THE ORIGINAL HARDCOVER EDITION.

A Fawcett Crest Book reprinted by arrangement with
William Morrow and Company, Inc.

Printed in the United States of America

First printing: March 1976

1 2 3 4 5 6 7 8 9 10

*For the feathered Caesar,
whose own forebears
were quite prominent
in Taylor Caldwell's Atlantis.*

"But now they desire a better country, that is, an heavenly: wherefore God is not ashamed to be called their God: for he hath prepared for them a city."

—HEBREWS 11:16

The Romance
of Atlantis

Foreword

AT THE age of twelve, Janet Taylor Caldwell wrote a romance of Atlantis, a presumably legendary land that she knew nothing about. Her father, a newspaper artist, was amazed by the perception in the manuscript, its detail and insight. He sent it to the child's grandfather, a book editor, in Philadelphia. The latter, promptly horrified, suggested the manuscript be destroyed immediately. He did not feel that any child could have produced so unusually mature a work, intellectually and philosophically. The only alternative that suggested itself was that she had borrowed freely elsewhere. In a way, he was right. She had borrowed from the past, not knowing herself how she was dredging up that past.

The manuscript lay fallow for sixty years. Then, on the strength of my collaboration with the novelist in *The Search for a Soul, The Psychic Lives of Taylor Caldwell,* I was given the task of readying the manuscript for publication. Provocative situations that Miss Caldwell had touched upon were amplified, some of the child's prose simplified; but the situations, descriptions, characters and story line remain prettty much as they inexplicably came from the pen of a twelve-year-old child. The insight, the wisdom, the biting wit, the disenchantment and yet the eternal optimism that intrigued and affected me are still there, together with an allegorical narrative that seems to fit our world with dramatic aptness. Indeed, it almost seems at times that the famous novelist as a child wrote this, her first novel, with prophetic insight. Judge for yourself.

J.S.

1

THE EMPEROR was two hundred years old, and even with the rejuvenation chamber few lived more than two hundred years in Atlantis. His fierce eyes were dimmed, lines of pain threaded the tired face. His forehead was beaded with sweat, which a dusky eunuch wiped at intervals with a silk cloth banded in gold. Around the Emperor's throat was a chain of gold, fastened in front with a crystalline seven-colored gem, which gave renewed energy to the weary. His hands, once powerful, were folded in resignation on his breast. A solemn-looking physician stood behind the Emperor's great bed, registering just the right note of concern. The Emperor had already sent for his two daughters. Salustra, the elder, was in the glorious dawn of ripening womanhood; Tyrhia was yet a child with a boy's figure. The father's fevered eyes turned to them with passionate intensity. Salustra! Was there anything more magnificent than this girl? She was not unlike her mother, thank the eternal gods! For her mother, the incomparable Maxima, had been an aristocrat to her impenetrable core. Salustra was tall for a woman, and her figure was such as to give the imagination pause. She had the Emperor's eyes, flashing with vitality. Her skin was pale and clear, with a birthmark high on the cheekbone which turned scarlet when she was aroused. Her mouth, though proud, was warm and inviting. Her tawny hair, reaching to her knees, glistened with a luster that seemed to catch the highlights of the sun. The white column of her throat, rising proudly from her marble shoulders, was strong and supple, giving her the carriage of a queen.

The dying Emperor sensed instinctively the feminine

glory Salustra would soon know. He noted the sinuous curve of her thigh and calf and, with satisfaction, the strength in the line of her jaw and the blue steel of her eyes. Perhaps she walked too confidently, too arrogantly for a woman, but the muscles under the shimmering skin were as sinewy as those of a man. Lazar smiled as he saw in Salustra his own indomitable will. As he looked at Tyrhia, the smile faded. Though actually but a few years younger than Salustra, she was still unformed, with a vapid, unclouded countenance. A circlet of gold dangling from her arm matched the yellow curls that framed her pretty face. Her hands were fluttering and white and somewhat helpless.

She was like her mother, the base-born Lahia. Seeing the child, the Emperor remembered the mother. She had been a slave of surpasssing beauty, a tribute from the petty kingdom of Mantius, to which he had granted independence, taking only the beautiful Lahia as a victor's spoils. Lahia had been weak, often vicious, constantly conniving. Nevertheless, Lazar, succumbing to the tyranny of the weak over the strong, loved her until his betrayal. Not until she carried his child did he discover that the Empress had plotted with an envoy from powerful Althrustri to poison his wine. Tyrhia was about due, and Lazar, who yearned for a son, had refrained from one word of rebuke. However, the Empress had guessed from his averted eyes that he knew, and she had literally died of fear after the child was born. Lazar had had her entombed with ceremony, and the world, aside from the Althrustri regime, was none the wiser. He had not thought about any of this for years. Now he held out a wavering hand to his children. Tyrhia, with the easy tears of the emotionally unstable, kneeled beside him, curling herself in the hollow of his wasted arm. Salustra stood looking at her father gravely, and waited. She was very white, and though her pale lips were set, they trembled slightly at the corners.

She bent closer to her father. At the touch of her fingers, it was as though under the smooth skin he had felt the sinew of steel. His eye notably brightened, and any misgivings he had vanished.

"My children," he said wistfully, "I am dying. But it is a natural and peaceful thing; where I go, you too will go one day. I am merely taking the path before you. I am accepting death as naturally as I have accepted life. It is but a phase of the human drama."

Tyrhia's sobs rent the air, causing the doctor to look at her reprovingly. Unheeding of her sister, Salustra gazed at her father, her dark eyes still and watchful.

"Salustra, my daughter." He motioned to her. She took the cloth from the eunuch and wiped the perspiration from the dying man's forehead. He drew a deep breath and closed his eyes as though willing his departing soul to halt its flight for a grudging moment.

"Salustra," he said, his voice hoarse with the effort of speaking, "in thy hands I leave my empire. Dost thou understand, girl?" He looked up into her face, and something he saw there gave him joy. "My time is near, Salustra," he said, "but what I have to say must be said. My empire is thine. Think of it! From east to west it extends three thousand miles sea to sea! From north to south, four thousand miles from icy glaciers to the tropic sands! A glorious heritage for him who merits it."

Salustra said nothing, but her eyes had begun to glitter. The sun, gleaming through the pillars, cast a golden glow over her features. A pulse leaped in the hollow of her throat. She fingered the chain on her father's neck and he nodded feebly for her to take it.

The Emperor groaned, and his head moved agonizingly on the silken pillows. Salustra laid a steady hand on his forehead. "Rest, my lord," she said quietly.

He turned his head slowly toward her and, his gaze again meeting that serene eye, his face brightened. His hand clutched hers "Thou art only a girl," he gasped. "But thou hast the wisdom of many wise men. Thou hast sat with me in the courts, and heard my judgments. Thou hast heard me attacked, and seen me fawned upon. As I hate a lie, so thou dost hate it. As I loathe injustice, so thou dost loathe it. Thou hast the vision which detects falsehood and dissimulation. Such vision normally is a curse; it bars one from even the semblance of friendship. But a ruler should have no friends. Friends lull one to false security. Hold thyself aloof, Salustra." He heaved a great sigh. "I need not speak to thee of the dull procedure of government which thou hast learnt at my knee, I speak to thee now of greater things, of the soul of government, of the heart of a people. Dost thou understand?"

Salustra inclined her head slightly.

"Once I yearned for a son! But no son could be more capable than thee. But thou art still a woman. Thy hands are soft and white, for all the steel underneath. Thou hast far more need of courage and wisdom than hath a male sovereign. But I feel the people will accept thee." His voice took on an almost prophetic note. "Approaching death is removing the veil from my vision. Listen well to these words, for they come as from beyond the grave. A ruler may make laws that are marvels of mechanical precision and justice, but he will still fail if he heeds not the hearts of those he rules. A fool, loved by his subjects, hath them always. A wise man, unloved, is met with stone ears."

His breath was labored, but he struggled on tenaciously. "How, thou wouldst ask, do I keep the love of my people? Not by loving them, my daughter. This incontinent people, decadent in their sophistry, can only be ruled by understanding their vices, insolences and ambitions. This is a nation in decay. We have reached the height of scientific achievement, but old morals, standards, codes and restraints have passed.

"The greater part of humanity is composed of greedy souls, disguising their lust in family love, hiding their lascivious lips under pious smiles, loving their neighbors outwardly but hating them in their hearts; shocked at vice but absorbed surreptitiously in lewdness.

"Take care, Salustra! Do not expect too much of these animals, who, though they no longer swing by their tails, feed their vanity even more than their mouths, and they will love and acclaim thee."

He looked at her intently to make sure she understood. The intelligent light in her eye reassured him. Tyrhia still sobbed against his breast. The physician bent down and touched the pulse of the dying man.

"Religion hath lost the power to hold them," went on the Emperor "They scoff at all things; they treasure the national religion, however, for it is a reassuring symbol of tradition. They deck the temples, and build great altars. They maintain a corrupt priesthood, seasoned in vice and licentiousness. They celebrate the birth of the goddess Sati, daughter of Chaos and Strife. But they perform their religious duties tongue in cheek. Not believing, yet they are intolerant of those honest enough to confess they do not believe. They laugh at the gods but would rend the first man to suggest abolishing them.

"I would advise thee, Salustra, to maintain the national religion. Young nations can survive the eruptive violence of new ideas; a fat and bloated nation, on the verge of disintegration, cannot withstand the constant jars of a virile assault on its crumbling institutions. This nation is much too old for new things.

"Pale thought doth ever numb the arm of ruddy action but the day of action has passed for this land. Do not use the atom-splitter in any way, lest it be used against you by a bolder enemy. Our people will capitulate rather than meet such a threat. We have grown too civilized with thought, too rich with conquest; too much success carries with it the very seed of destruction for that which nourished it. It is too late to turn back the clock. The damage is done; thou wilt be carried along with the tide." With a groan, he raised himself to an elbow. His eyes took on a prophetic gleam. "If the people should at any time demand thy abdication, if thou art of the opinion that thou hast been wise and courageous, hold fast to thy scepter and fight for it. The virus of democracy infects the very lifeblood of an imperial people. Whenever a nation is tired of self-restraint and discipline, it demands so-called liberation as a means of slipping the bonds of authority. Discourage democracy; it is thy foe, and the foe of thy people."

"And what of the external foe?" she asked intensely.

He sighed. "Look to the north, daughter. The Althrustri are a mighty nation, young and adventurous. Althrustri hath the spirit and enterprise we once owned. The Emperor Notar, I hated; he was crafty and cruel. He is dead, thank the gods! But beware the wolf's cub, the resourceful Signar. Watch him! I have sent him conciliatory messages, but he has not replied except to sow disloyalty in our ranks with his gold and promises."

He rested for a minute before going on. "At one time I thought to give him one of my daughters in marriage, but flinched from the thought of delivering any child of mine to such a savage.

"And now, thy dear self, my daughter, my beloved! Whatever thou dost, forswear the rejuvenation chamber. It is enough for man to live the natural span of seventy-five years. There are too many memories to live with when life is prolonged beyond what nature intended. We become jaded with the things that pleasured once, until we yearn for nothing but endless oblivion. Come not to that, dear daughter."

For a long time he lay in silence, his lidded eyes sunken in his gray face. Tyrhia sobbed afresh, but none heeded her. The physician shook his head, and moistened the dry lips with a wet cloth.

The Emperor was not through. He held up a finger. "But be jealous in how thou guardest the rejuvenation chamber. Hold it up as a constant reward for loyalty and achievement, but grant it only once in a lifetime, else in the experiencing it will lose its enchantment, and thou wilt no longer have this inducement to dangle before the ignorant."

Lazar stirred faintly. "My daughter," he went on, "thou mayest desire to marry. But think long before thou takest on so burdensome an anchor. Yet I would not advise a dull life of continence. Have thy lovers. Have thy lovers, indeed, but be judicious. Take only those thy equal in intelligence. To take less would be to court boredom and self-contempt. But marriage—ah, my daughter, I would not advise that for thee."

He fumbled for his younger daughter's hand. "Thy sister, my poor little Tyrhia, into thy hands I commend her, knowing thou wilt love her as I do.

"And now, Salustra, I have some hard-won philosophy to whisper to thee. Thou mayest scoff at it, but I have found it true after a double lifetime of power. Better to appreciate a sunset than to be lord of a thousand conquered cities. The man that can be moved by music is happier than he whose acclaim is shouted from the hilltops. The soul grows not by material things, but only by thought. If a man thinketh not, even though he sitteth upon a throne, his soul is still in embryo." He seemed to have come to the end of his valedictory. His breath rattled in his throat. She bent low to catch his last feeble word. "To thee, Salustra, I commend my people. If I know consciousness beyond that dark gulf yawning between us, I shall make every effort to see thee and to guide thy hand. For these are troubled times for our dear Atlantis."

With a sigh that was almost a groan, he fell back.

The doctor picked up the Emperor's limp wrist. He shook his head with an expression of grief. "The Emperor is no more," he said. "Long live the Empress."

It was not until the Emperor had died that Salustra wept. And then she threw her body over her father's and sobbed until it was time to carry him away. It was well that she did this, for it was the last time for years she was to know the luxury of tears. As she stood there, she knew not whether she mourned more her father's passing or the terrible responsibility that was now hers.

She had pleaded with her father to visit the rejuvenating Temple Beautiful once again, but he had explained it would be to no purpose. "The gods allow no man to live more than two centures. And it is well, for the gods know more than man." He had smiled thinly, as she recalled, saying, "When your time comes, daughter, you will better know what I mean." He had gestured to the heavens. "Who knows but what there is something better on the dark side of the sky, something that gives meaning to our empty pursuit of happiness?"

She had been too young to grasp the full portent of his words, and saw no reason why life's benefits should not be expanded indefinitely. As it was, only a favored few among the elite were even considered for Temple Beautiful and the special rays which reactivated the cells and restored the endocrine balance of the glands. Wrinkles disappeared, hair was restored, muscles and circulation renewed, and the years miraculously shorn away, except for what remained in the heart and mind. Lazar had received the rejuvenating rays first when he was seventy-five, and again at one hundred and forty. The second time, he was already tired of life and would have preferred the Unknown. But as yet then he had no heir.

No woman had ever achieved the Temple Beautiful, for none, until Salustra mounted the throne, had the opportunity to merit this reward. Salustra herself knew of nobody deserving this distinction, except old Mahius, her father's First Minister, and he soon pleaded for her not to prolong a life already freighted with one rejuvenation experience.

With tears in his eyes, he had appealed to her better nature. "I deserve better at your hands, Majesty."

"Where can I find another like you?" she had rejoined sadly. "Who but you will stand firm with me when the hordes descend from the north?"

2

HOW STUPID were these men, the Empress thought. For a week now, as a low, swirling mist hung over the land, Atlantis had been in the grip of a mysterious power shortage. Nothing operated by solar or nuclear energy could move—neither vessels of the sea nor land craft nor the ships of the air. All rapid communication via the vibrations of the atmosphere was at a halt, electrical energy was at a standstill, and it seemed as if the very empire must fall apart at the seams. And yet these men, these stupid men, were driveling nonsense for hours, inconsequential nonsense, which not only had no bearing on the present crisis but was also irrelevant to any of the immediate internal and external threats confronting the stricken nation.

As matters stood now, the Empress had been sitting in Council with the Nobles and Commoners for many hours, and the conversation had been more than usually oppressive. She moved restlessly upon her throne and tapped the floor irritably with a foot. Her eyes idly roamed the Council Chamber, passing from the walls of gleaming white marble to the tremendous soaring columns and the vaulted ceiling, so lofty that the upper pillars were lost in hazy shadows. Her gaze shifted to the center of the vast chamber, where a fountain featured a nymphlike figure holding aloft a torch so brilliant it illuminated the entire chamber. The Empress' eyes then returned to the twelve Nobles representing the aristocracy of the Twelve Provinces and the twelve Commoners representing the people of the Twelve Provinces. The Empress barely heard what they were saying. The Empress was unspeakably bored, her mind vaguely preoccupied with the power stoppage that threatened to paralyze the nation. Yet, as always, she looked serenely majestic. Her robes, heavily brocaded with gold, barely concealed the smooth roundness of her bosom and her gleaming shoulders. Her hair was lightly braided with pearls, and on her head rested the crown of Atlantis with its twelve points, one for each province. Her face, with its cold, indifferent beauty, gave the impression of an impassive nature. Against the pallor of her face, her full mouth provided an arresting touch of color. Her nose was a trifle too high and arrogant; the turn of her head expressed too obviously an easy imperiousness. Her frown perhaps was too pronounced. About her throat was her father's necklace, heavy links of polished gold fastened by the sparkling gem, which became a circle of fire in the warm hollow of her throat. Despite this energizer, stimulating the body, she was mentally very tired. One of the Nobles was speaking, his voice a dull drone in her ears. She looked beyond him to the slumbering Mount Atla. Through the blur of a heavy haze, a suggestion of red shone above the purple crags and peaks. Below, the blue bosom of the bay gently rose and fell, and great ships dipped and bowed at anchor while others dove underneath waves occasionally to mine the ocean floor for precious minerals, copper, uranium, nickel, cobalt, magnesium, gold, silver and many rare alloys. She turned her head, and the city struck her eye with a dazzling white light. The city climbed upward, until great pillars and walls and shining domes mingled together in a vast forest of gleaming stone. She frowned; she hated her capital of Lamora. Her best efforts had not been entirely successful in banishing dirt and disease and noisome spots. She remembered what her father had once told her: "One cannot teach courtesy to asses, nor cleanliness to hogs." So, despite the pearl-like whiteness of the city at a distance, she knew that narrow alleys and fetid streets lurked behind the pillars and domes and the shining walls. She had had great trees planted in the main streets and the vast parks, the fresh greenery making vivid patches in the glittering stone. But many died of the stagnant air and others became wilted through neglect. Above all, there came from the city a ceaseless murmur, a distinctive, throbbing hum, which reflected the soul of the inhabitants, ebbing and flowing like the changing sound of the sea.

As her eyes returned to the Council Chamber, she looked absently at a large relief map carved in color upon a marble wall. It showed a mighty continent. The whole continent was called Atlantis, but only the central section was really the nation of Atlantis. Mighty Althrustri, to the north and west, was as vast in territory as Atlantis but was a land of endless pine forests, frozen lakes, bleak mountains, breathtaking precipices and terrible stretches of virgin snow and ice. The upper fringe of the continent was white with snow for most of the year, but Atlantis proper had a versatile climate. It was livably cold in the north, with a pleasant summer, warm and temperate in the central portions, and hot and languorous in the south. In the south, in the First Province, was Lamora, the capital, with seven million inhabitants. South of Atlantis was a cluster of tiny island principalities, Mantius, Dimtri, Nahi, Letus, Antilla and Madura. The Emperor Lazar had guarded their independence as an indulgent lion would his cubs.

At one time Lazar had taken his daughters on a journey across the continent. They had visited all of the Twelve Provinces. Seven were industrious, with thriving cities and broad fertile areas. Some, distinctly urban, boasted large manufacturing centers. Others were agricultural, with small towns and hidden villages. Two were indolent, shiftless provinces, feeding on the rest. Two were thinly populated, with dense matted forests, rocky gorges and a sparse soil that made life too precarious for a soft generation. In a vast region comprising large parts of three provinces, there was an endless swamp and jungle. Here, baboons, monkeys, lions, crocodiles and elephants, which had somehow reappeared after the dinosaurs vanished, filled the tropic nights with their cries. Another province was a great, gray desert, unoccupied save for creatures of the sand.

Lamora, the bloated capital, felt vastly superior to its sister states. Life here was hectic, gay and abandoned. The other provinces called it the sewer of Atlantis, but to the Lamorans it was the center of the earth. Here abounded the most famous poets, artists, philosophers, the most accomplished mountebanks, the most profound scientists, the most beautiful courtesans. Its luxury was famous from the icy glaciers of Althrustri to the warm tropical waters of Letus. Each year, thousands of Althrustrians had seeped into the country, almost as an advance invasion force, lured by the wealth and comforts and opportunities of this favored land. Life was not hard and grim in Atlantis as it was in Althrustri, and laws here were more benign and tolerant. From other lands, too, the poorest class of immigrants flowed into Atlantis, the adventurers, the paupers, the incompetent, the biologically inferior, having found existence too strenuous in their own country.

Lazar, during the latter years of his life, had been concerned by this inferior bloodstream seeping across his borders. He had advocated a rigid immigration law, which would screen applicants for admission. But influential manufacturers, greedy for new markets, successfully protested this rigidity. Atlanteans demanded too large a wage scale, and profits were hardly more than two hundred percent. Lazar had spoken to Salustra about his proposed reform months before his death, but she had never mustered the votes to push the measure through the Council.

Salustra had been thinking about many things, none of them remotely touching the Noble Consul Lustri, of the Eighth Province, or anything that he was saying now. Her eyes rested upon him with a detached curiosity. Lustri was a handsome young man of the purest aristocracy, prominent in the licentious life of the city. He had great charm, a magnetic smile. His wealth was reputedly as limitless as his debaucheries. Rumor had it that he was the Empress' lover. But if so, she was already tired of his limited repertoire. Her nimble intellect demanded a kindred spirit. Lustri was a charming playmate, a delightful lover, a stimulating companion, but he could never breach the wall behind which Salustra suffered the isolation of the great.

She now caught a few words that Lustri was saying. He was standing before her throne, his dark eyes fixed upon her with confident boldness. Nobles and Commoners alike regarded him enviously. The Empress, they thought, could deny him nothing. Lustri represented the most dissolute elements of the turbulent Eighth Province, which experienced more crimes of violence than all the other provinces collectively. Each province made its own local laws, subject only to national statutes, and was authorized to raise taxes for the national treasury and to furnish a certain quota of men for the army.

There were two large cities in Lustri's state, and neither the national nor the local police body could effectively maintain order, as the poor were practically in a state of revolt. Because of widespread corruption of public officials, taxes were often extracted only by force, and rebellion, sparked by poverty, smoldered close to the surface. Tax monies were squandered illicitly, diverted from legitimate public projects. Roads had fallen into disrepair, thousands stood idle in the cities; vast agricultural regions lay fallow. The dissolute aristocracy found it impossible to gather taxes for the national treasury. They had induced Lustri, as their representative, to plead with the Empress for an emergency moratorium on taxes. The neighboring Ninth Province was industrious and prosperous, and the lords of the Eighth Province proposed that a larger tax be imposed on their more fortunate neighbor to make up their deficiency.

Lustri argued his case well, his smiling eyes fastened eloquently, as though sharing some special secret, on her Imperial Highness. As he smiled, he painted her a pathetic picture of the economic miseries of his Eighth Province. His lips openly called for a little more time; some understanding of the Eighth's problems and a larger imposition, only temporarily, to be sure, on the Ninth Province. Meanwhile, his eyes conveyed another message to this beautiful woman, as he remembered the hours when her bosom had been pressed to his, and he had felt the accelerated beat of her heart. He recalled the scent of her hair, the softness of her lips, and his glance let her know that. He was sure that she too remembered.

As he was speaking, one man in the Assembly had risen indignantly, restrained only by the forceful urging of his comrades. He was a tall, spare, middle-aged man, his blue eyes startlingly pale in a deeply tanned face. He was the Commoner from the Ninth Province.

Not missing any of this drama, the Empress raised her hand, and Lustri paused. Her manner was gentle and almost detached. As if ignoring the Commoner, she nodded to the Noble, Gatus, from the Ninth Province, kinsman to Lustri, and he came forward eagerly, kneeling gratefully to touch Salustra's golden slipper with his forehead.

"My Lord Gatus, thou hast heard the pleas of the Lord Lustri," she said. "What hast thou to say to this? Art thou and thy people willing that this should be so?"

Gatus looked at her closely, but her gaze was inscrutable. Lustri smiled inwardly, a confident and triumphant smile. He tried to catch the eye of the Empress for a secret glance of appreciation, but she did not look in his direction.

Gatus hesitated for a moment, apparently perplexed, then bowed in assent. Immediately, Publius, the Ninth Commoner, with an angry cry, broke from his comrades and sprang before the Empress' throne. His eyes flashed with righteous scorn as he glanced at the faintly smiling Gatus and Lustri. "Most gracious Majesty, I protest this rapacious assault on my people!" cried the Commoner. "We work too hard to be the object of such a conspiracy by the Nobles."

Salustra looked at the Commoner with surprise. Several Nobles stepped forward to join Lustri and Gatus, and, like their fellows, they held their hands lightly on their ceremonial swords, ready to avenge this boorish affront to their Empress.

Salustra motioned them back with a languid hand, leaving Lustri and Gatus and the Commoner standing before the throne.

She beckoned first to the Commoner. "Publius, come

forward, and tell me why I should not impose this tax upon thy more prospering people."

Lustri, supremely confident, toyed with the jeweled hilt of his sword. Gatus, smiling uneasily, traced the juncture of two marble sections in the floor with a nervous foot.

Publius stretched out his hands passionately. His voice rang with righteous wrath. "How unjust," he deplored, "for the industrious to pay the piper for the indolent. Why then should any man strive or labor, to what purpose?"

The Empress sat musing, her eyes fixed on the floor. She looked at neither Lustri nor Publius. Suddenly, she smote the side of her throne with her palm, her eyes flashed. "I deny the petition of the Lord Lustri," she said in a clear voice.

A subdued murmur, like a gathering wind, passed over the Assembly. The Nobles eyed each other in amazement: malignant glances previously concealed by fear were cast at the discomfited Lustri, who was staring at the Empress with dazed, unbelieving eyes.

Lustri was visibly trembling, and beads of sweat appeared on his forehead. He put out a quavering hand in a gesture almost of supplication. As she watched him with veiled eyes, her mouth curled a little.

"But most gracious Majesty," began Lustri in a subdued voice scarcely above a whisper. "I would implore further consideration. There must be a mistake!"

The Empress' hand moved slowly to her throat, and her slim fingers played with the gem there. She gave him a glance that reduced him to an awareness of the gulf between them.

"I have considered," she said dispassionately. "I do not understand why industry and prosperity should be penalized for inferiority and criminality. That is all."

Lustri looked stricken. "That is all?" he whispered, moistening his lips.

The Empress coldly inclined her head.

His face the color of chalk, Lustri bowed and withdrew to a bench, where a group of frozen-faced Nobles moved slightly away from him.

As though Lustri had never existed, the Empress took up a roll of parchment which lay in her lap and read it with a frown. "And now the rest," she said sharply. "Gatus, and thou, Publius, we grant you permission to build a provincial road joining the national road. You will impose taxes sufficient for the project. The national funds may be drawn on to ten percent of the local levies."

The routine business of the day proceeded. Salustra's mind swept over various proposals; she listened to the counsel of others, and made her decision. Her judgment was final. And so the day's trivial business was concluded.

For a decade she had ruled Atlantis, and during that time she had done her best to roll back an inevitable tide. Keen observer that she was, she knew the hour of decision was fast approaching for her country. In the back of her mind at all times were the rugged barbarians to the north. As a student of history, she knew that when a nation begins to decay inside, it is ripe for conquest from without.

Atlantis obeyed but did not love her. She had no room for sentimentalism. She knew, as her father had known, that men respect the hand that cracks a whip and discount gentleness in a sovereign as weakness. She knew that in the early history of a civilization men are simple and self-reliant, that nations sprout from the seeds of an older civilization, grow, wax vigorous, virile and superstitious, and finally absorb the decaying organism that gave them birth.

Tongue in cheek, they called her the Virgin Queen. She was a symbol of the final flowering of a dying civilization. To her subjects, she was Atlantis personified. They gossiped about her lovers, jesting that she chose only the strongest and youngest for her favors. On the intellectual side, scientists, philosophers, poets, artists found her a staunch friend. True worth did not languish unsung, even though she well knew that the brighter genius flames, the sooner it consumes itself.

"Better a day of radiant life than a century of darkness," she often mused.

Frequently she repeated to herself the cynical words of her Emperor father: "To think is to begin to die."

In an attempt to delay the decline, she had offered grants to Atlanteans of known ability to increase the size of their families, as one of the reasons Atlantis was dying was that men and women of accomplishment were practicing almost total birth control. It was so simple to sterilize either male or female with birth-control injections effective for six months that only the dull and the inferior, hoping to add excitement to their lives, were producing in excess of their death rate. There was another incentive as well. They could then apply to the national fund for additional welfare benefits. The very sensitivity of the superior conspired to hasten their end. Because they feared that they could not adequately insulate their children from a turbulent and debauched society, they refused to bear them. Salustra had attempted to persuade the ignorant and superstitious to practice birth control. But the religious groups headed by the priests protested loudly, and the ignorant and superstitious protested with them. What right had a mere temporal sovereign to order them to relinquish their divine right to spawn their feeble, mentally stunted, dependent, criminally inspired offspring?

Salustra had thought of invoking her archenemies, the members of the priesthood, to augment the birthrate among the upper classes by threatening them with untold future torments if they practiced birth control. Ironically, only the ignorant and the undesirables would listen to such absurdities.

Eventually, she hit upon a plan for penalizing aliens, paupers, dependent incompetents and inferiors for producing unrestrained numbers of children. She took them off welfare. Also, she prohibited unions of the diseased, the shiftless and the biologically inferior. She advocated intercourse between unmarried men of proven superiority and women of their choice, taking the children under the protection of the state. Illegitimacy was no disgrace. The priesthood, the pious and the righteous were outraged.

But these Salustra squelched with a firm hand. "These children are the state's," she said. "Atlantis is their father and mother."

Her enemies snickered openly. Advocating exceptional children, why did not she, the flower of Atlantis, set a notable example? The cream of a patriotic young manhood would be only too happy to cooperate for the public good. Salustra did nothing to dignify these sly barbs.

She rejoiced in her enemies, gauging the effectiveness of her laws by their opposition in certain quarters: the lords of industry, the indolent, the welfare recidivists and the criminal classes. Sometimes, obscene epigrams were scrawled on the walls of her Palace. Tales of her amorous hours were bandied about, encouraged by a malevolent priesthood. But the inarticulate majority trusted her cold intelligence.

She had few friends, and these stoutly maintained an attitude of belief in her virginity, as if to distinguish her from ordinary women. This naiveté annoyed while it amused her. She understood too clearly that they were mistakenly realizing in her the sentimental ideals of their own youthful fantasies. Clever and wise men were almost childlike in sexual matters. Only the cynical were totally emancipated from convention. "Cynicism is the boast of youth, the affectation of the mature, and the bitter tea of the aged," she would say.

3

SHE WAS rubbing her eyes drowsily as Mahius stood watching with a solemn expression.

"Why so long a face, Mahius?" she said. "How could today add anything more disagreeable than yesterday?"

Mahius' pained expression gave him the look of a squeezed-out sponge. "Majesty, the geologists report a huge rumble in the earth far to the north."

She sat up in her bed and looked impishly at her First Minister. "Look the other way, old man, while I climb out of bed. I wear nothing but my skin these nights; it is so beastly hot without the central air-cooling system. Why cannot our Palace generators, which still feed our lamps, be stimulated enough to send cooling air into my chambers?"

Mahius replied lamely, as he cast his eyes to the floor: "These generators have very little power, Majesty, sufficient only for partial illumination, and one can only speculate when this feeble trickle of energy gives out."

She now sat up on the edge of the bed, a shimmering vision in an abbreviated garment that began at the gentle swell of her breast and stopped at the hips.

Mahius coughed uncertainly.

"Now tell me of this earthquake, old man," said Salustra in a teasing tone.

Mahius' gaze was as close to a reprimand as it had ever been with his ebullient Empress. "It is nothing to jest about, Majesty, not when one considers the terrible situation we already find ourselves in."

Salustra became instantly attentive. "Speak without riddles, old man," she said sharply. "What dost thou mean to say?"

The old man gulped a few times. "This is no ordinary earthquake and there has been no such activity on the seismograph on Mount Atla since the last atom-splitter convinced our ancestors this was too devastating a weapon to be controlled by man."

Salustra now threw a colorful wrapper about herself, reached for her father's jeweled chain and stood up, immediately alert

"If we do not shatter the atom in the air because of what it may do to us, how can others safely use it?" She looked up, struck by a sudden thought. "To the north is only the land of the Althrustri, and they are much too backward to have developed nuclear energy."

Mahius waved his hand expressively. "Its manufacture is no secret, Majesty. Millions of Atlanteans have been concerned with its production and use, and some of these are Althrustrian-born, with a prior loyalty to their native land."

"What art thou suggesing, old man?"

He shrugged. "Like thyself, Majesty, I ask where they got it, and no reasonable answer, except one, suggests itself."

The Empress' eyes flashed. "I cannot accept the suggestion that any Atlantean, however discontented, could submit his country's fate to the whims of the barbarian."

Mahius sat silent for a few moments. "That is not my immediate concern, Majesty."

She looked up in surprise. "And what could that be?"

"We know the atom-splitter must be touched off deeply underground, lest it set up a chain reaction that could destroy the earth with its terrible heat."

She gave him an impatient glance. "Yes, man, go on."

"If the Althrustri have exploded the atom in the atmosphere, it could already, with its tremendous release of thermal energy, have begun a vaporizing action on mountains of solid ice at the pole."

She looked at him thoughtfully. "And if so, how would this first manifest itself?"

"It is too early to say, but as the heat chewed at the ice, there would be all the progressive elements of a great thaw; first, the pulverizing effect, and then as the radiation continues, a melting of an ice field as great as the Atlantic Ocean itself."

"That would certainly mean an end of the Althrustri."

He nodded gravely. "And perhaps of Atlantis, as the oracles have prophesied for centuries."

She spoke sharply. "They named no time, old man."

"Not quite so, Majesty." He repeated serenely, "When the land is so corrupt that even the beasts in the fields and the birds in the sky flee it, then shall we see the latter days and the vengeance of the gods."

Her lips curled in vexation. "Give me not the gods, Mahius. It is too early in the day for oracles. Besides—" she looked at a timepiece by her bed "—it is time to sit again with the Twelve Provinces. I must get ready for this meaningless sop to tradition."

Mahius rose with an effort, his old bones creaking more than their wont. "I will meet thee there, Majesty, perhaps with more information."

"Go to, old man," she said. "And let us face this more immediate ordeal of the provincial Assembly together."

Four times a year Salustra sat for three days with the representatives of the Twelve Provinces. The Commoner was chosen by popular referendum, the Noble by the aristocracy, each for six years, and none might serve longer without express consent of the sovereign. "In this way," Lazar had said, "corruption can be minimized. It takes three years to become vulnerable to graft, another two years to overcome the fear of being caught!"

The sovereign was the last authority, and the lowliest might appeal over the heads of the highest public official. Treachery and the betrayal of public trust were the most heinous crimes, punished by confiscation and death. The sons of convicted representatives were disenfranchised for ten years. Elections were supervised, and no more than a thousand decenari could be spent on any campaign—an inconsiderable amount. At one time there had been a movement to give women the right to vote. Salustra had vetoed the proposal. "They would vote in the beginning as do their fathers, their husbands and their sons," she said. "Therefore, there would be only a multiplication of the proportionate masculine vote. After a while, they would be governed by appearances and vote for only the handsomest and most personable men. They would all be actors or models."

She never thought of herself as a woman, and was considered colder, more ruthless and more indomitable than even her father. Occasionally, Lazar had been moved to pity and generosity. But not Salustra. A matter was right or wrong; either it was an infringement of the national law or it was not. Some declared her cruel; others defended her as hard but fair. And fairness without mercy can be a terrible thing. Just as she met with the provinces four times a year, she conferred for diplomatic reasons with the ambassadors of the small southern kingdoms and Althrustri. Althrustri's two ambassadors habitually wore an air of quiet defiance before the queen.

"Althrustri," they murmured, "is as great as Atlantis."

"The strong have no need of diplomacy," she said dryly, "certainly not such diplomats as you."

They reported back regularly to their master about this extraordinary woman. She had no illusions about the Emperor Signar's ambitions. She knew Althrustri to be younger, more vigorous, hungrier for dominion than Atlantis. She kept a wary eye to the north, she heard the protestations of friendship from Signar's ambassadors without comment. She bore no resentment. Signar merely represented the inevitable. As well resent the storm, earthquake or flood. Youth was always in hot pursuit of age. Atlantis had had her day: Althrustri's was coming. Nevertheless, she would delay the hour.

"Be peaceful," was her watchword. "Make no overt act, but let all see that your sword is well sharpened." Her ministers, save Mahius, had urged disarmament. To make a constant show of nuclear aircraft and ships and missiles, together with disintegrating rays, was to tempt war, they said. Let the northern neighbor see Atlantis disarm, and it would soon follow suit. Salustra had smiled incredulously. How could so-called wise men be so simple? "A disarmed man is a temptation to his enemies," she replied.

She told her people: "If you love Atlantis and would enjoy peace, arm to the teeth."

The people had so trusted her that they had voted a larger arsenal of weapons. Signar had been compelled to give Salustra a grudging accolade. "This is a leader," he told his distressed ambassadors, "though she leads a sick and craven flock."

The Althrustri were not sufficiently advanced technologically to match Atlantis in any nuclear race. But through espionage, through promises, to Atlantean malcontents and traitors, of petty principalities and high offices, they had stolen what they could not create. They had touched off their first blasts in the glacial wilderness north of their bleak capital city of Rayjava. Huge gaping holes had been torn into mountains of ice, and clouds of heavy mist had vaporized, hovering over the ice caps like a thick blanket. After a while, the water level immediately south of Althrustri had risen noticeably, but they thought nothing of this, not knowing enough of the weapons they had stolen to understand their long-range action. And in his contempt for the consequences, Signar made it clear he would not hesitate to use the atom in attack. "What other reason for weapons, but to subdue one's adversaries?"

He despised the Atlantean regime's reluctance to curb him when they had the chance. "Except for their Empress," he said scornfully, "they are all women."

Beyond his plan of annexing Atlantis, there was a mounting interest in this woman. When she apprehended his agents, he only laughed appreciatively. For his part, he caught a few of her spies and returned them to Atlantis with splendid gifts for the Empress. Salustra responded almost in kind. When the next Althrustrian spy was apprehended, she sent his head to Signar in a golden casket. The energy crisis was not so easily disposed of. With necessity the mother of invention, Atlantis over the centuries had harnessed the energy flow of the sun and the sea to become the greatest power on earth. Technologically, it was supreme. Its industries, homes, shops, vehicles, all had drawn on this apparently limitless reservoir of nature to maintain a complex system of production, transportation and communication.

But while this technology developed until Atlantis clearly dominated its neighbors, there was not a commensurate development in cultural and philosophical values. Indeed, the very abundance of energy, contributing to a leisure-time society that emphasized luxuries and creature comforts, served to hasten the decay of a society that knew the price of everything and the value of nothing.

Salustra was right in her estimate of her own people. Soft, indolent and self-indulgent, rotting at the core, they were ripe for a takeover by any adversary with sufficient cunning to perceive their internal corruption and the driving ambition to capitalize on this weakness.

The mysterious mist over the land, together with the power breakdown and ancient prophecies of destruction, had created a climate of confusion. Had it not been for drastic measures taken by Salustra and her ministers, the country would have been in chaos. Before meeting again with her National Assembly of Nobles and Commoners, Salustra had promptly summoned her Ministers for Transport, Communication, Atmosphere, Science, Solar Energy and National Preservation in secret session to meet Atlantis' most serious crisis since the old struggle for survival with the giant dinosaurs.

The Cabinet members had been as bewildered as the general populace, but Salustra, renewing her own flagging energies from the energizing jeweled amulet around her neck, had announced that they had no time for debate, as the country would soon be at a standstill, with food supplies spoiling in the fields or not getting produced or distributed.

She told Timeus, the Minister for Transport: "I give you twelve hours to restore the movement of goods and supplies on our roads and waterways." When Timeus, a lean man with a dark brow, opened his mouth to protest, the Empress held up a hand. "Don't tell me, Timeus," she said mockingly, "that you have already come up with a solution. Fine, we shall see evidence of it in the morning."

The ministers, convened in her private chambers, were looking most profound.

She gave them a steadfast look. "I need no ministers to tell me what can't be done, only what can be done."

"You, Fribian—" she pointed to the Minister for Solar Energy "—tell me why our crystal receptors and our radiating transmitters are neither receiving nor sending energy through the atmosphere."

Fribian, a strikingly young-looking man, stood up promptly and began to talk with the directness of youth. "We relate it to the mist, Majesty. Hours after the mist descended, we began to get word of stoppages in all solar-driven ships, aircraft, land wagons, which could not even send messages of their predicament. Our telesound and distant-pictures apparatus stopped simultaneously, as did all facilities depending on the transmission of electricity through the atmosphere."

Salustra nodded thoughtfully. "And what have you done, Fribian?"

The minister waved his hands expressively. "Short of moving the sun, I can only suggest."

"And what have you suggested?"

Fribian motioned curtly to Hammu, the Minister for Atmosphere, sitting opposite him, doodling with a pencil. "I discussed with Minister Hammu the possibility of dissolving the mist, as we have done with cloud banks when we felt a need for additional rain."

"Yes?" Salustra impatiently looked from one minister to the other.

Hammu was a stocky man, with a round face, dull brown eyes, and a truculent look. He was known as a great physicist. "It is easy to suggest, Majesty, but suggestions do not move the heavens."

The Empress gave him an imperious look. "What have you done, sir?"

"These clouds are different from any others, Majesty. We have stocked them with all types of water-producing chemicals, without the slightest effect. The mist only seems to get thicker, hanging lower in the atmosphere." He paused for a moment, and his eyes moved slowly around the table. His face was glum and his shoulders sagged. "The birds have all disappeared from the skies of Lamora, as if they had some foreknowledge of disaster."

Nothing he said could have more oppressed the minds of the assembled dignitaries, susceptible as they were to the astrologers' repeated portents of catastrophe.

But Salustra was quick to counteract Hammu's bombshell. "Bah," she exclaimed. "They were no doubt driven off by the noxious fumes; this mist reeks of sulfur."

Her eyes now rested on her supreme councillor, Mahius. "What sayest thou, dear friend, to this gloomy talk?"

Only Mahius dared speak his mind, not only because he was closest to the Empress but because two lifetimes had wearied him and he no longer aspired to the greatest reward a grateful Atlantis could conceive—the rejuvenation chamber. For this reason, too, Salustra, grown cynical with rule, knew she could count on him for an honest opinion. He had nothing to gain or lose.

"What sayest thou?" she repeated, as he remained rapt in thought.

He spoke slowly, with a solemn mien. "Majesty, just as Fribian cannot move the sun, Hammu cannot alter the atmosphere, and Timeus—" his head nodded toward the Minister of Transport "—cannot move the unmovable."

Her head bridled impatiently. "Then are we to sit around and do nothing, while the people starve and Signar moves in on fossil-fueled vessels and takes over all we have built over the centuries?"

There was the trace of a smile on Mahius' gray lips. "No, Majesty, but we can learn from the barbarian. We have our network of canals and fleets of smaller barges, some fitted for nuclear energy, others for the sun's rays. We can fit them overnight with sails and oars, and let them sweep over the waterways in the same way that our ancestors did centuries before. Meanwhile, we could scour the museums for the internal-combustion engines that our forefathers once used, and perhaps find fuel for them in the ground." He paused, as he saw her frown. "It would be a temporary expedient, Majesty, to move foods, perishable for lack of refrigeration, and to feed an empire, while your ministers apply themselves to this crisis."

With her knack for instant decisions, the Empress' head inclined. "Timeus, go to, and have these ships moving before daybreak."

Timeus had a sailor's keen eye. Small craft were his hobby. His eyes gleamed at these instructions. "It shall be done, Majesty, Lamora shall not starve. But I will need help."

He turned to the Minister for National Preservation, who until now had maintained an aloof somewhat disdainful attitude. "I will need Sabian's fullest cooperation for the required manpower."

The Empress' eyes focused on a short man, with a beefy face, who appeared vastly overdressed for so somber an occasion. "And what say you, Sabian?"

Sabian hesitated. "It will take time, Majesty, to collect so huge a force, considering the breakdown in the rapid-transit and communication systems."

The Empress' eyes blazed. "Dolt," she exploded. "Were these systems functioning would we be here at all, but rather out in the garden listening to the birds, which also are inoperative?"

The Minister for National Preservation visibly blanched before this assault.

"Atlantis can no longer afford you, Sabian. Too long hast thou allowed thy indolent fancies to make thy office that of a figurehead." Her eyes turned to the Minister for Transport. "Thou, Timeus, art now Minister for National Preservation as well."

Sabian had turned the color of chalk. The other ministers now avoided his gaze. He stammered a moment. "May I leave, Majesty?"

"None too soon to suit me. Go to, man. Thou canst not even preserve thyself."

Sabian seemed to dwindle in size as he slunk out of the room.

Hardly waiting for the door to close, Salustra turned to a tall, thin man with a nervous mouth. "And what say you, Matthias?"

The Minister for Communication was ready. "No sooner did reports come in, Majesty, that ships and vehicles of various types had lost power not only to navigate but to communicate than I established a system of couriers by foot and horse for land communication, and semaphores, used long ago by our ancestors, for sea communications. But, alas, we are handicapped at sea by the uncertainty of the sun playing on our mirrors, and by limited visibility. Meanwhile, we still try to penetrate the atmosphere, but our radio signals fall dead. It is as if the mist had laid a blanket on the atmosphere, blocking off all electrical frequencies by which the vibrations of sound, light and movement are carried through the atmosphere."

Salustra had listened intently. "You do well, Matthias. Others might take a lesson from thy resourcefulness."

Matthias made a modest inclination of his head. "I do what I can, Majesty, but a bold adversary could slip through our hampered defenses without our knowledge. Our advance-warning system is nonfunctional. Nothing shows on our telesound screens, not even the bouncing waves."

Grimly Salustra turned to her two Ministers for Science. They blandly expressed hope that the mist would soon dissipate and the sun once more show itself.

Salustra regarded these men of science dryly. "And what would you scientists recommend, that we appeal to the High Priestess Jupia, so that she may intercede with the gods in our behalf?"

The ministers blushed.

Bronko, the science coordinator, was a burly figure with a deep voice. "I will gladly resign if your Majesty thinks another may do better."

She gave him a friendly smile. "I do not blame any of you for that beyond thy sphere. But what can be done that thou dost not do I shall hold in account. Atlantis is still the last bastion of civilization, and must be preserved."

The ministers were seeing a side of the Empress that the revelers and libertines of the court had no inkling of.

"All will do the best they can," said Mahius, sounding the optimistic keynote.

"Go to, then, and show our adversaries that we are not yet ready to play dead."

As they filed out singly, the Empress motioned for old Mahius to remain.

She sipped slowly from a glass of wine.

"The seven-colored crystal my father bequeathed me," said she, indicating the jewel around her neck, "has been pressed to keep up to my own energy demands of late."

Mahius managed a smile, but he minced no words. "Even without Signar," said he soberly, "Atlantis is in a critical situation."

She looked at him thoughtfully. "We could always go back to fossil fuels—coal, oil and natural gas—even though these primitive carbons take up so much room and pollute the environment."

"It would mean bringing back the internal-combustion engine on a large scale, and other archaic mechanical devices powered by such fuels."

She nodded. "Then so be it—give the necessary instructions to Gobi, the Minister for Science. He added naught to the meeting today, and should be glad to prove that he is not as decadent as that precious sister of his, who is known far and wide for the calluses on her back."

Mahius suddenly felt drained. "Is there any more, Majesty?"

"Yes, I would have you make a tour of the city with me. Now that the land wagons are no longer functioning, we can travel in one of the ceremonial litters, without stirring the attention of the populace."

In keeping with ancient tradition, despite Atlantis' technological progress, the ceremonial litter had been retained, with its guards, as the only means for the reigning monarch to travel through the city, just as ceremonial swords were still maintained by the aristocracy as a symbol of their ancient tradition.

Mahius' face dropped. "I am an old man, Majesty, and fatigue has settled in my bones."

She gave him a mocking glance. "Perhaps we should put you back in the rejuvenation chamber."

Mahius' face contorted in horror. "Please, not that again, Majesty. Life already has too many memories for my overburdened brain."

Salustra smiled fondly at her loyal adviser. "I. was merely jesting. Go to, and I will find another companion for my tour."

With a grateful bow, Mahius backed out of the royal presence.

He was no sooner gone than the Empress rang for Creto, the young Prefect of her Palace Guard. He arrived in a few minutes, a burly young man with bulging muscles and a gleam in his eye. He bowed low, then gave his Empress an inquiring glance.

She smiled appreciatively for a moment, then her voice became crisp and businesslike.

"Summon a litter," she said, "and we will make an inspection of the city and its slumbering plants."

Creto looked up in surprise. "But it is late, Majesty, it will be dawn in a few hours."

She gave the splendidly muscled soldier a disarming smile. "And is the mighty Creto afraid of footpads? Fear not, the litter-bearers will protect thee."

Creto blushed to the roots of his wavy blond hair. "Thou knowest, Majesty, I would gladly give my life for thee."

"Better save it for me, my protector. Thou servest me better alive."

Salustra had the normal layman's curiosity about the ponderous power-producing machines, which seemed so intricate and all-powerful and yet were now powerless, sleeping giants. She had always mistrusted these machines, incongruously so much more powerful than their masters. She had long contended that the mind of man should be able to do directly whatever an extension of his mind could do.

"What an inanimate object can do," she insisted, "certainly the mind that conceived it can do."

She thought of all this as she began her tour of inspection. With the faithful Creto, she was borne but a short distance to one of the many waterways that formed a network of canals from one edge of the city to the other, and which fed into a great mile-wide moat of seawater that surrounded the city. Her barge, the first to be refitted with sails, floated her small party through the heavy night to a major water-pumping station at the harbor front. There, normally, the ocean water was forced through corrosion-proof conduits, creating the electrical energy for desalinization plants that freshened the seawater and filtered out its riches, at the same time collecting valuable elements from human-waste materials and churning the dross far out to sea.

The barge slowly entered the great moat, where it was suddenly carried along by a swiftly swirling current, formed by huge jetties thrust deep into the open sea.

The pumping station, one of many girdling the moat, appeared to be quiet, though oddly, despite the power breakdown, some lights shone bleakly through ground-floor windows.

Salustra was immediately recognized by guards, and the manager of the works promptly summoned. He was a sleepy-eyed man, with a bushy red moustache and eyebrows that contrasted oddly with his bald pate.

Salustra sized him up immediately as one of the small army of efficient civil servants which managed to keep her decaying empire outwardly intact.

"I have come," she announced, "to observe for myself. How dost thou have lights with the city in darkness?"

Minotaur, the manager, bowed low. "We have our own generator, for just such emergencies, as thou, Majesty, in thy Palace and the government chambers."

She pointed vaguely out a window. "I see the waves churning as before, taking energy from the tides, so why do not thy pumps churn with all this power?"

"Our pumps are powered, Majesty, by solar energy, from the vast solar center which circles the mountain, and for a reason we do not yet understand this energy flow has stopped."

"Is it not madness to rely on but one energy source

when the sea sits ready to do our bidding, a sea that no cloud can obscure?"

Minotaur hesitated, flustered under the Empress' stern gaze.

"Speak, man, this is no time for protocol. Why doth not the ocean move thy pumps?"

"Thy pardon, Majesty. We can normally generate enough sea power for a hundred and one household uses. This alternate program was intended to become operational when the sun hid behind the clouds for three days or more, and the solar supply dwindled." He shrugged unhappily. "With the sun obscured, tidal energy is being produced, as we can tell by our gauges, but it dissipates before our transformers can convert it to energy. It is a mystery."

"So how doth thy generator work?" The Empress glanced pointedly at the overhead lamp.

Minotaur was happy for an opportunity to have something explainable to discuss. "This functions on a limited range, Majesty, on a closed-circuit system, independent of atmospheric vibrations, but—" he frowned "—even so, we find the impulse weaker than usual, with some units losing power after a few hours."

Moved by the man's sincerity, Salustra laid a hand on his shoulder. "It is men like you, Minotaur, who make me feel that my efforts are worthwhile."

Minotaur blushed and bobbed his head. "This visit, Majesty, is reward enough for whatever service I perform."

She turned to the hovering Creto with a wave of her hand. "Now for the desalinization plant which is nearest us. Without fresh water," said she, "how long can we survive?"

"There is always the rainfall, Majesty, collecting in the mountain streams."

"Polluted, my dear Creto, with these insufferable fumes that smell of the sulfur that grows on gravestones."

The de-salting plant was a miracle of subterranean pipes, tubes and chambers, all intricately interwoven, so that minerals such as sodium, phosphorus, magnesium, calcium, cobalt, nickel, manganese were successively drained off from the churning seawater at different temperatures. Volatile elements such as chlorine, fluorine and iodine were distilled into massive chambers, and there refined for commercial use. Meanwhile, the freshened water, reinforced with certain beneficial minerals such as calcium, was drawn into great pipes and pumped into reservoirs throughout the city.

As at the pumping area, all activity had come to a halt. The foreman was in a nervous state, perspiring from the heat accumulating underground since the power failure.

The Empress felt faint with the heat. "How dost thou stand this temperature?" she asked.

The foreman was of the same stripe as Minotaur, loyal to his monarch and well trained for his particular task. He replied apologetically. "Our air-cooling machines require more power than the emergency generators can produce, and so we must stand this heat, Majesty, until we return to normal."

"And when will that be, Fresto?" she asked, picking up his name from a desk plate.

Fresto shrugged unhappily. "None can say, Majesty. The Minister for Science was here earlier and asked that very question."

Salustra's face was incredulous. "The minister asked thee? Then indeed we are in trouble."

Fresto looked at her blankly.

"And what say you to the waste-disposal system? Shall we strangle in our own offal?"

The foreman shook his head. "No, Majesty, the ocean tides, funneled in and out of the moat, still carry off the wastes, which flow by gravitation to the moat itself, are treated chemically in our purifying plants and the residue expunged. The great Lazar created this system with great foresight."

She looked at him sharply for an implied rebuke.

His face was noncommittal.

"Go to, Fresto," she said. "I interfere with thy work."

She looked at Creto with a sigh.

"It is almost dawn, Majesty," he said.

"How dost thou know in this devilish mist?" she said wearily.

She threw a cape over her shoulders as they stepped into the barge, and shivered. "If only I knew what to do."

Creto gave her his strong arm. "That is what thy ministers are for, Majesty."

"But the people will blame me, as honest Fresto did."

"I heard naught of blame," Creto staunchly replied.

"Oh, yes, why wasn't the daughter of Lazar equally vigilant?"

"But how couldst thou know the evil the gods would contrive?"

Salustra smiled mirthlessly. "My subjects, used to having things done for them, care not for excuses."

She reached out and touched Creto's cheek. "One more stop, dear protector, and we call it a night."

There was a flickering light in the solar-energy center, the most accessible of a chain of stations which spiraled laterally up the mountain so as to capture the arching sun at all times.

Guards posted at the entrance quickly stood aside on recognizing the Empress. The director came forward holding a candle in his hand. "If we had only had some inkling—" he began.

Salustra cut him off. "You would have had a larger candle, forsooth."

The manager had the intelligence to blush. "We do find ourselves in unaccustomed straits, Majesty."

She looked around a darkened chamber, toward an outside balcony. There, in the approaching dawn, she could see a series of giant rubylike crystals slanted toward the sky. "And what is being done to remove these straits?"

The manager, Zeno, was a product of the civil-servant system, like the others Salustra had encountered. He made no attempt to dissemble. "The Minister for Science just left, Majesty, and we are under his direct orders."

"And the orders?"

"That we remain on duty through the crisis."

"You may be here a long time, Zeno."

He bowed. "My staff and I stand ready to do what we can."

"That is very well, but meanwhile thou providest a spectacle of a solar-energy center without sufficient light to move around in. What has happened to thy independent generators, man, so thou canst at least see thy own shadow?"

For a moment he hesitated.

"Speak up, man."

"The Minister for Solar Energy, Majesty, has never encouraged any other energy."

"And why not?" Her voice was sharply insistent.

The manager suddenly became uncomfortable. "By the same reasoning," he said uncertainly, "that the Minister for Tidal Energy resisted our efforts to modernize our system."

"And what was that?"

"So that the one would not be more important than the other."

Salustra drew a deep breath, and her lips curled in disgust. "It is no wonder that we have no ready way of overcoming this crisis. We have blockheads for ministers."

She turned to Creto, but spoke almost as though to herself. "One knows a civilization is moribund when jackals quarrel over the first bite." Her eyes took on a look of brooding intensity. "Underneath our Mount Atla and a hundred other mountains simmers enough volcanic energy to heat ten million homes, fuel ten million land wagons and a thousand ships, and a hundred great pumps if need be. The scientists call it thermal energy: It is the earth's own steam heat, and yet we have done nothing with it because some thought it would spoil the aesthetic features of the mountain tops, while others have selfishly sought to make their department first." She sighed. "Whom the gods would destroy they first make brainless."

Her mood lifted, and her voice grew less intense as she

motioned to the crystal-like reflector jutting out over the balcony. "Tell me, Zeno, how this works, when it does work?"

Zeno seemed relieved to be on positive ground. "This is one of a large network of reflectors which capture the sun's latent power, then transform the limitless energy from the sun to relay centers around the country, sending varying impulses like a radio beam to ships, hovercraft, land wagons, and units of the city's rapid-transit system."

"What of our airplanes?" she said.

"As you know, Majesty, we have very few long-distance aircraft, as there is no civilization comparable to our own to journey to."

As she looked into the intelligent eyes, she felt an inclination to expand on the thoughts turning in her mind. "Dost thou know anything of history, Zeno?"

"Some, Majesty. I am Atlantean born, though my ancestors came from honorable Dimtri."

"Then thou must know that Atlantis faces its most serious crisis since the great dinosaurs overran the earth centuries ago and threatened our population. Having despoiled most of the earth's surface, except for Althrustri, which was too cold and forbidding even for these monsters, these armored dragons next fell on our people. The Atlanteans of that time had no weapons with which to repulse these formidable creatures, some standing several stories high and weighing hundreds of tons. What were spears, swords, axes, arrows, even catapults against monsters who could swallow up a roomful of men with a gulp? But, driven by necessity as urgent as today's, our ancestors devised new ways of defending themselves. First, there were flame-throwers, then explosives, but neither flames nor ordinary firearms could pierce hides two feet thick. So our ancestors, developing new sciences out of their extremity, experimented with the atmosphere and found they could draw vast streams of energy from the sun, capable of great explosive power when brought to atom-splitting heat. And so the nuclear atom-splitter was born. But even as it got rid of the beasts, it tore up forests, mountains and populated areas. But out of it all came the energy that gave Atlantis a technology never surpassed."

She fell silent, musing a moment, as both Creto and Zeno maintained an air of respectful attention.

"And what has it done for us? It made us affluent, and then soft and pleasure-loving."

Abruptly she shook her head. "Come, I keep you two awake, and myself as well. Let us—" she motioned to Creto "—bid good-bye to the worthy Zeno, who minds the lighthouse after the light has gone out."

It was already dawn, though the sun was nowhere to be seen, when the Empress finally got back to her Palace and her bed.

"Go to, Creto," she said playfully, giving him a fond tap on his head, "thou richly deservest thy own bed for thy services this night."

4

SALUSTRA conferred gravely with her minister and her representatives on an entirely new matter. A strange band of foreigners had recently appeared in Lamora. Who they were, and from whence they came, no one knew. They were dark men with hungry black eyes and large aquiline noses so unlike the fair, regular features of the Atlanteans. Atlantis traditionally granted peaceful residence to all, asking no questions, but this group had become a problem through arousing public resentment by their conspicuous lack of piety. The national religion of Atlantis involved the worship of Sati, the great goddess of wisdom and fertility. In the early life of the nation, she had also been the jealous patroness of agriculture. Salustra paid her homage tongue in cheek, but she recognized the wisdom of her father in upholding the national religion, to give the masses something they could feed on in time of stress. With the problems she already had she found this new problem most vexing. "Are these strange men peaceful?" she asked of Mahius.

The old man replied hesitantly. "They publicly declare they oppose conflict and dissension, but they refuse tribute to Sati, and never attend the temples, or celebrate the holidays. Also, they expound the tenets of their own faith to all who will listen."

"And what are these tenets?"

"They declare there is only one God, and He is not Sati. They declare Him just, virtuous, jealous, all-powerful when He wills; that He hates idols, intemperance, incontinence and pleasure of a worldly kind."

Salustra smiled cynically. "Atlantis has always granted religious sanctuary, provided the religionists do not meddle with affairs of state, blaspheme Sati, or cause public disturbance. From what thou hast told me, Mahius, they seem harmless enough, except I like not this all-powerful concept. It would not do to encourage this belief. New religions are poison in the bloodstream of an old nation. They cause division and lay authority open to attack." She looked off into the distance with narrowed eyes. "Pleasure!" she said. "Pleasure of whatever kind is the only thing that makes tolerable this most intolerable of all worlds. They must be corrupt who call pleasure sinful!"

The new religionists talked disturbingly about freedom. One million of Lamora's inhabitants, almost every fourth man, were slaves, and a million others from Althrustri maintained their old allegiance. The slaves were descendants of those impressed from the tropic islands near Atlantis at a time when Atlantis had been thinly populated and men were needed to fell the forests, tame the rivers, plant the plains. The slaves had multiplied and formed a formidable nation within a nation. The old Emperors had wanted to free them when the original purpose had been served, but the slaveholders objected, even though the state offered to reimburse them. For prestige was measured by the slaves one owned.

Salustra had hoped to return the slaves to their ancestral islands, but after hundreds of years few felt ties to the misty lands of their origin and most desperately clung to a desire to be taken care of.

Salustra saw the dangers of a large parasitic population. The slaves, backed by their masters, saw only the present urgency. "We have never provided for ourselves," they said, "and we dread the prospect of not being provided for."

Even as she thought of all this, and the representatives thought longingly of their perfumed baths and their female slaves softly massaging them with fragrant oils, Salustra watched the dark clouds against the dull outline of the sun. One formation startlingly resembled the Lamora skyline. Through a momentary gap in the perennial mist, the aurocalcric white pillars, towers, domes and walls of the city were momentarily splashed with color, and, too, the lofty peaks in the distance, as though a whole city were covered with blood.

Shaken by this vision, she rubbed her eyes uncertainly. She stood up abruptly, even as Mahius was speaking. "None of you has anything to say," she said impatiently. "In three months the Council will sit again. Tomorrow, ambassadors from the Emperor Signar of Althrustri bring an urgent message from their master, and it will be curious to note whether their urgency is also ours."

She stood impatiently as each representative approached to touch her foot with his forehead, a precedent that preserved the gulf between her and her advisers. By the time the last had departed, she was worn to a frazzle. But once alone, she lay back upon the cushions and closed her eyes gratefully. She was not only weary but sick in spirit, knowing in her heart what the future foretold for Atlantis.

I am soul-weary, she thought, as she stretched out upon a divan in the cool shadow of a chamber that opened out onto a roofless gallery.

From where Salustra lay, she could see the mist shrouding the normally purple sky and mountains. She closed her eyes and breathed deeply of the musky ambrosia from the lush gardens below. A slave touched a mechanism on the wall, and a round lamp on a slender golden pedestal filled the chamber with a soft light, which flickered for a moment before it stayed on. Thick crimson rugs were islands of color on the shining marble floor. Exquisite statues were half-glimpsed in the shadows of the stately pillars. Frescoes on the snowy walls peered out quietly in delicate hues. The arched ceiling was so high it was lost in a haze. Large vases, of beautiful symmetry even in their odd shapes, were decorated with masses of varicolored and fragrant flowers.

The slaves brought forward a little ivory table and noiselessly laid out the Empress' supper. She watched them listlessly. She had an increasingly terrible sense of unreality, a premonition of disaster. With an effort she turned to her food. The meal was simple: fruit, cheese, honey, wheaten cakes, a roasted bird, wine. She lifted a crystal goblet to her lips and frowned over its sparkling brim. With a curt gesture she motioned for all but one slave to leave. The girls exchanged furtive glances as they withdrew between the columns like white shadows. Some were trembling, for with the self-importance of the insignificant, they were sure her displeasure concerned them.

"What is wrong with me?" Salustra shook herself irritably. Bah! she thought. What I need is a new lover or a physic. But where shall I find him? We are a nation of monkeys. We chatter emptily of things, label wonders with words, and think that in this way we have pierced their mysteries. We call a mysterious force electricity, and are therefore content. We have given it a name! What more can be desired? We call our existence life and, once naming it, never ask what it is. Monkeys, without a monkey's peace of mind. Where is there a man who is not a fool? But perhaps I am the fool, after all.

She picked up a bunch of grapes and surveyed them with a critical eye. She had put one to her lip when a soft laugh interrupted her reverie. She frowned, looking up quickly. A slim girl stood at the foot of the divan, watching the Empress with dancing eyes. White flowers garlanded a crowd of golden hair, and dark-blue eyes looked brightly from under golden lashes. The soft lamplight, highlighting the gold in her hair, at the same time silhouetted the ripening curves of slim thighs and bosom.

Salustra's lip softened. She lifted herself on an elbow and held out her hand.

"Oh, Salustra," pouted the girl, "thou didst promise me that thou wouldst return early. Hast thou forgotten that this is my birthday? Already the guests begin to arrive, and thou art lying here!"

Salustra drew a blue cushion to her side and motioned the girl to seat herself. "Thou foolish little Tyrhia!" said the Empress fondly. "Dost think I have naught else to occupy me? I have not forgotten. But thy guests must wait. Who are they but virgin maids like thyself, and their beardless fondlers?"

Tyrhia's voice turned shrill. "Thou dost treat me as though I were a child, Salustra! And thou dost speak as if thou wert a crone with bleary eyes. Knowest thou not that I have invited Lustri?" She smiled with arch pride. "Didst thou think I had forgotten thee?"

Salustra frowned faintly, then smiled indulgently. "Lustri will not come," she said. "Ask me not how I know. Here, child, wilt thou have wine, or perhaps this orange is more to thy liking?"

Tyrhia scowled at her sister. "There are others, they always come," she went on in a sultry voice. "There are always thy friends, and Mahius, and the Council. Already they arrive."

Salustra's face hardened suddenly, and Tyrhia shivered a little. "Have I not told thee that thou art too young for such dissolute company? The Council! Debauchees! And, I suppose, in thy foolishness thou hast included the Senate. Monkeys. Hippopotami! Baboons! How didst thou dare?"

Tyrhia's lips trembled. "I am not a child!" she said sullenly.

Salustra shrugged. "Thou art a child." She touched the white flowers on the girl's head and adjusted a stray blossom with tender fingers, responding to the springlike radiance and untouched virginity of her sister.

After a moment, Tyrhia artfully began to chatter of the day's gossip, interrupting her own flow of words with supplications that Salustra hasten. "Dost thou know that foolish little Poymnia, Salustra? What dost thou think? She hath lost her heart to Licon, the son of Glaurus, that gilded butcher! Her father declares she shall enter the cloister of Sati if she doth not turn aside her eye, and she is defying him. Is it not absurd? She thinks herself a languishing heroine of the drama, dying of love. And absurdity of absurdities, Licon does not even know that she casts calf eyes upon him. He is serenely in love with Utanlia, and Utanlia hates him, which makes him love her the more. And, oh, dost thou remember Zutlia, whom thou didst call a little crocodile with her sleepy eyes and big sharp teeth? She is betrothed to Seneco, that fat old roué! He drips with jewels, and her father hath lost his fortune in sunken vessels and at the gaming table. So he sells Zutlia, who hath a voluptuous figure. But she is quite content to be sold. She is tired of having but one slave girl to attend her. She puts on such airs! Ludia was here today, also; she minces like a cat, and her mother purrs like one. They fawn when they speak of thee, but they shiver, too, in spite of their wealth. Ludia poked her fingers in the cage of my parrot, and got them well nipped. I laughed until I wept; they departed in high indignation. And today, Salustra, I saw the most entrancing necklace of sapphires; the stars shone in them. And only two thousand sallions! Seneco has them in his shop, and he dangled them for me to admire. Only two thousand sallions, Salustra! How they would glitter on thy neck!"

"Or on thine, little hypocrite." The Empress smiled, twining a yellow curl about her finger. "Go to! Send for the necklace now if thou so desirest. Seneco closes his shop at sundown, but he will gladly open it again. Let the necklace be my present to thee."

Tyrhia, with a cry of joy, kissed Salustra's hand. Salustra saw only the childlike blue of those eyes, the light in the eyes of a pleased child, so she considered. She saw nothing of Tyrhia's mother, Lahia, in her. She called for a messenger and dispatched him for the necklace.

Tyrhia prattled on, and Salustra listened, smilingly, as she continued to eat and drink. Then her smile faded and her brows drew together thoughtfully. Her eye moved over the radiant girl, speculatively, appraisingly. Her hand glided smoothly over that golden head, gently brushed the velvet of that girlish cheek. She broke into the girl's chatter. "Thou art no longer a child, Tyrhia," she said suddenly. "Hast thou ever thought of marriage?"

Tyrhia stared at Salustra, and slowly, under the other's gaze, her color changed. "No," she answered in a low voice.

"And thou hast no yearning for any youth?"

Tyrhia avoided her gaze. "No," she said.

Looking at her sister, Salustra was suddenly struck by an idea. "After all, thou art a princess, Tyrhia," she said briskly, "and must marry wherever it is politic. We live and marry not for ourselves, but for Atlantis." She quickly turned back the unspoken query. "I myself shall never marry. A queen can only reign alone. But thy children shall rule Atlantis."

With a flash of insight, Salustra had seen a way to save Atlantis for Lazar's line.

Not quite heeding her sister, her mind preoccupied with her party, Tyrhia stood at the window briefly and shuddered as a distasteful odor flooded into the gallery with a shift in the breeze. "When will it leave? My air-cooling device no longer works, and it becomes too humid to move a finger."

Salustra gave her an ironical smile. "And the aircraft, the ships of the sea, the pumps, the land wagons, the wireless, telesound, all things that depend on the electrical vibrations in the atmosphere, what of these, child? Does it not trouble thee that none of these work since the great cloud came?"

The Princess pouted prettily. "I am more concerned about my toilet," said she, "than the greatest ship at sea."

Salustra looked at her sister as if she were seeing her totally for the first time. "Dost thou put thy little conveniences ahead of thy proper concerns as one next to the throne?"

The Princess stifled a yawn. "Oh, sister mine, thou art but a handful of years older than I, and with the rejuvenation chamber, wilt go on forever." She frowned. "Besides, this is a mere atmospheric condition, and will pass soon. All say as much."

Salustra bit her lip. Her own propaganda, meant to quiet her people, ironically had boomeranged in the royal household. For a moment, she had the impulse to reveal her own vague uneasiness and that of her ministers, but one look at that vapid face convinced her that it would serve no useful purpose. Not for long did Tyrhia's thoughts stray from pleasures and comforts.

5

THE ROYAL Palace stood upon an eminence in a great park, with luxurious hanging gardens, replete with statues and fountains and small artificial lakes fed by Lamora's canals. From its south colonnade, a broad road ran from the great gates to the ocean moat. The road, over a mile long, provided a clear view of the ocean from the colonnade. Salustra had added a gallery to one of the upper floors, and here she often sought solitude.

While she carefully watched over Tyrhia, she was grateful they had different mothers. Her mother, Maxima, came of an older, more distinguished family than even her father's. Lazar, a warrior Noble from the Fifth Province, had been adopted by the childless Emperor Clito. Lazar came of a melancholy strain and Salustra sometimes wondered whether her growing ennui was part of his legacy.

Tonight her mood was more somber than usual. Having obtaining the guest list from a rebellious Tyrhia, she sent messages to the older and more sophisticated guests at the birthday party, bidding them remain after the younger fry had left.

It had occurred to her, disconcertingly, that she had no companion to share the later hours. She was almost tempted to recall Lustri. He had the faculty of arousing her to a superlative degree if she made her mind a perfect blank. She abandoned the thought with a sigh. How predictably tiresome he was. Then, who else? Mentally, she ran her eye over the guest roll, and her mouth drooped in distaste. Too young, too old, too anemic, too fat, too unsophisticated, too cynical, too ignorant, too desiccated by learning. Her mind even more than her body had to be intrigued, at least in the beginning.

She left the gallery for the banquet in bad humor. Fifty guests were awaiting the Empress' arrival in the ante-chamber leading to the grand ballroom. Most were young, sons and daughters of Nobles and friends of Tyrhia. These included the sons of Cicio, King of Dimtri, and the children of Patus, King of Nahi. The young men were in white tunics, cinched at the waist with golden girdles. The young women were in translucent robes, through which shapely limbs gleamed with a subtle sensuality. The older guests, all men, were grave in their purple togas. They talked seriously among themselves, while glancing occasionally in amused indulgence at the callow young men. The young women received a more searching scrutiny, as practiced eyes appraised the gentle swell of a maidenly breast or sweetly enticing thigh.

In the midst of this byplay, the great bronze door at the end of the chamber opened softly, and the Empress, alone, unattended, stood in the high arched doorway. The corridor behind her was dim, but the blazing light from within struck her with a dazzling effect. She wore a long trailing robe of brilliant gold, bunched about her waist with a gem-studded sash. Her hair was entirely concealed by a close-fitting helmet, from which twelve golden spikes sprang some two feet. The dark brilliance of her eyes and the voluptuous red of her mouth stood out in the cold pallor of her face.

Though they had seen their Empress many times, the guests stared in admiring awe. It was almost as though the goddess Sati had made an appearance. With every movement, every gesture, her person blazed like the very sun itself.

At the banquet tables, the seating was such that each man had a maiden at either hand. Salustra had arranged, with an eye to the midnight festivities, that the jaded tastes of the older guests might throb with the anticipation that the downy-haired maidens would be counted on to arouse in them; to be later gratified by more experienced females than these unsophisticated adolescents.

The older men were plainly bored with the younger men, but obviously enjoyed the young women, making a game of teasing and fondling them, as though it were an impersonal tribute from those detached by the disparity of years. The wine was weak, cooled with glittering cubes of ice. Rare pheasants, roasted in wine-flavored sauce, tongues of nightingales, sturgeon from the north, exotic fruits, olives, golden cakes, tiny fish in their own oil, and scented sweetmeats were brought in on heavily laden platters by beautiful slaves nude from the waist up.

Tyrhia sat opposite her sister at the main table, her voice a trifle shrill with excitement, as she bantered archly with a young man next to her, from time to time playfully slapping a too bold and experimental hand.

Salustra sat impassively in her chair. She smiled perfunctorily, and with a visible effort. She confined most of her remarks to Mahius, who sat at her left.

She spoke to him in an undertone, not wanting the others to overhear. "What do thy geologists and astronomers say of this cursed mist?"

"My scientists?" The minister sighed.

"Do not quibble," she snapped.

"Frankly, Majesty, like all who are confused, they talk a lot, without saying much. Molanti, the geologist, points out that this mist appeared a few days after a mysterious earth tremor to the north, picked up by the seismographs at the Geological Institute.

"In establishing a connection between that quake and the mist, Molanti believes he may yet account for the power failure."

She muttered darkly to herself. "Theories, always theories. Tell Molanti it is answers we need. And if he solves this mystery, I shall see that he is accorded the rare privilege of the rejuvenation chamber."

Mahius sighed heavily. "Are you so certain, Majesty, that this prolongation of life is a proper reward for such meritorious service?"

She smiled slyly. "Molanti, though a scientist, will consider this boon of youth worth more than a dozen palaces or the greenest grove. What do scientists know of life?"

"What do any of us know, Majesty?"

She smiled practically. "We know that life will be insufferable if we do not soon learn why the electricity normally conveyed through the atmosphere has dissipated." She drew her lips together reflectively. "What says the physicist Goleta? He already has earned nomination for the Temple Beautiful for his discovery of the health ray."

"Majesty, Goleta reports that the atmosphere is so lacking that the experimental electromagnetic signals he sends out produce not even the slightest static."

Salustra showed signs of mounting irritation. "Do not these fools know that we cannot long live in this primitive manner? We are not barbarians like the Althrustri."

Mahius shrugged as he pushed away his food, untasted. "Underrate not these barbarians, Majesty. They have the nuclear atmosphere-changer, and they will use it, if they can."

Salustra looked at him thoughtfully. "So you have said, but it may not even go off in this deadened atmosphere."

Mahius' face turned gray. "But can we take the chance, Majesty?"

She clenched her teeth, thinking of the treachery that had given Signar this weapon. "To turn against one's own country, it is unspeakable. Yet I am ever pleasantly surprised when a friend does not betray me." She put out a hand reassuringly as Mahius flinched. "They shall pay, either at my hand or Signar's. No ruler trusts him who betrays his own people."

"They are so numerous, Majesty."

"Yes, the rotten apple is not worth saving."

He laughed mirthlessly. "Thou dost agree with the High Priestess Jupia, who prophesies some terrible catastrophe."

The Empress snorted. "That old crone. She has been preaching doomsday ever since Sati closed her womb. How else can she express her frustrations?"

Her eyes ran over the glittering assemblage, lingering on the distinguished Nobles and Senators grouped around tables that had been lowered so that the feasting guests could sit or recline comfortably. They seemed oblivious of the multiplying threats to their country's very existence. Masking an expression of disgust, she turned back to Mahius. "What else say these scientists of thine?"

Mahius shrugged. "Goleta and Molanti agree that the recent tremor was responsible for not only this accursed heaviness in the air but certain erratic movements in the ocean tides, which may affect all electric output before long."

Salustra laughed bleakly.

"As any can see—" she pointed to slaves waving heavy fronds "—the palace cooling system has already stopped functioning." She rested her chin in her hand. "Knowest thou for sure whether this atom-breaker was exploded underground or in the atmosphere?"

He nodded soberly. "I cannot be sure, Majesty, but even underground, it still might generate enough heat to thaw the frozen sea and send it tumbling down on our heads."

She shook her head. "My scientists tell me that the subterranean earth mass safely contains an atomic blast and the ensuing radiation, but in the atmosphere there is a continuous chain reaction, with ever more heat and energy building up until the very skies take fire."

Mahius gave an expressive shrug. "As thou knowest, the Atlantean atmosphere-changer was used but once, on an invading army of marauding dinosaurs. They not only vanished, but the vast territory they foraged vanished with them."

Her brows knit together. "And how long ago was this, Mahius?"

"Many centuries, Majesty."

"And we have not used one since."

"We are too civilized, Majesty."

She made a wry face. "Not civilized, Mahius, decadent, degenerate, cowardly. We cannot stand the thought of inflicting death on millions, yet is it not as horrible to kill but one person? If that one life is of no importance, then a million times naught is no more important."

As usual when he sat long, the Minister's tired eyes became bleary and his gray head began to nod.

Tyrhia had looked up brightly from the young man so free with his hands.

"So solemn, Salustra, on my birthday?"

The incongruity of Tyrhia's demeanor, in the face of a very real national danger, nettled Salustra more than she would have thought. "How like her mother," she found herself thinking, even while admiring her brittle prettiness.

Before Salustra could frame a reply, a smoking brazier was thrust before her. She poured a goblet of wine upon it in honor of Sati. The fragrance of the perfumed libation hung in the warm atmosphere, as the shapely slaves, glistening in their nudity, moved on light feet to serve the guests.

Salustra continued to talk seriously to Mahius. She drank little of the weak wine, and then only with a wry mouth. "Thou wilt remain for the later feast, Mahius?"

He looked at the Empress with pleading eyes. "There will be women later, of course, Majesty?"

Salustra's lip curled a little, and she inclined her head. "No righteous virgins; no women with weak wine in their veins. But there will be females, I assure thee, Mahius."

Mahius looked at her directly, and there was something in that steadfast regard that caused her to drop her eyes.

She glanced around the room, at the older men, scientists, philosophers, writers, engineers, musicians, sculptors, dramatists. Already these distinguished men were bored by the simpering maidens on either side, especially as all their overtures had met with embarrassed giggles and shrinking withdrawals. The maidens did not shrink so obviously from the younger men, not even when a casual hand dropped to a soft breast. The elders began to talk soberly over the heads of the maidens, and to count the hours with impatience.

Noticing all this, Salustra smiled to herself, looking to an early end of Tyrhia's phase of the party.

"Thou wilt remain?" she insisted in that low and languid voice.

Mahius gave a troubled sigh. "Will it displease thy Majesty if I should refuse? I am very tired of late. I have a premonition of approaching disaster. I am not superstitious, but there is something in the air, something sinister. No, no! No human foe, no human danger, not this time. Forgive my drivelings, great Salustra. The forewarnings of those artful astrologers have always aroused in me the deepest ridicule. No, no! It is something else, something most awful . . ."

Salustra looked at him with incredulous eyes. Her bosom rose, as though with suppressed laughter. "With what childish fear we cower in the shelter of the known, hiding from the cold winds of the unknown! A thousand legions could not disturb thy iron equanimity, Mahius, but the first breath from the black and icy cavern of superstition freezes the very marrow in thy bones! Bah! I have a most efficacious powder which my physician hath given me. It is a splendid laxative; it stirs up the bowels like the lash of a whip. Religion and her twin, superstition, are naught but the phantoms of a sluggish liver, Mahius!"

Mahius winced but made no reply.

She touched his arm lightly. "There are three times in a man's life when he believes in the gods, Mahius. When he is a child, when well fed, and when he is old. Thou art old, dear friend. Thy blood no longer runs swift and hot; thy eye no longer wanders to virginal bosoms and young lips. Music fails to stir thee; thou wouldst return to thy books and to the grave contemplation of thy gods. The man who tells himself that he is old is old, no matter how few his years: the white-haired grandsire who assures himself that he is young is truly young."

Mahius looked at her almost sadly. "I am old, Majesty," he said quietly, "and thou are eternally young. Perhaps it is because I am old that I am afraid, that I feel something insidious in the air. Age is always apprehensive, I know. But when I look at thee, I am affrighted. It is as though I see a huge shadow over thee. Thou knowest how I love thee, and how I loved thy father, and thou canst judge how thought of danger to thee fills me with dread and confusion. Fear! I, who have never felt fear before, fear now, and its icy wind causes my teeth to chatter and my heart to chill." So earnest, so urgent was his voice that the quiet smile faded from Salustra's lips.

She reacted defiantly, affected more than she would admit. "Fear!" she said contemptuously. "Sati, I believe, can find it possible to forgive the fool, the adulterer, the liar and the traitor. She may even find extenuating circumstances for the hypocrite, for where is there one of us but is forced to dissemble in some manner? But I doubt that she can forgive the coward, who fills the dim and lofty halls of heaven with his pusillanimous cries and disturbs the most high Herself with his craven bleatings. And I, have I ever feared? Nay, fear hath never touched me with her shriveling hand. I come not of the blood of cowards, my Mahius!"

She touched her minister upon the cheek with the back of her hand, and then, as her mood swiftly changed, she experienced a sudden wave of melancholy. "This city, I loathe it, and I am weary. Dost know why those barbarian envoys of Signar's have requested a special audience tomorrow?"

Mahius' gray brows contracted in deep thought.

Salustra spread out her hands with a careless gesture. "I would like thee to come to my apartments for a few moments. These children will not miss us."

She would have risen had not her eye suddenly been caught by another's. A young man, of twenty-seven or eight, perhaps a trifle younger than herself, was peering at her intently over the brim of a goblet, from the far end of the table. She had never seen him before. As their eyes held, she saw a finely molded head and sensitive blue eyes. As she gazed at him, he put down the goblet slowly, revealing a straight, sculptured nose and a strong, yet delicate mouth. Her eye quickly took in the sturdy throat, wide shoulders, bare, sinewy arms and artistic hands. She studied him with a sense of growing excitement, and he returned her gaze breathlessly, yet with an air of confidence. She looked again at his face, and he smiled, inclining his head respectfully. He had an air of distinction so different from the youth of Lamora.

Mahius had been watching this little drama with a

sense of weariness. He looked at the young man and frowned.

Salustra leaned back in her chair. A faint smile touched her lips. Her breast rose quickly with quickened breath. She was herself again.

"That, radiant Majesty, is a cousin of Cicio, King of Dimtri," anticipated Mahius in a dry voice. "He beseeched me only this morning to request an interview for him. He is a poet of great renown in his country, and he seeks thy patronage, knowing thou art a devotee of the arts. His name is Erato."

Salustra nodded slowly, keeping her eyes on the poet, who was now smiling quizzically. He lifted his goblet to his lips again, and on his hand a great ruby, like a ribald eye, winked brightly at her. Salustra smiled. "He must remain for the later banquet, Mahius. We are always willing to serve Poetry, expecially when she hath so gallant and handsome an advocate."

Salustra now rose, and the startled guests rose with her. She made a gesture with her jeweled hand. "We shall return," she said and glided from the chamber, followed by the old minister. The poet smiled, and nervously drummed on the table with his fingers.

6

FAR BELOW lay the city. The streets were veiled in a yellowish gloom through which the lofty domes and tall pillars gleamed grotesquely in the obscure moonlight. It was a city of illusion, its distant confines hidden by the thick curtain that hung over the city like a pall. The air was hot, motionless, languid, causing men to breathe laboriously in a depressed atmosphere and the animal life to scurry about in aimless apprehension.

Mahius, wondering at this sudden conference, glanced furtively at the Empress. Her profile held the eye with its pride and strength. She began to speak uncertainly, in a low voice, as though in a dream. "Wert thou ever afflicted with this strange emotion, Mahius? I am not a fanciful woman, or a morbid one. But I feel an awful sense of fatality upon me; the world has receded into unreality and illusion. I am a shadow moving amongst shadows."

Mahius was silent for a moment, and then he replied quietly: "I have felt so often myself. Life fluctuates, flows, ebbs, comes from the shadows and returns to them. Only the gods remain, ever present and eternal."

Salustra gave a weary gesture. "Bah! Gods! To think that in this world today, this ribald, jeering and cynical world, there should be some that believe that the great Unknown has cognizance of us! Only the frail, the feeble, the cowardly can have such faith. Faith is the trademark of the pusillanimous. Unable to fight life adequately, they feel the need of a supernatural ally, compelled to encase themselves in armor against a predatory world; otherwise raw and violent life would be unendurable. Some armor themselves with faith, and hide behind the shadowy image

67

of the gods. Some encase themselves in philosophy, and look with a tranquil eye upon the combat, disdaining, however, to take part in it. Some arm themselves with cynicism and refuse to believe anything, even that they do not believe anything. Some saturate themselves with sentiment and observe life through deliciously maudlin tears. Some arm themselves with the stern ax of a self-inflicted duty, and call themselves brave when they are merely acquiescent. Nearly all justify life in terms of empty platitudes. If man did not lie to himself he could not live."

Mahius looked at her kindly. "Thou art so young to have reached so final a conclusion, Salustra. But when thou art older thou wilt no longer feel so keenly. Thou wilt accept life tranquilly, without fear and without hope. The small child and the old man are the wisest philosophers."

Salustra shrugged. "We need no armor against life, no philosophy," she said somewhat sullenly. Then she laughed shortly. "We need truth. But what is true and what is false? What is brave and what is cowardly? What is vice, and what virtue? All we know is that we are here, and that tomorrow we shall be gone. From whence we came, and whither we go, no man can tell. Like shadows we come, like shadows we go, and the familiar places know us no more. When man speaks of the gods, he babbles like a monkey at the moon."

Mahius bowed and relapsed into silence. But his eyes were sad. Salustra began her pacing on the colonnade. She halted abruptly and spoke in her usual imperative manner. "Tomorrow the ambassadors of Althrustri speak confidentially with me. I already know their errand, though I did not let on before. They bring a suit from their Emperor, seeking my hand in marriage. If it would save Atlantis, I would accept, much as I shudder at the thought of contact with that barbarian. But it would not save her. He would be Emperor of both nations."

Mahius looked at her in mute distress. She lifted her hand as though to prevent him from speaking. "He is thinking of his sons, yet unborn," she went on. "He covets Atlantis for their heritage. Even the most ambitious men are mere tools in the grip of biological forces. And, indeed, I admire him for it. It is inevitable that the blood of Signar be in the veins of the man who will one day sit upon the throne of my country. I am content; I hold no grudge against him. The sun sets; tomorrow a new sun rises in the east. It is natural and inevitable, and who am I to quarrel with nature?"

Mahius was plainly puzzled by this new turn of events.

"I repeat, he desires Atlantis for his sons, as well as himself," went on the Empress calmly. "They shall have it, but only when I am dead. While I live, Atlantis is mine. But how shall I prevent war that would wipe out our world? Simple, my friend! I shall give Signar my sister Tyrhia in marriage. Their oldest son shall inherit Atlantis, provided that I have Signar's solemn oath that the two empires be not combined during my lifetime."

She looked up and saw Mahius regarding her with narrowed eyes. She tapped him lightly on the arm. "Come, thou hast something to say, dear friend and teacher. Fear not. What is it?"

The minister spoke in a low but urgent voice. "I too, have my spies. They tell me that Signar desires one thing even above Atlantis."

"And what may that be?"

He wet his lips, and then said simply, "Thee."

Salustra's face went rigid with indignation, then broke into a jeering smile. "Thou poor old man!" she exclaimed. "Thy senility is indeed upon thee! He desires me only because I am Empress of Atlantis, and through me he hopes to conquer painlessly. I, too, have my spies. They tell me how Signar makes jest of me, and they speak of the ribald stories he enjoys about me." She shrugged. "I tell thee, dear old foolish friend, that he desires only Atlantis. And when he sees my innocent and virginal Tyrhia, he will be only too glad to take her."

Mahius' air of not being convinced irritated Salustra. "I have never seen him, but I loathe him! Althrustri is a fierce and backward land. And Signar is fit Emperor of it. But it is a virile land. I shall be glad that the son of Signar shall inherit Atlantis peacefully." She leaned over the marble balustrade and her eyes grew soft for a moment. "My country!" she murmured. "My splendid and decaying heritage! I shall rest in my grave, secure in the knowledge that thy corruption is preserved, that thy incontinence shall continue."

She sighed. "My father told me that when a nation reaches a certain stage of gilded rottenness it is afflicted with all the depraved appetites of a morally and mentally perverted man. And at that time it is feverish for new sensations. Thus, some look to an alien leader like Signar, others prattle of a freedom they label democracy. Bah! The very name *democracy* is a denial in terms. Men are never fundamentally democratic. Nature herself makes them unequal. A republic is the most autocratic form of government. One monarch is preferable to a multiple monarchy of rapacious men, who, having but a short time in office, rob and ravage with feverish dexterity and without scruple. Atlantis has reached the stage where she is beginning to think of a republic out of boredom. Loud is the expression of love for me, but let the wind blow strongly enough in the direction of republicanism, they would spill my blood with the same cheerfulness with which they now hail me. Signar is not as patient as I. He will give these democrats short shrift."

Mahius began to speak gently, hoping to penetrate Salustra's shell. "Didst thou say thou wilt never marry, Salustra?"

She shook her head impatiently. "There is no season for marriage even if I willed it. If I should marry a prince of Dimtri, Nahi, Madura, Antilla or Letus, my children would become the Emperors of Atlantis. And Signar would not endure that. He wants what he wants now. Besides, I have no desire to marry. Why should I?"

"And thou hast no desire for love, Majesty? Only in love do we approach the gods. Love explains all things, interprets all things, is the keystone of all things. Love is life. I would not have thee miss that!"

Salustra laughed with genuine enjoyment. She tapped the old man playfully. "Poor Mahius!" she exclaimed. "What hast thou now? A delicious slave girl from the Island of Lusi? And has thou found in her arms what thou hast not found in the arms of thy old wife? Go to! When a man speaks of love, he is not thinking of his lawful spouse!" Her laughter ceased suddenly and her lip curled. "Love is the greatest force in the world, so say the sentimentally ignorant. Nay, I say that hatred is omnipotent—hatred, the ruler of all destiny, vigorous, fiery, gratifying. Love is death; hatred is life. When a nation begins to drool of love, she is in her dotage. Love is parasitic; all hatred enterprising, ambitious. Hatred builds new empires. Love, by weakening the logic, destroys them. Hatred is the conquering warrior; love, the camp follower. If I could do so, I would raise a temple to hatred. When nations loudly prate of their love for each other, they are secretly sharpening their swords. When men and women speak together of love, they are merely attiring naked lust in becoming modesty."

Mahius kept his eyes on the floor throughout this tirade, until Salustra finally began to speak of other things. "The day after tomorrow, the National Assembly meets," said the Empress. "It will be a wearisome day. Those old Senators, quarrelsome and petty! They all have a personal ax to sharpen, and a private coffer to fill, and they talk of patriotism and a desire to serve the people. Why cannot they be honest?"

"If they were honest, they would not trust themselves," said Mahius dryly.

"My father used to say: 'Art thou honest? If thou dost answer yes, I will call thee a liar!'" She smiled. "If we were entirely honest, we would find life insupportable. We need a delicately colored mist to soften the hard and naked crags of truth."

A laughing murmur was heard below in the gardens. Litters were arriving for the young guests. The two were suddenly aware that time had passed rapidly. Still Salustra lingered. She looked at the heavens. Mahius' eyes followed hers. Even as they watched, an ominous cloud, shaped like an enormous hand with hooked fingers, approached the hazy moon. So like a human hand was the cloud that Salustra and Mahius were involuntarily startled. They watched, almost breathlessly. Slowly the cloud-hand lifted, reached upward; and before their astonished eyes, the fingers curled, the wrist twisted, and the fingers stretched like rapacious talons. A moment later it had clutched the pale outline of the moon, and the moon vanished completely behind its curtain of mist. A chilling breath of air caused them to shiver momentarily. A dark shadow, in the shape of an enormous hooked hand, passed over the city.

Salustra tried to smile, to force a gay word past her lips. But no sound came from them.

Silently, preoccupied with their own dark thoughts, they went into the Palace. In the marble corridor stood her Prefect of the Guards, that handsome and vigorous young man who, it was rumored, had served the Empress well during the dark lonely hours. Abstracted, she favored him with the same glance she would a useful piece of furniture, and moved on with an absorbed air. She arrived in time to bid farewell to the youthful guests. Tyrhia was frankly weary, the white flowers looking wilted on her touseled head. Meanwhile, additional guests were already arriving, Senators, Nobles and others from the idle aristocracy of Lamora. Salustra bade her sister a perfunctory good-night and then looked for the young poet, Erato. As her eyes found his, Mahius again begged permission to retire, and Salustra carelessly gave her consent. There were fifty men already present, including some earlier guests and the young poet who had been especially bidden to remain.

Wreaths of red roses, fresh with the evening dew, were placed in fun upon the heads of the guests. Salustra's shrewd eye traveled over each face. They all said something to her. Fat Senators, with lascivious mouths and puffy eyes, exchanged obscene quips and looked boldly about them. The semi-nude slaves had been replaced by a crew of totally nude nymphets of surpassing beauty, their fair hands appearing almost too delicate for their task of filling and refilling the goblets of shimmering wine.

There were as many of these slim, rosy-skinned sirens as there were guests, and they blushed occasionally at the unmistakable attentions of these lecherous elders.

There was something forced about the festal mood, for there were none there, not even the plotting Senator Divona, who could lift themselves totally out of the depression that the stifling mist seemed to lay over the city. They had been flung into confusion by the sudden disruption of electrical facilities and were increasingly concerned by the dark forecasts of the astrologers.

But now all took their cue from the Empress. For though many secretly hated her, she was still the hub around which all revolved. They saw that she was apparently unconcerned, immersed in a new admirer, and they took heart. Salustra was very conscious of all this. By her command the poet Erato sat at the right hand of the Empress. At her other hand sat Pellanius, ambassador-in-chief to Althrustri. Erato's hand trembled as he lifted his goblet to his lips, his eyes never leaving Salustra.

Salustra had thrown off her golden robe; she was now revealed to be almost nude, except for breast plates of delicate gold filigree and a scanty golden garment about her hips. Her body glistened like marble under the changing lights from an overhead crystal. Her headdress with its twelve points glowed radiantly. There was no nymphet in the room, however young and beautiful, whose face or form could rival the Empress! She was a perfect expression of seductive femininity, appearing suddenly unattainable in her regal splendor.

The air became heavy with perfume and the aroma of food and drink. The laughter of the guests became louder. Some men sprawled on divans, ogling the passing nymphets, their wreaths awry over sweating foreheads. Occasionally, a beautiful slave sprayed them with fragrant perfumes, which lent an additional heaviness to the humid air.

Salustra had, as yet, exchanged but few words with Erato, but she leaned toward him from time to time, and smiled to see how he quivered as her bare thigh brushed against his hand.

The Noble Gatus was speaking, his mouth twisted with humor, his eyes dancing. "Listen to this!" he shouted. "I vouch on my word of honor that it is true."

Salustra laughed. "Art thou certain thou hast a word of honor, Gatus? Thou wert willing to sell thy province today, if I remember rightly."

Gatus scowled, then quickly regained his gaiety. "I have heard this story from one in a position to know. It seems that Seneco, that old swindler of a jeweler, became much enamored of the beautiful young bride of a noble in Lamora. She shall be nameless, of course. Her husband is very devoted, but somewhat abstracted at times. No! Ask me not who she is! It seems that one day she was in Seneco's shop, and he displayed an entrancing diamond anklet for her delectation. She was immediately fascinated. She slipped it on a delicate ankle, and Seneco assured her that it was designed with such an ankle in view. At last, with a sigh, she confessed that she could not buy it; her husband had told her that she had sufficient jewels for any woman."

A gray-haired man with his wreath dropped over one eye stood up drunkenly. "What cruelty!" exclaimed Pellanius. "Whisper the name of the lady to me, and I shall buy the anklet for her. Youth should be adorned with jewels."

Pellanius sat down to shouts of silence and Gatus was urged to continue. "The poor girl was indeed grief-stricken," Gatus went on, smiling. "She wept in Seneco's arms, and allowed him to manually explore the supple softness of her body. At length he told her how tenderly he adored her. He importuned her to allow him to bring the anklet to her home the next day, when her husband was absent on business. The girl hesitated coyly. She murmured something about virtue and matronly chastity; Seneco convinced her that diamonds had greater permanence than chastity."

There was another interruption. "Bah! No woman is worth a diamond," said the Senator Divona, who had once aspired to the Empress and, having been rejected, never lost an opportunity to deride her sex in her presence. "A bit of crystal, a delicate turquoise, perhaps, but not a diamond. Women are too easy to come by."

Salustra smiled indolently. She laid her hand negligently on Erato's shoulder, and he kissed it solemnly. She brought her goblet to his lips, bade him drink, then drank herself. The young man shivered with delight. Salustra motioned for Gatus to get on with his story.

"Finally," Gatus continued, "the young matron consented that old Seneco might visit her the next day. He came, full of love and wine, bearing the anklet. An hour later he left, minus the anklet, and some of his ardor." He chuckled. "That night, the husband returned home. The lady had discreetly hidden the bauble. However, looking at her sharply, the husband asked if Seneco had visited her that afternoon and had left an anklet for her. She confessed the visit, full of terror, not knowing how he had guessed her secret. She would have thrown herself at his feet and begged for mercy but was paralyzed with fright. Not seeing this, however, the husband explained with smiles and caresses that he himself had bought the anklet for her the day before, and that Seneco had promised to deliver it to the lady in person today!"

The gale of laughter that ensued caused the overhead lamps to vibrate. The Empress joined in gaily, enjoying the story more than most because it confirmed her belief that treachery was a popular commodity. "These women!" shouted Pellanius. "But it is not often that we can trick them that way! I'll wager the lady does not often wear the anklet in public."

Other stories followed, becoming more ribald as the wine circulated. Some guests had captured the slave girls, and playfully held them prisoner on the silken divans, kissing them awkwardly as they twisted in their captors' arms. Great laughter followed when a doughty young girl, resisting certain liberties, deliberately poured a goblet of wine over the old Senator Contani. The wine dripped over his sodden face, and he shook his head like an old boar to clear his glazed eyes.

"Spit him!" shouted Patios, the youngest Senator. "We shall then have pork in the Palace tomorrow!" The party progressed. A singer, a man of effeminate beauty, emerged from an alcove and began to sing an obscene lyric. When the singer retired to considerable applause, Patios stepped forward to take his place. But upon being drenched in turn with a bowl of wine, he retired with drunken dignity to a fountain in the center of the room. Amid shouts of laughter, he solemnly stepped into the pool, ardently embracing one of the marble statues.

"He thinks she is his wife," remarked Divona in a scornful voice.

"The statue is more responsive than she," muttered Noble Glarus aloud.

In the midst of this revelry, the Prefect of the Guard appeared suddenly at the side of the Empress. He held a roll of parchment in his hand and was apparently ill at ease. "I am sorry to disturb thy Majesty," he said in an undertone. "But this was left with urgent supplications that it be delivered at once."

With a frown, Salustra unrolled the paper. She gave a sharp exclamation. It was from the disgraced Lustri.

"When thou dost read this, illustrious Salustra, thy poor Lustri will be dead. When thou didst dismiss him from thee, thou didst dismiss him from life. I have chosen the wiser part; to live without thy smile is worse than death. Memory would be torment. I leave thee now. Perhaps thou wilt have one last thought of kindness for me."

The hand that held the message was steady and strong. "Lustri is dead, the fool!" she exclaimed.

A pall suddenly fell over the gathering. The guests looked at each other uneasily, avoiding the Empress' gaze.

Gatus, kinsman to Lustri, rose at last, his face white and his eyes flashing. "Thou wilt allow me to retire, Majesty?" he said, his voice trembling. "Lustri was my bride's brother."

The uneasiness deepened. Only Salustra appeared amused. She allowed Gatus to stand for several moments before she replied. "Go if thou likest," she said carelessly. The others suddenly sobered, looked about uncertainly.

"Thou wilt permit him a public funeral?" said the Noble Glarus hesitantly.

She fixed Glarus with a frown. "Why should I deny him a public funeral? Dost think I fear the mob of Lamora? I prefer their open enmity to sly whispers that I ordered a private funeral because I feared them. Go to, Glarus!"

The chill that had fallen over the festivities lifted.

"At dawn, thou shalt whisper thy poems to me in secret," murmured Salustra to Erato.

Lustri was already forgotten, and the malicious gossip continued.

"Has anyone seen the house Consilini is building for his mistress in the suburb of Conla?" demanded the Senator Sicilo. "It is a villa of extreme delicacy, and he is lavishing his fortune upon it. They say Galo is furnishing the statues, and Stanti the frescoes. The gardens are little gems of beauty. I asked him today why he lavished all that on one woman, and he replied that his wife objects to his maintaining his mistresses in the city, so to oblige her he is building the villa as temporary residence for his various loves. They say he is tired of Guhliana, and is looking for a likely successor. Brittulia perhaps."

Noisy laughter and obscene comments greeted this sly reference. Brittulia was a notorious virgin, a beautiful young woman of Salustra's age. She was said to shudder at the approach of a man. Her house was a tomb in which she moved among her women slaves. No male was allowed upon the premises. Some wags declared that she ate meat only from female animals. "I have heard that she will eat only vegetables whose female sex can be proved," said Utanlio, the Noble from the Third Province.

"I heard she discards garments that have brushed against men in public places," said Glarus. "She cannot even endure eunuchs, and sold the one her mother had left to her."

"She is a female eunuch," grunted Divona.

"How canst thou prove that?" demanded Patios. He had removed his wet tunic, and now lay naked on the pink breast of a nude girl.

"She is a beautiful woman," said Pellanius thoughtfully. "But she turns pale at the sight of a man. I have seen that myself. It is not affectation."

"Perhaps she dare not trust herself," said Salustra. "I have invited her to my feasts, and she begged me upon her knees not to insist upon her presence. I rallied her a little, telling her she would never taste full delight until she slept in a man's arms. She fainted away."

"Poor soul," said Erato, bidding for Salustra's approval. "She has suppressed her inner and secret fires until they are consuming her."

All seemed to enjoy ridiculing the poor virgin for a lack of virtue. "Women like that are fearful and unbridled courtesans at heart," said Patios. "They are afraid of themselves. They can maintain their virtue only by strict seclusion. If they could ever be induced to surrender their chastity, their appetites would slay them."

"Sometime I shall invite her to the Palace and trick her into a walled and soundless chamber with an ardent young man," said Salustra. "And then let the men of Lamora beware afterward!"

They laughed uproariously. The name of the chaste Brittulia continued to be bandied about for some little time.

"We must not call to her attention that she herself is the result of spontaneous conception. Otherwise, she will commit suicide," said the Noble Utanlio.

"Perhaps she believes she is air-born, like Nehlia," said Erato, referring to the chaste female deity of his country.

Salustra shrugged. "There is nothing viler than a deliberately chaste woman," she said. "Their spiritual unchastity is revolting."

They continued to drink. The nude girls no longer waited upon the guests but sat or lay next to them, suiting the guests' pleasure. Salustra leaned casually on the breast of Erato, her eyes half closed, her red mouth curved in a sensuous smile.

The Empress lifted a languid hand, and the banquet hall was plunged into darkness. The soft whispers of women mingled seductively with the excited panting of men. The orgy had begun, but without the Empress. Salustra had disappeared, and Erato with her.

7

SALUSTRA still reclined upon her couch, though it was nearly noon. Deep shadows lay under her eyes, her face was drawn, her lips almost colorless in the remorseless light of day. She lifted her hand in languid acknowledgment of the High Priestess Jupia's obeisance. Jupia was an extremely tall woman. She did not seem to possess the body of a woman, so straight and spare were the lines of her figure. She wore a headdress of crimson silk, which entirely concealed her gray hair and framed a gaunt face with expressionless steel-blue eyes. She held her hands concealed in the wide, gold-banded sleeves of her red robes. She was attended by two virgins in blue robes. The obeisance she gave the Empress had in it a contemptuous deference, as though her spirit protested the honor. Salustra listlessly giving permission, Jupia seated herself near the Empress' couch, her virgin escort standing motionless behind her chair.

"I grant thee fifteen minutes, Jupia," said the Empress coldly. "So get to the point."

A slave girl stood behind the Empress, waving a huge fan; another handmaiden knelt beside the couch and brushed Salustra's hair to a lustrous sheen. Another attended her nails, rubbing a perfumed liquid upon the finger tips. Jupia surveyed her mistress with barely concealed disapproval, her eye moving slowly from the beautiful face to the half-naked body.

"What I have to say, Majesty, will not take long," she said stiffly.

Salustra yawned deliberately. "That wine!" she exclaimed. "The grapes must have been breathed upon by Loti. At any rate, her sour breath was evident in it."

Sati, the supreme deity, had a multitude of earthly lovers and offspring. Her children were Loti, queen of the unrepentant dead; the gentle Mayhita, patroness of chaste women and little children; Detria, goddess of the harvest; Parenalia, goddess of earthly love; the virginal Denia, patroness of the arts and sciences; and Iberia, goddess of war and virility. There were three supernatural regions in religious lore. One was Drulla, the place of anguish and fire, over which Loti presided in her castle of flame, attended by her handmaidens, Hatred, Fear, Debauchery and Crime. To that dread abode went the wicked, the unrepentant, the cowards and the traitors. The second region was Crystu, land of spirits who had not finished their work on earth or who, proven worthy, prepared themselves for eternal bliss in the halls of Litia, where they would bask forever in the glorious light of Sati, whose palace was the sun. None falling into the flames and icy blackness of Drulla could ever escape. Few went directly to Litia. Those few were brave and gallant men who died in war, chaste and holy virgins, the High Priestess, women who died in childbirth, and the imperial family. All deities were feminine, but all had earthly lovers, except Denia. Masculinity was never deified. The pontiff was always a woman, her attendants always virgins. She ruled a priesthood of celibate men, and to these subordinates she assigned the lesser duties of cajoling the faithful.

Jupia lived in a dark palace within the shadow of the glittering Temple of Sati. She was never seen upon the streets except closely veiled and in her ceremonial litter. Before her litter walked the priests in their black and crimson robes, their heads bent, their hands folded on their breasts. It was considered a mortal offense to pry with curious eyes into the interior of the litter, and it was the most evil luck to listen, even casually, to the chanting of the priests in public places. Jupia moved in a cloud of superstition and fear. Her priestly attributes were wisdom, symbolized by a staff entwined by a green serpent; chastity, symbolized by the doves that flew unmolested through the temple; and immortality, exemplified by an eternal flame in the temple altar.

All this was so much mumbo jumbo to Salustra, and Jupia well knew this, as she examined the Empress' remark for a hidden meaning.

"The wine was from the grapes in my own garden, great Salustra," said the High Priestess in a sadly reproving tone.

"Then I know that Loti breathed upon them!" exclaimed Salustra with a wry face. "Bah! Do not look so outraged, Jupia. Dost think I am insinuating thou didst poison them for my special benefit?"

Jupia's pale lips moved as though she were intoning a silent prayer.

Salustra gave her an impatient smile. "Art praying for my soul, Jupia? Do not, I implore thee! Loti already hath first claim upon it, and thy prayers will merely heighten the flames. What is thy business with me?"

"What I have to say will not take long, great Salustra," repeated Jupia in a harsh voice. "But thy mighty father was always willing to listen to my prophecies and to my advice. What he did, thou mightst well do."

Salustra inclined her head impatiently without speaking.

"Two nights ago I had an awful dream," went on the Priestess, "but it was more like a vision. The air was hot, sultry, molten—"

"The heat was intense. No wonder thou didst have a bad dream."

For a moment hatred, unconcealed, shone in Jupia's eyes.

"Thy spare diet is enough to give thee a thousand horrors." The Empress yawned.

Jupia's thin hands clenched under her red robe. "I am not given to either horrors or bad dreams, Majesty," she said harshly. "My conscience is clean, my life chaste, my thoughts virtuous, my couch unpolluted—"

"Then I should have your nightmares." Salustra smiled. "But I swear to thee that I sleep like a babe on its mother's bosom."

The two women regarded each other intently, Salustra

faintly smiling, the Priestess rigid and silent. Then Jupia resumed, in a controlled monotone. "The night was sultry. It seemed that I drowsed, and yet in a moment I was awake again, my blood running like ice through my veins." She paused. Salustra made a gesture for her to continue. "And then, in a cloud of light, I saw thy glorious father, the mighty Lazar."

She paused again and gave Salustra a glance.

The Empress lay back on her cushion and yawned once more. "I shall have the walls of his tomb examined," she said dryly.

Jupia's eyes flashed. "I saw him," she repeated. "He was wearing the twelve-pointed crown of Atlantis, and there was a star on each point, glittering like points of flame. His face was majestic, but there were tears in his eyes. The dim light shone on him as it would have shone on a mortal." Her face was pale and she visibly trembled.

Salustra frowned and motioned her to go on.

"I can still hear his voice. It sounded like a voice coming through a thick wall, but every word was recognizable. 'Jupia,' he said, 'I have tried to talk to my beloved daughter, Salustra, but she hears me not. But she feels my presence, the urging of my voice, the touch of my hand. I have talked to her soul; it hears my voice but still cannot accept my presence. That is why she hath been distracted, weary and sad for many days.' "

Salustra raised herself upon her elbow. The smile had gone from her face. She looked at Jupia suspiciously.

The High Priestess did not flinch. "Because he could not make thee hear, he came to me. And he hath a message for thee. As he spoke, he held out his sword, and lo, it was broken off but a few inches below the hilt. And then I looked at his crown, and it was no longer a crown. It was a wreath of roses, and they dripped blood. 'Tell Salustra that such is Atlantis,' he said. 'Tell her that its sword is broken and its crown a faded wreath. Tell her that its hour draws near, and that already the halls of Loti open for it.' "

Salustra's face for a moment revealed something akin to dread. But she said nothing.

Jupia smiled to herself. "He would save thee, he said. But he could tell thee nothing but this: 'When destruction comes from the north, flee east or west.'"

Salustra quickly recovered. She threw back her head and laughed. "Go to! Dost think, Jupia, thou canst frighten me with thy dreams? Tell thy prophecies to the mooning crowds in the temple; frighten them into bringing greater sacrifices to the altar. I wager after such a story thy coffers will ring again."

As though stung, Jupia quickly sprang up. Her tall, gaunt body quivered like a barren tree in a storm. She lifted her hand in a compelling gesture. "I have given thee warning," she said coldly. "I can do no more. My duty is done. Thy fate is with the gods." Without the customary obeisance, she turned abruptly and stalked from the chamber, followed closely by her virgins.

Salustra gave her a scornful glance. "Perfume the air!" she cried to her slaves. "The old crone hath left a stench of death in it!"

True, she had felt the presence of her father at times, but put it down to an active imagination induced by his dying suggestion. She wished for his love, strength and counsel. And so she saw his familiar face and form. It was no more. Drulla, Crystu, Litia—they were all of one's own making.

Salustra had more compelling things to think about. An hour after Jupia's departure, she sat in secret council with the ambassadors from the court of Althrustri. Her ennui was evident in her every look and gesture. And even her trusted councillor, Mahius, appeared to reflect this weariness with diplomatic deviousness.

Tellan, the ambassador-in-chief, was accompanied by his aide, the wily and crafty Zoni. Salustra, watching the pair, smiled faintly. Her hand played with the gem at her throat, and it flashed with a ruby-red glow. The ambassador held a golden casket in his hand, which he extended reverently as he spoke.

Salustra ignored the casket. "Surely the great Signar did not have thee ask for a private interview for the purpose of giving me presents, Tellan. Out with it! What hast thou to say to me?"

Tellan glanced at Zoni, who lifted his brows, then with a bow extended the golden casket to the Empress.

"Our Emperor begs that thou wilt accept this humble gift, which, radiant though it is, cannot approach thy radiance."

"A pretty speech," said Salustra carelessly. "I'll wager Signar did not compose that himself."

She opened the casket and brought out a dazzling collar made of gems. It was composed of hundreds of magnificent stones, perfectly cut, splendidly matched. She lifted the collar and weighed it abstractedly, admiring its rainbow glow. Tellan and Zoni exchanged secret smiles of satisfaction.

"I am incapable of expressing my pleasure at such a gift," she said slowly. She lifted her eyes sardonically. "What does Signar expect for this, my lords?"

Her frankness momentarily disconcerted the ambassadors.

Tellan bowed again, his head dropping to Salustra's shining slipper. "Thy Majesty doth ask an honest question," he murmured. "And it deserves an honest answer." He stood erect and looked at the Empress admiringly. "Thou dost ask what our lord desires, Majesty. He desires thee."

Salustra was silent for a second, remembering now what Mahius had said, then gave a cold and mirthless laugh of contempt. "Thou dost mean he desires Atlantis," she said with a withering look.

"Nay, great Majesty," broke in Zoni eagerly, "he desires only thee. He did say to us, 'I want the beautiful Salustra for my bride; to be my Empress and the mother of my children.'"

Salustra laughed again in derision. "I am only an appendage to the Empire he covets. If I were to offer him Atlantis alone, he would seize it with never a glance for me. Go to! Let us be frank. He is willing to be reasonable and to try a peaceful conquest. But what if I should send him this reply: 'Salustra is flattered and overcome by the honor Signar doth pay her, but she must decline it'? What then, Tellan?"

Tellan smiled coldly, but made no reply.

Salustra toyed languidly with Signar's gift. "And if I should send Signar that reply, it would be war?"

"Did I say so, Majesty?" Tellan asked in a mocking voice.

"No, thou didst merely imply it, Tellan. But come, we made a bargain to be frank. I have known for some time that Signar covets Atlantis, and that it is inevitable that he attempt conquest. He has stolen our atom-breaker, and does not hesitate to use it, thinking we are too civilized to strike first. But can he be sure I might not give the signal that would destroy millions? So he decides upon a peaceful method of gaining the same end. He will marry Salustra! Atlantis intact, not a smoldering ruin to be avoided because of dangerous radiation, will then be his. For such a prize he can even endure the Virgin Empress!"

Tellan's mouth twitched. He looked at Zoni, whose face reflected his own discomfiture.

Salustra saw their concern, and amusement lurked in her eyes. "I should have your heads," she said with a mocking smile.

The silent Mahius gave the envoys a reassuring glance.

"Signar's ambitions are worthy of him," said Salustra, enjoying their surprise. She toyed with the glittering collar on her knee. "He is of the bold blood that makes empires. I could wish no better than that a son of his should sit upon the throne of Atlantis. And so I intend it."

Tellan stared at her incredulously; Zoni's mouth fell open.

The Empress smiled enigmatically. "But I shall not marry him," she continued. "What! Look not so dismayed, my lords!" She leaned forward in her chair. "This is the message you may take to him: The Empress Salustra declines his hand, feeling herself unworthy of the honor. But Salustra offers instead, in marriage, the lovely and gentle Tyrhia. There is a bride worthy of him, a chaste and virginal princess, who will bring no dishonor upon him. Tell him that Salustra will never marry; that no son of hers will wield the scepter over Atlantis; and that she will keep her Empire safe for the son of Signar and Tyrhia."

The ambassadors looked at each other in stupefaction.

Salustra slid back in her chair, and waited with a faint smile.

"That is thy decision, great Empress?" finally cried a baffled Tellan.

Salustra inclined her head. "Let Signar consider my offer well. If he declines, then let it be war. I know that his legions will be mobilized, and the flag of war unfurled."

Zoni raised a protesting hand. "Our lord," he said passionately, "does not desire war with Atlantis. Thou hast been frank; we will be so too. It had been his dream, frankly, as that of his father, to annex Atlantis to Althrustri. He felt the day was inevitable when the two nations would come to a death grapple. He awaited that day. But now Atlantis is no longer his prior desire. Above his desire for conquest, above the joining of the two great nations, he desires thee and thee alone."

Salustra rose impatiently. "Absurd!" she exclaimed. "How doth he know that he desires me? He hath never seen me! Go to!" She would have stepped down from her dais, but Tellan lifted a restraining hand.

"He hath many accounts of thee," he said. "And they have made him desire thee, above all other things, as a regal figure uniquely to his liking."

"The accounts lie," said Salustra contemptuously. "Had they been truthful, he would not desire me."

She would have withdrawn but Tellan's eyes stopped her. "Thy Majesty's decision is final?"

Salustra nodded shortly.

"We have but one thing to add, Majesty," said Tellan. "A messenger arrived today in Lamora to announce the Emperor will arrive three days hence. He will take his answer himself."

Salustra's blandness suddenly deserted her. The color

drained from her face, and she brushed past the envoys without a word. Mahius trailed after her. "He is on the way to Atlantis now, Mahius," she said fiercely. "It is war!"

8

THE National Assembly, composed of Senators and the Commoners and Nobles on the Council, gathered in the huge Hall of Law adjoining the royal Palace. Before the towering bronze doors, under tremendous white columns, stood the two giant lions of Atlantis. So cunningly were these figures carved, so lifelike, so fiery their phosphorescent eyes, that at a distance one could not distinguish them from actual animals of gigantic proportions. Inside the marble dome drooped the scarlet banners of Atlantis, bearing upon them the national coat of arms, crossed swords behind a lion rampant. A rigid line of ceremonial soldiery, helmeted and armored, massed around the circular marble walls. Their captain, the handsome Creto, stood directly behind Salustra's throne.

The Senators sat upon cushioned benches to the right of the Empress. At her left were the twenty-four Commoners and Nobles of the Twelve Provinces, and twenty-four royal Representatives. In ivory chairs between the two groups sat three representatives of the capital, Lamora.

The heat and the haze disturbed them all more than they would acknowledge, but they tried to remain calm and deliberate, as befitted an august body.

The heat was intense, a strange heat, brazen, sultry, smoky. The Noble Gatus spoke of feeling the earth tremble the night before, but he was laughed down. Then Utanlio claimed that if one would listen, the sea had a strange sound, as though a great sea serpent growled beneath the waters. He had heard, also, that the tide had not come in as far as usual for the past few days; indeed, each day it had receded a little farther than the day before. The sun, barely outlined, was surrounded by a smoky ring of fire, and the orb itself was molten brass behind the unusual haze.

While awaiting the Empress, the solons went out onto the portico and stared up at the sky. Some shook their heads and looked uneasy, vaguely recalling an ancient prophecy. One day Sati would become weary of the crimes of Atlantis, and that day she would bid the waters of the sea to roll over it, and the living would know it no more. The aristocrat Contalio mentioned the prophecy, but was shouted down with laughter and ridicule.

"Is it possible that superstition still lingers amongst us?" exclaimed the plebeian Marati.

"Religion could not survive without superstition," said the Senator Tilus, who was also a philosopher of renown.

"Religion!" exclaimed the Senator Vilio. "What religion? We still have its shadow, it is true, but the substance is gone."

Gatus mockingly asked the question that Salustra asked herself so often. "What is truth?"

This question aroused great mirth, signaling as it did the entrance of the Empress.

At a great blare of trumpets, the councillors hastened back to their places. The bronze doors swung open, and Salustra emerged in her purple-and-white ceremonial robes, with the twelve-pointed crown of Atlantis. She moved with a stately step to her throne, Mahius a step behind.

Before she seated herself, a massive slave, naked except for a loin cloth and sporting pendants of linked gold in his ears, knelt before the Empress holding in his hands a brazier of hot coals. Mahius handed a red silken bag to the Empress. It contained portions of finely sifted earth from each of the Twelve Provinces. The assemblage knelt in conventional reverence as the Empress unfastened the bag and poured the contents upon the hot brazier. Immediately a pungent cloud of smoke leaped from the coals, spreading upward like a startled serpent.

The Empress lifted her hand and began to speak.

Every corner of the chamber ran with the sound of her voice. It was a twice-repeated welcoming, traditional for centuries, giving imperial sanction for the Assembly to sit. Then Mahius rose and hesitantly pointed out that the national treasury needed replenishing. He called for proposals. At this, Zanius, the Noble representing Lamora, rose with a plan, a tax on the private income of the owners of mills, factories, shops and ships.

Salustra listened, frowning. "No," she said firmly. "That would be inflicting another injustice on the already overburdened middle class. Who would suffer from such a tax? Not the incompetent and shiftless poor; they are beyond such a tax. Not the independently wealthy, for they are not engaged in industry and trade and manufacturing but live off the investments of the past. As it is, we are becoming a nation of paupers, slaves and enormously wealthy aristocrats. Such a condition cannot long endure without a resulting discontent, chaos, revolution and national disaster."

The subject was closed.

Another Noble confidently rose to lay a petition of a different nature before the Empress, a sweeping law to suppress treason by proclaiming an emergency. Government spies had unearthed widespread plots to overthrow Salustra and create a republic.

Salustra's lips curled with derision. "How great your anxiety for me!" she exclaimed, her eye flashing with scorn. "I am moved to the heart. Consider me overcome with the evidence of your love and devotion.

"Use no oily hypocrisy with me, noble sirs!" she added contemptuously. "Tell me, like men, that you are afraid for yourselves, for your own positions, for your own lives. You petition me for aid to suppress the revolutionists, the radicals, the protesters against your own rapacity. You would have me bypass normal civil rights and throw the dissidents into prison, take their lives, stop their tongues, torture them, confiscate their property. Go to, fools!

When national wrongs begin to boil in a caldron of injustice and hatred, it is rank folly to clamp the lid upon it. Let the steam escape. When men talk, they lose energy to act. Let their tongues wag; let their pens write. Suppress them, and the steam blows off the lid."

She passed on to other proposals, vetoing some, granting others. The Senator Toliti, a well-meaning, if narrow-minded, man, complained that the people were no longer reverent. The majority failed to attend the services in the temples, and ignored public holidays honoring the gods. Obscene epigrams had been written on their very statues. "Let the iron hand of the law descend upon this licentious people, and force them into godly worship," he said solemnly.

Salustra shook her head wearily, "We will make Atlantis virtuous in spite of herself, eh? I'll wager Jupia's shadow is behind thee, Toliti; perhaps even her gold jingles in thy purse at this moment. If Atlantis does not worship her gods, is it the fault of the people or the interpreters—the priests who say do as I preach, not as I do?"

Because of the appalling increase of crime, one Noble proposed more rigid punishments.

Salustra was silent for some time before she spoke. "Why not look for the cause before attempting drastic treatment? Law is held in disrespect. Why? Our courts are slow, unwieldy. Punishment is uncertain. Immunity from justice is a matter of money and influence. Find out, my lords, what is polluting the bloodstream of Atlantis, and you will not have to worry about the increase of crime. Is it undesirable aliens, unjust laws, poverty? Is it overpopulation, congested cities, a trend away from honest labor, a too artificial and sophisticated life? Is crime the passionate protest of the adventurous human animal against the miserable drabness of his existence? Or is it unemployment, the multiplication of the inferior, with no wit for anything but theft and skulduggery? Find out, my lords. I shall hold you responsible for a prompt report."

In the face of this sardonic inventory, the great hall was silent. The representatives were all too well aware of these ingredients in Atlantis' decay. During the lull Salustra spoke to Mahius in an aside for several moments. Finally, she came forward a few steps, tall, commanding, vibrant. From her manner, all realized that she had something of importance to communicate.

"Noble sirs, I will recount what would have saved Atlantis. The wealth of the nation should not have been concentrated in the cities but spread over the country. Men's bodies and spirits should not have been exploited for the sake of amassing fortunes for the aristocratic few. We should have allowed no religion to pollute the air with superstition. We should have prevented the propagation of the unfit, allowing only the superior to procreate. But we didn't do all this and we have failed!"

The Assembly regarded her with uneasy astonishment.

She raised her hand eloquently. "The hour of reckoning is upon us. Do you know, my lords, that Signar of Althrustri is now approaching Lamora with a great fleet?"

Had the walls of the Hall of Law fallen upon them, the Assembly could have displayed no greater consternation. Voices, shrill, incoherent, merged in a babble of speculation. Where were the legions and the fleet? Why had not Signar been halted before entering Atlantean waters?

Salustra smiled grimly. She said in a low voice to Mahius, "Where is their stoicism now, their smiling indulgence?"

She stood forward and again lifted her hand. "Sirs," said the Empress with quiet contempt. "You have lived up to my expectations. This panic is what I anticipated." She paused a moment. Something in her manner made them suddenly hopeful. "I said, sirs," she repeated with a smile of derision, "I said that we had failed, that the hour had arrived, that Signar was already in Atlantis. It is all true. But he comes with peace in his hand and war in his heart. His primitively powered ships have slipped like a shadow between the vessels of my stationary fleet mysteriously made immobile, as have been our aircraft and land wagons. Even our warning system failed to function in this accursed fog."

Dismay would again have overwhelmed the Assembly,

but Salustra, with an imperative gesture, calmed the group.

"Fortunately, he comes on an ostensibly peaceful mission. Sirs, he hath asked my hand in marriage. In doing so, he states his determination to annex Atlantis peacefully, if need be."

Hope again surged through them. She saw this, and something akin to contempt again welled up in her.

"I promised my father that I would attempt to preserve the integrity of Atlantis. Could I, by marrying Signar, maintain that integrity, I would gladly marry him. But should I marry him, Atlantis as a nation would disappear."

She paused dramatically. "But I shall offer him my sister, Tyrhia, in marriage. After my death, his son shall sit upon my throne, and Atlantis will still be a separate nation."

An awkward silence fell over the hall. Now that the threat of immediate danger seemed past, shame took possession of many.

"If I were in a position to do so," she continued, "I should attempt to stop Signar. But Atlantis would crumble before him like a rotten melon. He has a weapon that would kindle all of Atlantis. And it was we who gave it to him—traitors here in this Assembly who feel they will be a part of Signar's new order. They are not only traitors but fools."

Those like Divona who were guilty all craned their necks as if trying to ferret out the traitors. But for the most part, hope, like a cool wind, blew over the Assembly. The members whispered together in excited tones, ignoring that quiet figure in the shadow of the throne.

She looked down on them as if they were chattering magpies. "You ask yourselves why we do not blast Signar's empire with our atom-splitter. It is a barren waste, and with it we would only bring the glaciers down upon us." She smiled bitterly. "Signar hath not the same problem as Atlantis. The beggar hath naught to lose, and so can gamble all on a reckless throw of the dice."

For the first time the Assembly even considered there

was such a person as Tyrhia. Better that she be sacrificed than they. They looked upon Salustra warmly, even affectionately.

She returned their regard in grave silence. "We must deck Lamora as for the visit of a beloved friend," she said dryly at last. "We will pretend, with him, that he is here on a friendly mission. That is the way of diplomacy."

9

THE EMPRESS strolled into the imperial gardens alone. Under the heavy haze, the great trees formed a rustic pattern of ordered greenery. Marble statues dotted the heavy foliage and the rolling lawns; fountains splashed their perfumed spray into marble basins, the water running off into artificial lakes on which floated regal white swans. The sun, obscured by the endless cloud, barely filtered through the boughs.

At a distance she spied Tyrhia tossing a golden ball with her friends Zutlia, Utanlia and Ludia. Their movements were graceful, their young bodies lithe, full of delicate promise. Their white garments swirled seductively about them with every sudden movement.

Salustra paused in the shade of a tree, watching the frolicking maidens with an amused smile.

Tyrhia pouted when she missed the ball, and angrily accused her companions of deliberately misthrowing it. They deferred to her openly, but Salustra saw the wry smiles they covertly exchanged with each other. She frowned. That babe! she thought to herself. I am beginning to wonder whether I am being just to Signar. Will he crush her fluttering little heart, or will she, like many trivial women, wind the superior male about her fingers, in still another classic example of the tyranny of the weak over the strong? It did not once occur to Salustra that Signar would not grasp at Tyrhia eagerly as a means to what he wanted most—Atlantis. She fell into a reverie. Would Signar's sons inherit their father's ambition and enterprise, or would they, as did so many sons, inherit their mother's softness and smallness?

At this moment, the gamboling maidens caught sight of

that majestic figure. Tyrhia, turning swiftly, ran to her with a little exclamation of surprise. Salustra, smiling rather perfunctorily, put her arm about the girl. She looked down into the charming face. With a careless hand, she pushed aside the tendrils of golden hair which curled down on the white forehead. "Thou art warm, little one," she said. "Thou shouldst be resting, not tripping about in the heat."

"One has to do something," responded Tyrhia, a litttle petulantly.

"Well, where are thy books, thy music, thy birds?"

"Books!" exclaimed Tyrhia. "I am weary of books! Thou art always urging me to them, Salustra, and despite what thou dost explain to me of them, they fill me with yawns. I cannot understand them; they are so stupid. Besides, men do not like clever women."

Salustra laughed suddenly. "And where didst thou acquire thy great knowledge of men, child?"

Tyrhia looked at the Empress slyly. "There are enough of them in the Palace. They wait on thy slightest move like dogs fawning for a bone."

Salustra laid her hand upon the girl's shoulder, her face suddenly solemn. "Tonight, Tyrhia, I wish thy presence in my apartments. I have something of moment to impart to thee." Her hand fell to her side, and with a glance she took in the maidens, who had respectfully hung back a few steps. She extended her hand to them and they kissed it reverently. She stood conversing awhile, listening to their eager remarks. She patted a rosy cheek or two, smoothed a head with an affectionate hand, and then, feeling suddenly old and drained, she slowly moved off. When Tyrhia would have joined her, she lifted her hand, and the girl fell back. They watched her tall figure, deep in thought, moving toward the Palace. She was thinking somewhat bitterly that, unlike Tyrhia and her friends, she had never been young

10

THE CHASTITY of Brittulia, daughter of the philosopher Zahti, was by no means accidental. Zahti, after a brief plunge from ascetism which had resulted in his marriage to the frigid daughter of Pletis, Consul of the Fourth Province, had retired gratefully to his bare chamber and his philosophic treatises. It was rumored slyly that after six months of marriage he and his wife had agreed to absolute chastity. Whether the rumor was true or not, they had no more children after Brittulia, nor did the older Brittulia need resort to the clever physician Nulah, the helpful accomplice of all wealthy matrons desirous of avoiding maternity.

The senior Brittulia had died after four years of connubial continence amid whispers she had succumbed to madness begot by frustration. She left a sizable fortune to her only child and namesake. Zahti had little affection, obviously, for his daughter. He saw her upon few occasions and seemed to possess the same morbid aversion for women which she later professed for men. After his death, the girl was kept secluded in the care of her father's sister, a frigid termagaent. Taught from childhood that chastity was the only desirable condition for a woman, the girl had no male teachers, no male companions. She was closely veiled against men's defiling glances. Even the household slaves were exclusively female.

Brittulia, now the age of Salustra, was beautiful with the small-breasted meager beauty of the overripe virgin. Despite some shortcomings, her frosty beauty intrigued many men who would have been pleased to relieve her unfortunate condition. Brittulia, like many virgins no longer in bloom, was concerned much with religion. She was devoted to the goddess of the arts and sciences and regularly paid homage to the High Priestess. Jupia yearly enriched her coffers with gold from Brittulia's considerable store. As a noblewoman, she was obliged by tradition to visit the royal Palace once a year to pay her respects to the sovereign. After the brief formalities, she would leave with impassioned haste, as though she could not stand the perfumed pollution of Salustra's presence.

"This woman will bite herself in frustrated passion one day," wryly observed Salustra on one occasion.

In view of her attitude, it was not surprising that Brittulia was thrown into a panic when the Prefect of the Guards appeared at her secluded house and brusquely advised her that the Empress intended to visit her before sundown. The very appearance of the formidably masculine Creto was enough to cause her consternation. She had the overwrought imagination of the secluded, and fancied reasons for the unusual visit crowded her mind. Was there to be a casual suggestion that she commit suicide, a harsh demand for her fortune or a spiteful command to attend some super-orgy? She spent the hours before Salustra's visit in a darkened chamber, silently praying to the goddesses she had supported so handsomely.

However, when the Empress, attended only by a small detachment of guards, finally appeared, Brittulia's despair had turned to a cold resignation that gave her an outer appearance of composure. She perfunctorily kissed the Empress' hand, as her eyes searched Salustra's for a sign of her fate. She saw only a pale, rather grave Salustra, who looked about the house, which she had never before visited, with feminine curiosity.

"Thou hast a charming house, Brittulia. Why have I never been extended an invitation before?"

"I am delighted that you found your way here at last, Majesty."

"Come, Brittulia," rejoined the Empress, "I thought not to find thee a victim of the common malady, hypocrisy. Tell me, frankly, after I am gone wilt thou scour the very chairs in which I have sat, and fumigate the rooms?

Tell me that thou dost consider my breath an abomination, my words brazen cymbals in a sacred tomb, my smiles degradation, my very presence anathema. I will not think less of thee for being honest."

Brittulia shuddered slightly, her eyes shrinking yet proud, asking the reason for the visit. But Salustra was obviously in no hurry.

"One naked truth," observed the Empress, indolently leaning back in a chair, "is worth a thousand gorgeously attired lies." She looked directly at Brittulia, who this time did not flinch. "Even fools serve a purpose. They are the dull background against which the brilliant shine the more brightly."

Salustra studied her hostess with drooping eyes. Yet even in her negligent attitude there was a suggestion of supine strength. Brittulia, with her acute sensitiveness, felt this, and her apprehension increased.

Suddenly Salustra's casual manner vanished. She leaned forward in her chair, her hands gripping the arms. "I could spend hours with thee, Brittulia, exchanging polite inanities, but I have no time. Let me say directly I have a favor to ask of thee."

Brittulia stared at the Empress fearfully, her face paling still more. She had not erred, then, in her apprehensions.

Salustra saw her fear, and her lip curled, but she betrayed no emotion. "In all Lamora, with the exception of Mahius, I can trust neither man nor woman in this matter but thee. Thy virtue has kept thee free of treachery. Swear now that what I say to thee will go no further."

Brittulia put a trembling hand to her modest breast. "Illustrious one, death would not wring one word of thine from me."

Salustra studied her with narrowed eyes. "I will come to the point. My sister, the Princess Tyrhia, I intend to betroth to the Emperor Signar of Althrustri, who is presently at our gates."

Brittulia uttered a faint cry of surprise.

"Tyrhia," continued the Empress in her sharp, direct manner, "is a child. I have kept her secluded, because I did not wish her to be contaminated. I could consign her to the care of a hundred matrons in this city. I could surround her with the fawning daughters of noble families. I want none of these. Signar will demand the most snowy innocence in his bride, worthy in every way to be his consort. Tyrhia is both chaste and innocent, but she is very naive. Knowledge had no easy path through that pretty and unsophisticated little head. I am not especially concerned with that at this time. But I do wish that she could have with her a noble lady of unquestioned virtue. I wish that lady to be in constant attendance, be guardian, teacher and friend." She gave the dumbstruck Brittulia a penetrating look. "Thou are that lady, Brittulia."

An involuntary groan passed Brittulia's lips.

"Thou hast till tomorrow to consider it," said Salustra. "Tomorrow, thou wilt appear at the Palace with thy answer. I trust it will be affirmative."

Before the Empress' regard, Brittulia felt hopelessly trapped. "And must I live at the Palace, noble Salustra?" she murmured. "And for how long?"

"Only until such time as my sister is married. Thou shalt spend every moment with that child who has the body and tastes of a woman. Thou shalt let her be approached by no man or woman. Heretofore, she has been almost as secluded as thou. I wish her now to see the world, to see Lamora, so that she will become familiar with life. But not life as I know it, more as thou wouldst have it be."

"And if I should refuse?" whispered the stricken Brittulia.

Salustra shrugged and spread out her hands. "Thou art a free woman, Brittulia."

Brittulia wet her lips, and her famished soul looked hungrily into a forbidden world that she could safely enter under the guise of helping her country. Salustra clearly understood what was passing in the other woman's mind. She made a gesture to Creto and he handed her a small gemmed casket. Salustra drew forth a magnificent necklace of opals. She held them delicately on the end of a finger, and surveyed them with critical pleasure. Then she carelessly tossed the necklace into the other's lap. "This puts thee under no obligation, Brittulia," she said, watching the other woman languidly. "Accept this merely as a token of the new direction thy life may henceforth take."

Brittulia's pale face flushed. She clasped the opals about her neck, and looked involuntarily at the Empress for her reaction.

"They suit thee marvelously, Brittulia," said Salustra with a friendly manner. But her lips curled with a secret smile, and her eyes were faintly contemptuous. "They are as chaste as thou, yet under their modest opacity glows a smoldering fire. Who knows but that they resemble thee in this also?"

"Thou art too charitable, Majesty," said a quivering Brittulia.

Salustra nodded carelessly. "I hope thy decision will be favorable, Brittulia. But that thou must decide thyself. Have I not told thee that thou art a free woman?" She looked about her benignly. "Oft have I heard my father speak of thy learned sire, Zahti. He spoke with great enthusiasm of Zahti as a logician and philosopher. I am interested in both logic and metaphysical philosophy. May I see his famed library?"

Brittulia bowed low. "My poor library is honored," she said. She led the way to her father's library. In the displaying of Zahti's literary treasures, Brittulia regained a measure of composure. She knew logic almost as well as her father had known it. She could prattle of universals and particulars, syllogisms, deduction, induction and chain analogy. But though she had the volubility of a parrot, she could parrot only what she had so often heard, without any real understanding.

"My father," said Brittulia, "dreamed of perfection; he thought that every true argument could be reduced to a valid syllogism. If it could not be so reduced, it was not truth."

"There is no naiveté as complete as the naivieté of the savant," said Salustra. "I was about to say the wise. But the wise are seldom pedants. Perhaps their wisdom prevents them from so becoming."

Brittulia felt vaguely confused. "My father said that nothing in this world was worth the having but wisdom, and no pursuit satisfying but that of truth."

The Empress smiled. "He gave his life to the pursuit of a shadow. Truth means something eternally true, an immutable fact. There are no eternal, fixed or immutable facts; therefore, there is no truth. What may be true today may be false tomorrow. However, that it is false tomorrow does not mean that it is not true today. Therefore, he who speaks of the immutability of truth, knowing the future may make it a lie, is a wise man. Few philosophers are wise."

Without meaning to, Salustra had allowed her own inclination to philosophize to extend the meeting beyond what she had intended. But she felt an inexplicable affinity for this woman so different from herself. Or was she really that much different?

Brittulia was bewildered. Few philosophers are wise—that was absurd. Had not her father been the wisest of men? The whole world had acknowledged that.

"Philosophers play with fantasies, suppositions and theories," said the Empress. "They spend their lives among shadows and obscure hypotheses. They quarrel with each other's armchair theories until they become ridiculous. They contribute nothing to the happiness of men. They advise tranquility. What they mean is death in life, for life is not tranquil, and he who is tranquil is not alive. Some advise love for humanity. They say, 'Love thy neighbor.' Bah! Know thy neighbor, and refrain from hating him if thou canst! Philosophers are the most slothful of men. When one has neither the desire for life nor courage nor health nor virility, he becomes a philosopher, and deals in dead things! I believe in thought; one would not wish to emulate the beasts. But I only believe in the thought which has a direct bearing on immediate life and its problems. It should teach us how to derive the utmost pleasure from daily existence, the least pain, the greatest comfort. The philosopher does not deal in life. He is a dull bystander, taking the crumbs that fall from the banquet table of the active and the virile."

Brittulia was horrified by such sacrilege. "But some philosophers have been martyred for speaking great truths."

"Those men were not philosophers," said the Empress, smiling. "They acted."

So offended was Brittulia, she dared not speak without deliberately framing her thoughts.

"A true philosopher is a parasite," went on Salustra. "He spends his life trying to fit together haphazard parts of a meaningless puzzle. Some speak of good and evil, especially those who are pious. As if there are such things as good and evil! Nothing is fixed or stable, not even virtue, not even the gods. Philosophy is a frustrating plaything."

"Thy Majesty must pardon me for differing," said Brittulia, with a light of fanatical determination in her eyes, "but virtue is unchangeable. It is a fact. Virtue is life, and vice, death."

"And of what does virtue consist?" asked Salustra. "Certainly not a sterile, fruitless, frustrated virginity."

Brittulia hesitated for a moment. "Virtue," she said thoughtfully, "is humility, penitence, chastity, mercy, honor, charity, honesty."

Salustra laughed. "How hagridden thou art with the morals of an antique order, Brittulia. Dost thou not know that virtue, as thou dost express it, was imposed by the strong upon the weak? The strong are few in number; the weak many. The strong, to maintain their supremacy, invented virtue. Not for their own use, however. The strong have no need of virtue. But imposing it upon the credulous, who are many, they rob them of thought, courage and ambition."

She laid her hand kindly upon Brittulia's shoulder, smiling grimly at the virgin's involuntary shrinking, as though at the touch of a serpent. "Thou art too strong, Brittulia," she said, "to be virtuous, too noble to be humble, too honest to need a conscience, too clean to wallow in remorse. Only the feeble, the incompetent, the subjected have need of virtue."

They went out into the gardens, which, though smaller,

were not surpassed by the luxurious gardens of the Palace. Salustra, with a passion for roses, was delighted at the many rare varieties. Brittulia, preening with a collector's pleasure, cut a particularly large rose for Salustra. The Empress inhaled the scent with gratification. "Thank you," she said. "This I call a virtue."

Tears of relief filled Brittulia's eyes when the Empress took her departure. Brittulia went back into her garden, alone. On a graveled path lay the dying rose, which had fallen from Salustra's hand. Brittulia shuddered, stepped aside as though a serpent had risen in her path.

"Loti has been here," she said aloud. She began to think. I saw a threat in her eyes, she thought. She smiled, but under that smile her words were flavored with gall and poison. She tells me that I am a free woman; free now, but how free for the future?

She put her hand to her throat; her fingers closed about the opal necklace, and for a moment her muscles tensed as though she contemplated wrenching the Empress' gift from her flesh. She moved to a mirror and stared at herself intently. She saw a pale, tight-lipped woman, small-breasted, too thin perhaps, but there was a hint of beauty in the wide blue eyes and the thick bronze hair. Her neck was a downy white, the rainbowed opals blending with the warm ivory of her skin. She touched the gems again, but this time her touch was gently appraising, soft, tender.

She again relapsed into thought. If she consented to Salustra's request, she would be forced into a world she loathed, a world of cynicism, impiety, incontinence, lust, greed, indecency, luxury. She recoiled at the thought, even though her slumbering blood tingled with a terrible and secret desire.

However, she was too repressed to acknowledge the rising clamor of natural desires. She was struck only with her own burning virtue. She knew that Tyrhia was still innocent; it would be her duty to preserve that virtue even while she guided Tyrhia through the contamination of the city. Was it not a task worthy of a dedicated virgin? Sati would never forgive her if she refused. What, turn an innocent girl over to dissolute companions, when she, Brittulia, could save her? What folly, what cruelty, what wickedness! She began to long for the morrow feverishly.

The vision of the Empress rose before her mind's eye. She remembered, now, the weariness of that haggard face, the beautiful eyes so tragic and bitter behind that mocking smile. A rare emotion befell Brittulia. A wave of pity swept over that frozen heart, and its locked gates stirred, moved ajar. The Empress, in her wisdom, had recognized virtue for the mutable thing it was.

11

TYRHIA found the Empress and Mahius waiting in the dimness of Salustra's apartment. A breeze blew in from the sea, carrying with it the ceaseless murmur of the breaking tide and eddies of mist.

Salustra smiled cheerfully at her sister and made her comfortable. "Dost thou have any inkling why I have called thee here, Tyrhia?" she asked.

"None, Salustra," answered the girl, revealing in that instant how totally insulated she was from the flood of state affairs. A sense of uneasiness took possession of her, and her eyes wavered uncertainly.

Salustra held her sister's hand between hers. "I have told thee from childhood, Tyrhia, that we do not live for ourselves but for Atlantis, and that when it was politic I would give thee in marriage to one worthy of thee." She paused dramatically. "I have found that one."

Tyrhia stared stonily at the Empress, and her jaw tightened. "And suppose I should refuse?"

Salustra laughed involuntarily. "Refuse? Thou? Poor child, what hast thou to say about what I decide for thee? But, come, thou hast not yet asked me for whom I destine thee?"

Her expression was so kind, so gentle, that Tyrhia was suddenly suffused with a wild and delirious hope. She well knew that little escaped that keen eye. Could it be possible that the Empress had guessed her secret?

"In two days the Emperor Signar will be in Lamora," said Salustra. "And to him I shall betroth thee. What aileth thee, girl?"

For Tyrhia had leapt to her feet, her face white and convulsed. She stretched out trembling hands to Salustra.

"No, no, not he, Salustra!" she cried. "I cannot leave La-mora, I cannot go into that frozen wilderness. Wouldst send me away friendless, alone, at the mercy of a barbarian? Oh, Salustra, if thou didst ever love me . . ." She faltered, and began to sob silently.

Salustra regarded her without emotion but with a mild sort of curiosity. She turned to the ubiquitous Mahius. "The chit loves someone in Lamora," she said coldly.

Tyrhia stood as though stricken to stone.

"Whom dost thou love, Tyrhia?" asked Salustra in amusement.

Tyrhia continued to weep, her slight figure racked with sobs, her hands covering her face. Salustra waited, unmoved, indifferent. After a few moments, Tyrhia stopped sobbing and looked appealingly to her sister.

"Whom dost thou love?" Salustra repeated.

Tyrhia gulped. "He is worthy of me, Salustra," she said. "He is of royal blood, cousin to the King of Dimtri. He would bring no dishonor upon me. He is Erato, the poet."

Mahius, hitherto an uneasy bystander, gave vent to a muffled cry of horror. He looked at Salustra. The birthmark on her cheek had turned scarlet, but her mouth was a thin, colorless line.

Tyrhia shrank back in fear, her hands extended as though she would ward off a blow. She sank to her knees and knelt quaking before Salustra.

For moments absolute silence reigned in the chamber, then Mahius spoke earnestly. "Great Majesty," he murmured, "have mercy upon this child, who, like thee, is a daughter of the great Lazar."

Salustra made an impatient gesture. She laid her hand upon Tyrhia's shoulder and shook her. "Cease thy quaking, little fool," she said roughly. She seized the girl's slender wrists. "Look at me! Hath that man spoken one word of love to thee?"

The girl's hand fell upon her breast. "Not one word," she cried brokenly. "He does not even know that I love him."

Salustra flung the girl from her contemptuously, and

Tyrhia lay where she fell, in a sobbing heap. "If I thought that he had tampered with the little idiot, I would have him drawn and quartered." She began to pace the chamber floor. Mahius, gaunt in his crimson robes, waited in silence. At length, she stopped beside Tyrhia and touched her disdainfully with her foot. "Cease thy maudlin tears, Tyrhia," she said imperiously. "What canst thou know of love, little virgin? And mark this, Tyrhia, if thou shouldst as much as look upon that man so that he may know of thy delirium for him, I shall have him summarily removed. Dost thou understand me?"

The girl pushed herself to her knees. Her hair fell over her tearful face in a golden shower. She nodded her head weakly. After a moment, she rose, tears still streaming from her eyes. But as she turned her head, her eyes began to shine with a new determination.

12

THE DAY before Signar's arrival, Lamora hummed with speculation. A few looked with troubled eyes at the Palace gleaming proudly on its eminence. Who was to blame, they asked, for this calamity about to befall them? The heat was intense, the sky brazen, the sea swelling uncertainly, the mountain tops aswim in a molten yellow mist. The streets sent up rank odors from every dark alley and court. Already unnerved by the ceaseless fog and the power breakdown, crowds jostled each other uneasily in the main thoroughfares, ignoring the cries of vendors and street entertainers and the whine of beggars, in their single-minded reaction to the press of events. Slaves were forced to beat their way through the wedged masses of sweating humanity to make a passage for their languid lords. Everywhere, the restless river of life constantly moved and flowed from one thoroughfare to the other—tall and sturdy men from Althrustri with the barbarian's direct eye and swinging step; the small and scrambling men from Antilla, Letus, Nahi and Modura, with darting black eyes, curling dark hair, and the stamp of roguery upon every feature. They were interspersed here and there with giant blond natives of Gonelid, a far Arctic province subject to Althrustri, a land of six months' night and six months' sun. The shops blazed with light and color. Floated to market on barges, heaps of fruit—peaches, plums, grapes, oranges, lemons, apples, raisins, bananas, all kinds of melons—glowed in their stalls, attracting swarms of flies. Here, another shop displayed small, handwoven rugs, still another dealt in cheap jewelry; others attracted throngs with cheap wine and unsweetened cakes, displayed sandals and knives and saddles and belts studded with brass nailheads, or sold sweetmeats and pastries and cuts of juicy meat fresh from open ovens. Some featured dolls for children, and other play-things. The largest crowd had gathered around a vendor who shouted of the vast sexual benefit to be obtained from a certain potion. Everywhere, there was noise, dust, heat, confusion. Lean dogs and cats sniffed at the heels of the mob. But these familiar pets were the only animals in sight, for all the feathered creatures, except those in cages, and all other wild life, from the wolves and jackals in the outlying forests to the mountain lions and bears, had already mysteriously disappeared in recent days.

Although Lamora's welfare benefits were notoriously liberal, beggars in droves, some blind and crippled, added their plaintive cries to those of the hawkers of goods. They angrily jostled a timid girl with a pinched pale face, meekly offering bunches of fresh wild flowers to the indif-ferent throngs, chiding her for not begging like them-selves.

This sea of life surged about the impassive walls of the Palace amid rumors that its royal occupant was in a bad humor. It was whispered she had refused to see anyone that day. Messengers from the Nobles came and went without seeing anybody but her guards; Mahius himself could not gain an audience.

Toward sundown, as the milling throngs moved home-ward for the evening meal, the western gate of the Palace, rarely used by the Empress, swung open, and a detach-ment of burly guards appeared with a heavily curtained litter.

In a short time, so rapidly did they move, they were at the portals of the Temple of Sati, in the shadow of a giant dome supported by a colonnade of great pillars, two hundred feet in height, with elaborately carved symbols of Atlantis' history decorating their surfaces. Before bronze doors, fully fifty feet high, stood two enormous lions of Atlantis, so huge six men could sit side by side on each massive head.

Inside the temple, in the very center of the circular vastness, stood the altar with its eternal fire of Sati, attended by relays of silent, expressionless blue-clad vestals. So vast was the interior that men and women appeared like dolls under the arching gloom of the lofty dome. The altar fire gave off a spiral of thin blue smoke that heightened the senses.

As the great bronze doors opened noiselessly, a woman entered. For a moment, she hesitated, looking about her. The temple was empty, as usual at sunset, save for the guardians of the flame, for then Sati went to her rest. After that momentary hesitation, the visitor moved slowly to the altar. The vestals, visibly startled, made obeisance, then returned mechanically to their duties.

As Salustra knelt before the altar, the cloak fell from her and lay like a pool of blood upon the marble floor. At the altar, two virgins stood immobile, hands folded like pale lilies across their breasts, their eyes downcast, the pristine pallor of their faces the color of white stone. The altar flame rose like a restless serpent in a spiral of pungent smoke.

Salustra knelt, motionless. Why had she come here? She had no faith, no prayer to make to those in whom she professed not to believe. Was it because her heart ached with a nameless longing, and in her loneliness she had reverted to the comforting patterns of childhood? Or was it because only here could she find the quiet of the grave and the peace that passeth understanding?

She sighed, half-mockingly. The pious might say that my sins are consuming me, she thought, smiling a little. But I am conscious of no guilt. So why have I come?

She was aware in that instant of a sudden pang in her breast. She clenched her hands so tightly that the nails dug into the flesh. She was aware, too, of an instant's sickness of soul, a sort of deadly disgust and loathing of everything, including herself. The attack was so intense that it dried her lips and filled her mouth with the taste of ashes; it was profound, prostrating. Her heart thudded against her chest. She raised her eyes to the altar flame.

Ah, could I but rise above the world's lusts, passions, lies and hypocrisies, she thought passionately. But I am chained like others to the flesh. I am a prisoner in my own body. And while I am such a prisoner I must partake of the fare of my prison, and propitiate my jailers!

She was tired, disconsolate, discouraged. She longed for the peace of oblivion. Could it be found in death? No one had returned from the other side of that shadowy wall, and, though Jupia spoke of Lazar's presence, she had dismissed any feeling she herself had as imagination. No voice had called from beyond, no warm and loving hand had made a signal. Not even an echo reached the fearful watchers here. Was the mystery of death too great for the comprehension of mortals? Were the gods beyond their understanding, as the sun is beyond the comprehension of a beetle? Or was there simply nothing? Was there only a void, a silence, a funnel of darkness? And all our religions, our elaborate rituals, our priests and our temples, they have taught us nothing, thought Salustra bitterly. Is it because we instinctively know that it is a sham, a puny effort to comfortably fill the black void? Is it because we realize that religion is merely a man-made fancy, sublimating his corrosive fear of utter annihilation? If we believe what we desire to believe, is religion then only the result of our wish that death not be the end?

She was suddenly overwhelmed at the excursion her mind had taken. I am maudlin, she thought angrily. She looked at the altar, and a black wave of despair assailed her. The gods! she thought. What gods?!

Her body seemed to droop, her fingers listlessly brushed the floor. For a while she knelt there, and then, suddenly sensing another presence, she looked up, startled. In forbidding rigidity beside her stood the High Priestess, Jupia.

The long robes and high headdress of the Priestess made her appear incredibly tall and cadaverous in the gloom, the flickering flame from the altar casting ghostly shadows over her gaunt features.

As though recognizing the hidden drama in this unexpected confrontation, Jupia made a half-mocking obeisance. "It is strange to find thee in the temple, Majesty," she said in her flat voice.

Salustra quickly recovered her composure. "Yes." She shrugged noncommittally.

"The Temple of Sati is honored," said Jupia, and this time the sarcasm was unmistakable.

Salustra's eyes gleamed with sardonic amusement. She rose to leave. "Perhaps Sati will demonstrate her gratitude with a propitious tomorrow. Thou dost know that the Emperor Signar arrives in Lamora at that time."

As she swept past the High Priestess without another glance, the leaping flame seemed to lend a malevolent cast to Jupia's face.

At the bronze doors, Salustra turned and looked back. Jupia was still standing before the altar, her face and arms raised as though in supplication. She is death personified! thought the Empress with a shudder.

In a few minutes, she was in the solitude of her apartment, and stepped out onto the colonnade overlooking the mist-shrouded city. Sighing, she heard a sound behind her and, turning, saw that she was no longer alone. The poet Erato, a privileged companion since their first night together, stood beside her. She smiled and gave him her hand. Her eyes passed over him appreciatively, reveling in the breadth of his shoulders, his slenderness, grace, the handsome, sensitive face. She leaned her head on his shoulder and her hair brushed against his lips. For a long time they stood thus, looking silently out on the city.

"Is thy land as fair as Atlantis, Erato?" asked the Empress at last.

"Nay," he answered gallantly, "for it doth not boast thee."

She touched his cheek lightly. "Be not a courtier. There are too many jackasses in court now; do not begin to bray with them."

"I despair of doing thee justice in mere words, beautiful Empress. Today I tried to write a poem to thee; my pen stammered, could not move. Words! How inadequate!"

"How horrible to think that I have robbed thee of thy fire, Erato!" she said banteringly. "And what have I given thee in exchange? Nothing!"

He fell to his knees and raised the hem of her gown to his lips. "Thou art my soul," he cried.

"May the gods help thee!" she said.

He rose again, looked into her eyes, then kissed her passionately. She leaned forward in his arms, her eyes closed. Finally she stirred, and he released her.

She took his hand and held it to her cheek, "Thou art so young, Erato," she said.

"So very little younger than thee, Salustra," he replied quickly.

She smiled. "I am countless eons older than thee. Years are nothing. Only the soul must be reckoned, and my soul was born old and sad."

He held a lock of her hair to his lips. "Thou art Sati then. For thou didst give me my soul." His blue eyes glowed with tenderness.

"Thou art an idealist, Erato. Poets are poets only when they are young and in love and the world is all perfect sunsets and beauty."

Erato released Salustra's hand, but his eyes did not leave her face.

"Assuredly, it will be better for thee to die young," said the Empress. "When beauty has gone, death comes as a kindly friend, bearing a crystal cup filled with the blessed waters of forgetfulness."

Erato frowned in his concern. "Thou art sad tonight, Salustra."

"Nay, I am but learning of life. With such learning comes much grief. A man has two choices, he may be either ignorant and happy, or wise and sad. If he is ignorant, he accepts life complacently, rejoicing that the sun warms him, and that his dinner of bread and stew is forthcoming, and that his wife hath a tender bosom. He does not think; therefore, he is content. But the knowledgeable man cannot be happy, otherwise he would not be knowledgeable. He cannot satisfy himself all is well so long as his digestive and sexual organs are functioning. He cannot understand why a man should be given consciousness to know suffering, and then merely die. He sees life as it is, a huge hoax. How, therefore, can he be happy?"

"Is happiness incompatible with wisdom?" asked Erato, smiling gently.

"Most assuredly. I favor eliminating *happiness* from the national language. In its place there shall be the word *ignorance*. Therefore, one will not say, 'Behold, a happy man.' He will say, 'Lo, an ignorant man.' "

"Wouldst have us full of perpetual gloom and sadness, Salustra?" asked Erato wistfully. "The man who causes us to laugh, be the jest ever so vulgar, is thrice blessed compared with those who make us weep at some sublime tragedy."

Erato fell into the brooding reverie of tormented love, his sad eyes upon the floor. Salustra was conscious of a faint pity akin to what a mother feels when she first tells her child of the pitfalls lurking in an evil world.

He finally raised his head. "Thou art so sure, Salustra," he said slowly. "I should die if I were so sure that there was nothing here for us but ugliness and strife, that this world offers nothing but injustice, tragedy and despair. What hast thou then to sustain thee in the darkness of thy spirit?"

"Courage!" she replied. "Courage is the one virtue in this vile world. Courage is what keeps the knowledgeable from gibbering like apes in their agony of knowledge. To meet life gallantly, to smile gaily at its threats, to hope nothing, fear nothing, to fence with its manifold obstacles, laughing merrily the while. Ah! Only a great soul can manage that!"

"Then," said Erato quietly, "thy philosophy is courage; mine, beauty. To me, they seem the same."

He caught her hands and kissed them with renewed

passion. "How could I do otherwise than believe that beauty still matters in a world which thou dost grace?"

There was a sudden dimness in her eyes. "Kiss me—" she smiled "—if thou hast the courage."

13

THEY CAME out of their ships like conquerors, though there were only a few hundred of them. They trampled over garlands of flowers with arrogant strides. They lifted welcoming hands of salute to the hysterical hails of an Althrustrian vanguard gone mad at the sight of their Emperor. The harbor rang with their welcome, and the multitude churned like a veritable whirlpool, thousands pushing in every direction for a better view of Signar and his men.

Salustra turned her restless eyes for a glimpse of the Emperor and his barbaric followers. Tyrhia stood by her side, holding tightly her sister's arm. Behind Salustra stood the uneasy Senators, lords, Nobles and their curious wives.

Her eyes finally found the figure they were seeking, a figure that rose imperially above the others, tall and herculean, with the winged helmet of Althrustri glittering on a proud head. Soon, she became aware that the group had paused before her. She felt a current of incredible vitality, as she felt her hand taken and a man's rough lips upon that hand. The man now raised his head, and was looking down into her face. She saw, with an inexplicable thrill, a rugged countenance, almost the hue of copper. His magnificent figure was cloaked in a brilliant phosphorescent cloth, embroidered with blazing colors. His giant arms were banded with gold, and his fingers glittered with rare gems.

Behold the conqueror of Atlantis! whispered a mocking voice within her. She gave Signar a penetrating look. She saw, behind the dark eyes, a spirit as indomitable as her own. Black brows, almost meeting, gave those eyes a commanding fierceness. Boldly returning her gaze, he spoke for the first time, in the Atlantean tongue. His voice was surprisingly soft. "Thy pictures have not lied of thee, Salustra."

She smiled faintly. "But pictures have not done thee justice, Signar." She gave him her hand again, and he held it, as she felt an unaccountable tingle up her spine. "Atlantis welcomes thee, Signar. More, I cannot say."

Signar's eyes moved over her confidently, lingering on every gentle swell and curve under the crimson robe.

Feeling herself blushing, Salustra turned slightly and brought Tyrhia forward. The girl shrank as Signar kissed her hand. Signar appeared not to notice, but the Empress' face darkened.

The crowd broke into new acclamations as the imperial party slowly moved to the Palace. Signar lifted his hand at intervals as he walked between the rigid lines of soldiery, but Salustra seemed oddly distracted. Behind the royal pair streamed a queue of lords and Nobles. And bringing up the rear, Signar's personal guards, helmets gleaming in the mist, fierce faces frankly showing their contempt for these soft southerners.

They had made the voyage in primitive vessels, powered by archaic fossil fuels laboriously extracted from the frozen tundra of Althrustri. The fleet, led by Signar's flagship, the *Postia,* numbered five other vessels of a minor category and fire power, using explosives the Atlantaens had discarded for nuclear energy centuries before.

Signar had been distracted en route by the murky atmosphere that hung like a gray mantle over the sea. "A cheerless sky was our companion," said he, as they walked together, "and I saw not the sun until I looked on thy radiant countenance."

Salustra, surprised at his turn of a phrase, dismissed what she took for flattery, but picked up on the rest of his statement. "What thinkest thee of these clouds, Sire?"

He frowned for a moment. "A most strange occurrence; for with it our air seemed warmer, even without the sun, and the falling snow melted almost in the air.

Our wise men know not what to make of it, but for what are wise men except to mystify?"

She looked at him sharply. "Dost know that our wise men relate the gray mist to our unprecedented stoppage of solar power?"

"I knew not the reason," said Signar candidly, "only that the Atlantean technology had failed her at last."

She could find no trace of triumph or elation in his face. "And so you considered the season propitious for your visit?"

"Thou givest thyself too little credit," he said with a bow. "Thou alone art worth the voyage."

She gave him an ironic glance. "In this weightless murk, the atom-splitter may not go off and thou losest thy advantage of caring not for human life."

He shrugged. "Who determines of what importance life is? The dinosaurs had life and thy ancestors destroyed them with these fearsome weapons. Was not the dinosaur's life as important to him as that of any ruler, councillor of state, doctor or shopkeeper?"

"Canst thou compare human life with that of animals?" Her voice was sharper than usual.

He gazed at her gravely. "This is a problem not of predicate but subject. Thou hast failed because thou hast not used thy power to properly protect thyself. Were it not for this nice sensitivity, we would not have made our move. And when the gods permitted the collapse of thy communication systems, they were surely giving us a message."

She was amazed at his candor. "A ruler," she said, "can go no further than his people."

"Exactly." He clapped his hands in vigorous assent. "And thine are a people corrupt and cowardly, looking to be fed, sheltered, entertained and otherwise provided for from the cradle to the grave—a welfare state of parasites looking to enjoy the fruits of others' labors."

She smiled wryly to herself. "How well he knows us."

14

"WHAT thinkest thou of him, Mahius?"

The old man spread out his hands and his expression was one of sadness.

She struck her hands together. "At least he is a man."

"Greater praise apparently cannot be given," replied the Minister dryly.

Salustra burst into a peal of laughter. "His ministers are now advising him of my decision," she cried. "Watchest thou tonight, Mahius!"

The Palace shone brightly against the dark sky. The moon was obscured, as usual recently, by the unexplained vapors. From the sea came a restless growl, like the sound of a ravenous beast. A wind blowing uneasily from the sea brought a breeze at one moment cool, another as scorching as though it had passed over coals.

Tables with rare dainties had been spread in the great banquet hall. An army of slaves moved like graceful messengers, anticipating each little want. A broad stage had been erected in the center of the great circle of tables and awaited the players who were to entertain for this notable occasion.

All the nobility of Atlantis seemed on hand. The hall rang with music, laughter, gaiety, as the guests settled down to the festivities on soft divans and ivory chairs, as suited their pleasure.

At Salustra's table sat the Empeor Signar, his own principal minister, and an intimate friend or two. The others were the cream of Lamora's wit, intelligence and nobility. The Senator Toliti served as the arbiter of the feast, and the Senator Divona, famed for his cynicism, kept the conversation flowing. At this table were also Jesico, celebrated for his collections of mosaics and exquisite statuettes; Zutlian, with a legion of mistresses and a manner of lofty purity; Jupian, whose female slaves were unrivaled for beauty and sundry accomplishments; Poltrius, whose books were for only the lascivious; Ludian, the most notorious debauchee in Lamora, who could always be counted upon for the most provocative stories when exhilarated by wine. Here were also the most renowned scientists and philosophers: Yonis, the idealist; Sodoti, the vitalist; his bitter rival, Everus, the mechanist, who insisted man was an animated machine; Talius, whose philosophy was ruthlessly masculine (he being a sickly man with a meager frame and an effeminate face); Zetan, calm and kind and very wise; Lodiso, always seething with plans for an ideal state; and Morti, of whom it was said that he laughed at everything, including himself. Here were also Torili, the musician; Galo, whose statues were living fire; and Stanti, whose frescoes were marvels of licentiousness.

Signar was at Salustra's right. At her left sat Tyrhia, wearing in her hair a circlet of stars. Beyond Tyrhia slumped the dwindling figure of old Mahius, gaunt in his white robes. Salustra, clad in smooth and shimmering robes of silver, Signar's jeweled collar around her throat, next to her own precious chain, seemed strangely aloof. Beyond Signar sat Erato, somewhat abstracted. At intervals, he would glance gravely at his imperial inamorata over the rim of his goblet. His slim fingers drummed restlessly on the table. Upon one thumb glittered an imposing yellow gem, the gift of Salustra. Beside the vital, mature presence of Signar, he seemed a callow youth. He was none too happy with the situation. He had already conceived an intense dislike for Signar, and Signar made no attempt to conceal his contempt for the poet.

"We have few poets in Althrustri," he said, looking at Salustra, "and these sing only great songs of our warlike history."

Erato retorted boldly. "One bloody war is the same as

another, varying only slightly in circumstance. Therefore he only is a poet who sings of subtle things, of beauty and of the glory and the subtleties of the souls of men."

Signar smiled disdainfully. "Subtleties! It is evident thou dost know little of men! Men are but beasts, greater than the ordinary beasts only because they are more cunning."

"Then thou dost not believe in the soul, great Emperor?" asked Erato, smiling faintly.

Salustra turned her eyes upon the two men and listened. It amused her that Erato's little philosophic tidbits were being made the butt of Signar's wit, but she was also annoyed. She saw herself being attacked under cover of the attack upon Erato.

"Soul," rejoined Signar, turning his goblet about in his fingers. "What dost thou mean by the soul, dreamy youth? I confess that I have never seen a soul, but perhaps thy experience hath been broader than mine. I have dealt only with men's bodies and minds, and have found them perplexing enough. But I am always willing to learn. Of what substance is the soul, what texture? What is its appearance?"

Erato looked at him steadily. "No man hath seen the soul, except perhaps the very pure, or very wise."

Signar broke into laughter. "The very pure!" mimicking Erato's soft voice. "What are the pure? Starved creatures, without lust for life. A wise man? Wise men are fools, too craven to do aught but prattle or scribble."

Salustra found herself nodding at this echoing of her own earlier remarks to Erato.

Erato's slim hand tightened on the table. A little burst of applause rose from the others.

Signar shrugged carelessly. He sprawled upon the divan, the hard lines of his powerful figure revealed under his tunic. His lips brushed Salustra's bare shoulder. His fingers dropped to her hand and closed upon it.

For a moment she attempted to disengage her hand, but his grip only tightened. She pointedly leaned across the table that she might catch a remark of Lodiso's. This philosopher had now a new shadowy paradise in mind and was enthusiastically sketching it for the benefit of his listeners.

"Sex should be a national concern, not an individual one," Lodiso was saying. "Children would be bred only from the finest, and upon birth removed from their mothers and nurtured by the state. Men would not be bound to one woman, nor women to one man. Continual intercourse between the individual man and woman would be discouraged for the good of the state."

Signar moved even closer to the Empress. "That would not please us, eh, Salustra?" he whispered. His lips touched her cheek and his arm moved about her waist possessively. Erato saw the angry protest on Salustra's lips, the flash of her eye. He saw Signar's hand holding down the fingers of the Empress, then suddenly releasing her hand to fiddle with the stem of his goblet, as though he were bored by the conversation. Erato chose this moment to lean forward across the table. He swayed, unaccountably, and his goblet struck that of Signar's, knocking it out of his hand and dashing the wine over the Emperor's robe and person.

Signar sat upright, turning his face furiously upon the poet. Erato displayed the utmost concern and anxiety. "Pardon, a thousand times, my lord!" He lifted a corner of the cloth and would have wiped the wine from Signar's hand. But the Emperor, drawing back, coldly flicked the remaining wine into the poet's face. Erato calmly wiped the wine from his pale cheek.

"Dolt! Fool!" the Emperor's voice rose above the music, and the others at the table stared uneasily. Signar turned wrathfully to the Empress. "How came this emasculated child at thy table?"

The occupants of the other tables, as though touched by a chilling wind, froze into silence. Even the music died away. Hundreds of faces were turned uncertainly in the direction of the imperial table.

Salustra glanced beyond Signar to Erato. The poet's eyes met hers and saw in them, beyond the assumed frown, gratitude, even amusement.

"Erato," she said reprovingly, "thy carelessness is inexcusable. Thou wilt oblige me by awaiting my orders in the Great Hall."

Erato bowed profoundly and with an unhurried step left the scene. He had only a short while to wait. After a time, a slave appeared from beyond the mighty columns and approached him, handing him with a bow a roll of parchment. With trembling fingers, the poet unrolled the missive. He strained his eyes in the uncertain light of the flickering lamps.

"Impulsive poet," Salustra had written, "be at the foot of the great stairway in the gardens before dawn, and I will be there to reprimand thee."

15

AT ONE table a certain constraint followed the dismissal of Erato. "I like not the barbarian's impudence," whispered Toliti to Senator Divona. "Gods! He acts as if he hath already conquered Atlantis!"

Divona smiled faintly, shrugged and spread out his hands. His glance moved rapidly over the table. "Conqueror!" he whispered in return. "Who knows? Look at Salustra. She smiles now at Signar as though she were indeed about to wed him."

"But look at Mahius!" said Toliti. "He looks as though he were contemplating his own grave."

"Old croaker!" said Divona contemptuously. "He trembles at the songs of birds!"

Contani, fat, greasy, old, with a cherubic face that hid a cunning mind, leaned toward them. "I wonder how long it will be before we are stuck like goats? I like not the look of things. These barbarians have too insolent an air. Have I not two of his crude generals billeted in my house? One broke a crystal and gold vase that my father did leave me, and I would not have taken the ransom of Mantius for it!"

"Evil days are upon us," said Toliti solemnly.

Contani groaned, shaking his huge head. "Evil days, indeed. I never thought that the glory of Atlantis would be forced to greet as equals barbarians such as these! Watch yonder hog thrust handfuls of roast kid into his mouth, and gulp down the horror with huge drafts of wine!"

Divona's smile was enigmatic. "Remember, they are our guests," he whispered.

The uproar of music and laughter drowned out any further conversation of this nature.

Signar was drinking freely. He was still somewhat sullen. He ignored Salustra and devoted his attention to a fair young courtesan in his entourage, who seemed to melt at this mark of favoritism. The rest of his party followed his lead, insolently ignoring their hosts, shouting over the music and mawkishly commenting upon the effeteness of their hosts. Salustra smiled tolerantly, as a mother might smile at the antics of unruly children. The Atlanteans, observing their Empress' manner, for the most part maintained an uneasy composure. There was a fixed smile on Salustra's face now. It was as though she had hung that smile upon her lips and then had retreated behind it. She drank little, ate less. At times she spoke gently to Tyrhia or laughed at some remark of a Senator's. She studiously ignored Signar's apparent preoccupation with another woman, who was obviously little more than a camp-follower.

At this point, typically, two dreamy-eyed philosophers, with characteristic academic naiveté, were engaged in an earnest discussion that had no relevance to the realities of the situation.

"I cannot agree with thee that truth is purely subjective," said Yonis, the earnest-eyed spinner of philosophic fables. "I say that truth is objective, and within the reach of man. There are certain fixed facts which even the most cynical must recognize."

"There is no truth," rejoined Morti with a smile. "War, violence, revolution, all result from a foolish conviction of objective truth. If we acknowledge that all truth is subjective, we should have a tolerant and understanding world, a world able to laugh at itself! Man takes himself too seriously. In himself he sees the center of the universe and in this misconception has built a civilization full of falseness, lies and hypocrisies. As part of this lie, man considers the prospect of living eternally. He frets and fumes through life, half hoping there is more than he sees ahead, rather than just concentrating on enjoying himself before plunging into the unthinking gloom from whence he emerged."

Pausing in his own enjoyment, Signar looked at the philosopher intently and then announced: "Thou talkest too much. Thou shouldst take thy own advice, and laugh at thyself."

Signar smote his hands together approvingly.

But Yonis was too much the philosopher to allow himself to be so easily routed. He leaned forward, moving a finger solemnly as he spoke. "We were speaking of truth. And truth is a somber thing, not to be approached with laughter. Man's mission should be to discover truth . . ."

"Why?" interrupted Signar blandly.

Yonis was disconcerted. "Why?" he repeated lamely. "Is not knowledge the only desirable thing in this world?"

"We do not live forever," said Signar. "Why acquire profound knowledge when we must only carry it to the grave with us? Why not simply be happy?"

"But in knowledge is happiness," insisted Yonis. "With increased knowledge come increased beauty and fullness of life. The lower animals are happier than we. They pursue desires without a thought for the future. But who would be an animal?"

Signar clapped his hands disdainfully. "Keep debating the mysteries of life, and as you do, we will resolve them for you."

Saustra now chose to join the conversation. "Thou art weary, my lord?" she asked. Their eyes locked for a moment. And then Signar burst into a loud laugh.

"Who could be weary beside thee? Thou art a veritable pool of pulchritude, in which I would be happy to drown myself while others talk on."

In the same vein, she lifted her goblet to her lips with a smile and drank with him. "Thou hast apparently spared time from more energetic pursuits to learn the useful art of flattery, my lord."

"Nay, lady, libel not truth with the name of flattery."

"Thou dost underestimate my intelligence, my lord," she said in a voice of velvet.

At this moment a blare of trumpets pierced the air. As

though dropping from the sky, the famed dancer, Ostasi, suddenly appeared on an illuminated stage. He was a beautiful youth, combining the delicacy of a girl with the lithe strength of a young and joyous man. He was naked, and his hair, short and curling, was a crown of pale light. Exultation, sensuality, passion glittered upon his delicate face. The music fell into a soft and insidious murmur, which stirred the blood and quickened the pulses. The dancer moved softly about the stage, swaying dreamily, his hands negligently upon narrow hips. A pale violet light fell upon him, so that he seemed to move in amethystine mists of illusion, and simultaneously all the lamps dimmed. Softer and more sensuous sounded the music as the dancer swayed through the violet light like a statue drifting through sun-touched water. A profound silence fell upon the diners, and no sound, save the music, the murmur of the sea, and the soughing of the trees, disturbed the deep night.

The music, heretofore languid, now began to take on a quicker note, and then, like a flame, a young girl appeared upon the stage, naked except for the long duskiness of her shining hair. Her body was slim, white, airy and delicate, and with her appearance the lights changed to a deep rose. The youth, as though stricken immobile with admiration at her appearance, stood in the center of the stage in an attitude of reverence. The girl floated about him, like a white rose petal drifting before a scented wind. Her hair flowed about her hips, half concealing her enticing beauty. Joy, innocence, mirth, provocative childishness glimmered on her small and lovely face. She seemed a child, innocently dancing in the light of the dying sun to the tune of her own inner harmony.

The music became quicker, and then, like a statue leaping to life, the young man stirred, and with movements of extraordinary grace began an eager pursuit of the retreating girl.

Salustra, smiling, watched the dancers. Her lips barely moved in a reply to Tyrhia. The young princess turned to Brittulia, and the elder virgin took her charge's hand with a gesture of despair.

The dance became wilder, gayer, madder. Colors flowed into each other; the dancers were drowned in blue light like the shadow of the moon, which then flowed into scarlet, into gold, into green like shimmering water, and then scarlet again. So deep were the colors that the dancers were barely seen as flashing white limbs, and then, as though wary and desirous of surrender, the girl fell into her pursuer's arms. Immediately, the great hall was plunged into darkness, the music ceased. There was an ominous rumble in the distance, and the building shook. For a moment profound silence fell upon the stupefied assembly, and then pandemonium prevailed.

Salustra reached a hand toward Tyrhia, but the girl had shrunk from her. And then a smothered cry burst from the Empress. She was seized in a viselike grip. As she struggled, the silver robes were almost torn from her body. She was crushed against a man's breast, and her cries silenced by hard, devouring lips. She could not move; her hair fell about her, and her senses dimmed. She lay, half fainting, in shock. She felt the ravenous lips leave her own and move on to her throat, shoulders, breasts. Dim mists floated past her closed eyes, and great drums roared in her ears. And then, as abruptly as she had been seized, Salustra was released. Her trembling hands adjusted her torn garments automatically.

In a few moments the lights came on. Salustra, still shaken, pushed her hair from her face, and turned angrily on Signar. He was half reclining beside her, smiling and composed. Salustra put her hand to her throat. The jeweled collar, Signar's gift, had been torn loose and now lay between Signar and herself, like a miniature cluster of fallen stars. Signar picked it up, then looked at Salustra sardonically. "What a misfortune if it had been lost!" he said softly. He would have clasped it about her throat, but with firm fingers she took it from his hand and laid it on the table.

"Yes," she said quietly. "It would have been a misfortune. It is the ransom of an empire."

He raised his brows. "Ransom?"

They looked at each other intently.

He made a deprecating gesture. Salustra pushed the collar from her. With an air of indulgence, Signar lifted the collar negligently with one finger, then let it drop upon the table with a clang. "That for the ransom," he said.

The performance continued as if nothing had happened. Others now appeared upon the stage: Serto, the noted weightlifter, Lelia, Atlantis' most famous singer, Noti, the mighty pugilist, Torili, a divine musician. But the artists performed almost unnoticed. The wine, together with the suggestive dance, had done its work, and in this new climate the spectators were looking to new titillating diversions. Men and women seemed to merge as one in the dim light. A cry rose from Brittulia's direction. Siton, Signar's burly General-in-chief, was now forcing his embraces upon the daughter of Zahti. Brittulia, half-insane with fear, was struggling, as if for her life.

Salustra stretched out her hand with a gesture of command. Then her hand fell helplessly to her side. Slowly her gaze moved to Signar. Signar dropped his chin in his hand, and watched with an air of amused interest.

"Is this the approved approach in Althrustri?" she asked in suppressed rage.

Signar turned to her with assumed surprise. "Thou art displeased?" he exclaimed ironically.

Salustra flushed. "Order thy savage to release that woman."

"It displeases thee?" he repeated, with a smile.

She stared at him, the muscles twitching in her cheeks. "As do thee," she said quietly.

Signar waved at his general. "Siton!" he commanded sternly.

The burly giant dropped his prey and started to his feet. Signar made a curt gesture, and the man, his face flushed with wine, obediently backed off and disappeared into the shadows.

Salustra rose, and all Atlanteans rose with her. Signar continued to sit and smile as though at some private jest.

Salustra gazed at him, and he returned her gaze evenly, his eyes dancing with unconcealed irony. She held up a hand. "The reception for our distinguished guest is ended. All are dismissed."

16

SIGNAR stood upon the terrace outside his apartments. A faint breeze stirred his hair. Here, in Atlantis, he found what he had always soberly sought: beauty, refinement, delicate glory. He thought of Althrustri and its bleak barrenness and felt secretly ashamed. The vital blood of his own country would pour through the decaying veins of Atlantis. Both would gain. There would be one mighty empire. From the marriage bed of barbarian Althrustri and dying Atlantis would arise a new world, full of vitality, beauty and dignity.

His mind was alive with ideas. He laughed as a vision of Salustra drifted before his mental eye. Her courage and resourcefulness stirred his admiration, and her beauty formed a constant image in his mind. As he thought of the Empress, Signar began to pace quickly up and down the terrace. Though he was a man of heroic proportions, his step was light and springy. Some forty Althrustrian summers had taken their toll, but he had the animal vitality of the barbarian at an age when dissipated Atlanteans were already growing weary.

He ceased his pacing abruptly. At the end of the terrace, where a broad marble staircase with wide steps and carved balustrades led down into the gardens, he had seen a white shadow move from the cloistered dimness of the palace and emerge upon the colonnade. He saw, by the pale and uncertain light, that it was a woman. Moreover, he saw that it was Salustra. She was in a transparent white gown, and her unbound hair cascaded in tawny waves to her knees.

She seemed to hesitate. She approached the stairway, then leaned against a pillar. She stood in profile before

Signar, and the cool wind, ending the oppressive heat of the day, lifted her hair and tumbled it about. Unconscious of any other presence, she stood with bowed head in an attitude of dejection. She fixed her gaze upon the livid sky and her lips moved as though she prayed.

"Oh thou most terrible Sati, if thou art, hearken unto my prayer. To thee only would I confess that I am sore afraid. Last night I sat among my people and smiled in the face of ruin. I have hated many of them, but now I have felt their spirit upholding me, gallantly, because I am their queen." She groaned, keeping her eyes to the sky. "Oh, thou great Unknown, to which man hath ever prayed, hearken unto me! Whatever thou art, be thou whatsoever thou mayest be, listen unto my first prayer to thee! Help me to save Atlantis!" she was silent a moment, then laughed bitterly. "Have I fallen so low that I must pray to a nebulous hypothesis for help?" She clenched her hands slowly, and her nostrils dilated. "Nay, as ever, Atlantis is my strength, and I hers. We need no other."

Hearing all this, Signar smiled. Having bent forward not to miss anything as Salustra moved, the Emperor now fell back into the shadows. She began to walk slowly down the stairway. At the foot of the stairs she paused and looked about her. Signar stared. For from the shadows emerged another figure, that of a young man. Signar, with a muttered oath, saw that it was Erato.

The poet fell to his knees before the Empress and brought her hands to his lips, kissing them over and over. She bent and pressed her lips to his head. He cried out passionately. "Ah, Salustra, tell me thou art not angered with me!"

As she sighed, Erato, taking courage, rose and took her in his arms. Signar stiffened and laid his hand upon his sword, but before he could make a move, the two, speaking softly, strolled arm in arm toward a cluster of trees and disappeared.

Signar waited a moment, then leapt down the stairway after them. He slipped from tree to tree, straining his vision in the night. The trees emptied suddenly into a large clearing. Signar, stepping carefully, saw that Salustra was now sitting on a small marble seat. Erato was kneeling beside her in an attitude of supplication. "Salustra," the young man was pleading. "Fly with me to Dimtri. My cousin, the King, will receive thee with reverence and respect."

Salustra ran her fingers through the young man's tousled hair. "And knowest thou what would happen? If thy King gave me shelter, Signar would crush little Dimtri in the hollow of his hand."

The light faded from Erato's face, and his head fell upon his breast.

"Look not so despondent," she said more lightly. "All is not lost. The strongest ship is helpless without its pilot." She rose abruptly and shivered a little. Through the mists, as day broke, the white columns and domes of Lamora started to take shape and the earth awoke.

Signar lurked behind the trees as Salustra and Erato, clasping each other's waists, walked slowly past him.

"Worry not about Signar," she said. "His days are numbered."

Signar, concealed by the thick shrubs, had heard every word.

17

THE EMPRESS sat upon her throne in the Council Chamber, arrayed in her robes of state. Beside her sat Tyrhia, still shaken from the previous night's experience. And behind Salustra stood Mahius, older and more bent over than ever.

As the minutes passed, Salustra lightly conversed with her sister and her minister. They were waiting uneasily for Signar. Finally, there came the sudden high note of a trumpet. The great bronze doors swung open, and Signar entered with his general, Siton, and his minister, Ganto. He moved toward the Empress and, without kneeling, kissed the hand she extended.

She regarded him in silence for some moments. "We need waste no time in elaborate and meaningless ceremony, my lord," she said. "Let us be frank."

She casually lifted a roll of parchment and studied it with an air of great interest. "I have from thee, my lord, an offer of marriage. Is it not so?"

Signar bowed again. His eyes gleamed as though he were inwardly amused.

Salustra rerolled the parchment and gave it to Mahius. She leaned on the arm of her throne and regarded Signar with an air of candor. "It is unnecessary for me to express my surprise and gratitude," she said quietly. "I am frankly overwhelmed."

Signar's smile broadened. "In other words, lady, thou dost refuse."

"I am unworthy to be thy Empress," said Salustra gently. "I am no longer young. Nigh on thirty summers have passed heavily over me. I am old in the ways of the world, and not untouched by it. There are fairer and nobler than I."

"We promised to be frank," interrupted Signar softly. He came closer to the Empress, placed a foot on the lower step of the throne and rested his elbow upon his knee. He smiled up into Salustra's eyes, and under his steady regard she flushed.

"I am telling thee frankly my reasons for declining such an honor."

Signar continued to regard her intently. "Thou hast something beyond that."

Salustra gave Tyrhia her hand, and the two women rose. Tryhia's golden hair had been braided with pearls and lay upon her white neck in shining clusters. Her yellow lashes half hid eyes of the palest blue, and her robe modestly revealed the virginal swell of her bosom.

"I offer thee my sister, the Princess Tyrhia, in marriage, my lord," Salustra said simply.

Signar turned and studied Tyrhia with the same interest with which he might have inspected a slave girl in a public marketplace. His glance moved from her small and lovely face to her throat and bosom, and lingered over the gentle swell of her hips, then moved slightly as though to obtain a better perspective. Tyrhia visibly shrank. The birthmark on the Empress' cheek turned a dark crimson, but she showed no sign of emotion.

"And what will be the dowry of the Princess?" asked Signar with a mocking air.

Salustra inclined her head. "With her, in trust for her children, she will bring Atlantis."

"In trust?" he said doubtfully.

"I will bequeath Atlantis to thy son, my lord. More, not even thou canst ask." The flush had faded from Salustra's face, leaving her pale.

Signar clasped his hands lightly on his knee, then smiled and made a profound obeisance. "Lady, I understand thee well. Thou dost fear the absorption of Atlantis by Althrustri, and so refuse my offer for thyself. Is it not so?"

Salustra's lips parted, but before Signar's mocking regard she fell into silence.

Again his eyes subjected Tyrhia to a thorough inspection. Then he bowed again. "If I should refuse, what then, Majesty?"

As Salustra shrugged her slim shoulders, Signar slowly and easily mounted the steps of the throne and took Tyrhia's trembling hand. Salustra moved slightly, but in no other way betrayed a loss of composure. "I accept the Princess Tyrhia as my bride," he said quietly.

The blue gloom broke into scattered fragments of laughter and relief. Mahius leaned against Salustra's throne. He saw Signar kiss Tyrhia's pale cheek, saw Salustra's smiling urbanity, heard her murmuring something. His own hand was seized by Ganto, who affected to be highly delighted. He watched Signar courteously lead Tyrhia from the chamber, followed by his minister and the general, and then he and Salustra were alone.

The Empress sank into her seat again. She leaned her forehead upon the back of her hand and closed her eyes. Mahius knelt beside her and kissed one limp hand that lay upon her knee. "Thou hast won, Majesty," he said.

She lifted her hand. "I do not trust him," she murmured. "He is too crafty. I followed his thoughts through dark caverns of guile. I shall never feel safe, not even if he marries Tyrhia."

"But he hath accepted the Princess," said Mahius. "Is not that what thou didst desire? And in accepting her, he accepted thy conditions. Thou hast surely won."

She regarded him steadily, her face grim and very pale. "Nay," she said simply. "I have lost."

18

THE FESTIVITIES that marked the engagement of Signar and Tyrhia were unequaled in the history of Atlantis. The streets about the Palace were teeming with throngs anxious to catch a glimpse of the betrothed. The mist was forgotten.

And in that Palace, amid all the gaiety, beyond all that noise and uproar, a man and woman smiled, moved about graciously and kept their thoughts to themselves.

On the third day after the betrothal, Mahius was summoned by the Empress. It was a gray day. The great sea was liquid steel, heaving uneasily under a pale sky. The mountains were hidden in glowering banks of purple, the city shrouded in a stifling fog that seemed thicker by the day.

Mahius found Salustra alone in her chamber. She barely glanced up as the old man entered. She motioned him to approach the table and a huge map spread out before her. Never had she seemed so much like her father to the minister. Her manner was intent and sure, her hand steady. As he stood by the table, she moved a light forward so that he might better see the map.

"Mahius," she said abruptly, "how many of Althrustri lineage are there in Lamora, including those born in Atlantis?"

"The population of Lamora is seven million," he said gravely. "Of that number there are one million native Althrustrians and children of Althrustrians born in Atlantis."

She pushed the map from her. "So now we reap the result of unrestricted immigration! One in seven! And does the same ratio extend throughout Atlantis?"

He shook his head. "No, through the western and more southern provinces the population is almost purely Atlantean. It is only along the east coast, and in the thickly populated cities, that this dangerous ratio exists. Overall, I would estimate a nationwide ratio of ten percent."

"Ten percent," she repeated sardonically. She rose and began a fevered pacing through the chamber, muttering to herself as she paced.

"Would they be loyal to me, these hungry wolves that crept starving and gaunt from Althrustri to enjoy the plenitude of Atlantis, which hath sheltered them and fed them and allowed them to pursue their lives like free men?"

A low exclamation burst from Mahius. "But, Majesty, what dost thou care whether they be loyal to thee or not? Only in war dost thou need loyalty. And there is no war. Is not Signar betrothed to thy sister?"

Salustra stared incredulously and then burst into a loud and bitter laugh. She moved to the old man, and still laughing, struck him lightly upon the shoulder. "Fatuous old fool! Dost thou not know that Signar still nurses his original intention? But fortune loves the resourceful. I have a plan."

She leaned upon the table and pointed to the map with a long white finger. She traced the northern outline of Atlantis. "Send a message in code to the northern solar stations, Mahius, so that none may know the message save the recipients," she said in a low voice. "Call an alert along the border, quietly, secretly. Call the fleet home from all foreign stations and distribute it along our coast."

Mahius regarded her with a shrug. "Thou forgettest that normal fleet movements and communications have stopped." He looked at the map, which gave the disposition of all Atlantean forces. "We can send couriers to stations close by and perhaps achieve the same result."

"But these forces," she said, "are foreign mixture and of uncertain loyalty."

Again his shoulders moved. "We have no choice, Majesty."

She came to a decision. "So be it, and in the meanwhile send agents through Lamora, and through the neighboring provinces, and find out the spirit of the people. Discover focuses of disaffection. And find for me if the Atlantean-born children of Althrustrians will be loyal to me."

Concern spread over Mahius' thin features, but he said nothing.

"And increase the guard about the Palace," said Salustra. She stood upright, her face stony, her eyes shining with grim resolution.

Mahius laid his hand on Salustra's arm. "And what of the Senate?" he asked. "Thou dost know that thou canst not legally move without their affirmative vote."

Salustra lifted her head haughtily. "I am the Senate in this matter."

"And Signar?" he whispered uneasily.

"I shall strike alone. Thus, if I fail, only I shall suffer. But I shall not fail. In the meanwhile, he is our dear brother, he shall be lulled into a sense of security. And then when he is totally disarmed—"

"Thou wouldst murder a guest?" said Mahius, shrinking involuntarily.

Salustra laid her hand upon his lips. "Hark, fool! Who knows what enemies are about us? Ask no further questions. Am I less than the child of my father?"

Before the day had passed, the Empress' plans were proceeding. Masses of troops swung toward the northern borders, others ranged out to sea for the mighty ships being refitted for action along the densely populated coasts. And through the silent night sped messages in code. All persons entering the Palace to seek an audience with Signar were minutely scrutinized. Spies swarmed about them. The guard of courtesy about Signar was augmented for his own protection. And for every Althrustrian soldier billeted in Lamora, two fully armed Atlanteans were assigned to watch him.

19

IT WAS twilight. Through one dusky crack in the clouds an evening star looked down bleakly upon mist-capped Mount Atla and an ominously quiet city.

In a mood as gray as the twilight, Salustra entered Tyrhia's apartments. She found her sister, Signar and Brittulia together in a charming little court that commanded an unbroken view of the turbulent sea.

Tyrhia's soft laugh quivered in the warm and perfumed air as she stood before a bird cage. With a finger, inserted through the bars, she prodded the bird gently, laughing joyously at its terror. Beside her stood Signar, his eyes moving speculatively over her pretty figure. Brittulia was stringing a broken necklace of Tyrhia's on a golden chain, happily oblivious of the conflict going on around her.

Salustra moved toward her sister, and then a faint frown touched her forehead. "Thou art frightening the poor wretch, Tyrhia," she said sharply. "Hast thou naught to do but torment the helpless?"

Tyrhia's eyes flashed, and her pink lips pouted mutinously. Brittulia, her head lowered in an attitude of resignation, continued to string the shining beads.

"It is easy enough to imprison the weak, then make game of them," said the Empress coldly. She glanced at Signar. He was regarding her intently, a faint smile on his lips. At that smile a chill passed over her. His strength, his magnetic eyes, his calm face stirred her unexpectedly. And he, in turn, studied her appreciatively. Here, in this perfumed silence, filled with the twittering of imprisoned birds, a man and a woman of the same stripe suddenly recognized each other for what they were.

To her consternation, Salustra began to tremble. She put her hand to her throat with her accustomed gesture and her fingers closed over the gem that clasped her father's necklace.

Signar looked at the jewel flashing between her fingers. "A magnificent stone!" he said softly.

"It belonged to my father," she answered abstractedly. Her hand tightened over the necklace, as though this alone gave her renewed strength.

"I have heard of thy father, Lazar, from mine," he said in a low voice. "The great Lazar doth live again in his daughter."

"He loved Atlantis," she answered.

"And I . . . I love Althrustri," said Signar, his voice hardening.

Salustra looked out at the sea and the rolling waves. Beyond those waves, thought Salustra, were riding the hopes of Atlantis, refitted ships plodding with reconverted engines toward the coast; and to the north, legions marching to the border. She drew away a little distance from the Princess and Brittulia, so she and Signar could speak alone. "What thinkest thou of my crippled empire, Sire?"

"There is none greater," he answered, "even now."

She touched him playfully on his bare arm. "What! Dost thou not consider Althrustri greater?"

"I am not a fool, lady."

"Will it not make a splendid heritage for thy son, my lord?"

"Thou art too generous, lady," he said ironically. "I am overcome. But what of thy son? Wilt thou leave him without an empire?"

She shrugged. "I shall have no son. I shall never marry." She glanced at him sharply.

He was still smiling, again with that quietly superior smile that irritated her so. "What! Dost thou expect to live out thy life without love?"

"Is love synonymous with marriage?" she returned carelessly. "I have never loved."

"Never loved!" he exclaimed, as though incredulous.

She smiled lightly. "Thou dost confuse love with passion."

"Are they not one and the same? Only poets and fools, who are sometimes identical, believe in love. They rebel from the reality of lust and so dress it in delicate garments."

In moving leisurely about the garden, they paused before a cage that held a large black bird with a flaming red crest. Signar casually poked a finger through the gilded bars and whistled at the creature. It paused, surveying him with bright and savage eyes, and then, without warning, flew at the finger and struck it cruelly with its flashing beak.

The Emperor gave an angry cry of pain and quickly withdrew his finger. It was bleeding profusely. Several red drops inadvertently fell upon Salustra's white robe. She shrank visibly.

Seeing her gesture, Signar regarded her with suddenly dancing eyes. "Behold, Salustra, my blood is upon thee!" he mocked. " 'Tis a bad omen!"

She shuddered involuntarily.

Tyrhia and Brittulia, startled, came up to join them. The young Princess cried aloud and closed her eyes, but Brittulia calmly wiped the blood from Signar's hand with her own kerchief. She examined the wound dispassionately. "It is nothing, my lord," she said. "It will soon heal."

The brightly plumaged bird was shrilling excitedly in its cage, and the Emperor laughingly shook his fist at it. "The captive creature can strike back savagely, lady," he said, turning again to the Empress.

"Quite true," she murmured. She gave Tyrhia and Signar a fleeting glance. "You would perhaps like to discuss the nuptials privately."

"As you say, lady." He gave her a low bow.

With a brief nod for the group, Salustra turned and went back into her chamber. She tossed her robe upon a divan, and the stains suddenly seemed to leap at her. She lifted the robe and stared at the dried blood somberly. A bad omen, he had said. He knew not, indeed, how bad an omen it was.

20

IN THE Palace apartments provided by his host, Signar sat in grave counsel with General Siton and Minister Ganto and several others of his entourage. Ganto had just finished speaking, and the Emperor sat in silence, his chin in his hand.

"I suspected that she might try some treachery," he said thoughtfully. "But never so obviously. There, she betrays her sex. Her courage is equaled only by her naiveté. We have honeycombed her nation with traitors and no word of it has heretofore reached her ears. However, with but a small force of our own, we are in a precarious position until the hour arrives when we may safely strike. Until then, it is essential that we know her every move." He turned to Siton. "Has she no political intimate, no man in her confidence, whom we may seduce?"

"There is Mahius," the general said doubtfully.

Signar shook his head in disgust. "That fool is too old to be bought."

Ganto spoke eagerly. "Lord, there is such a one close to her, the Senator Divona with whom we have already profitably dealt. We first approached him when we learned that she deprived him of a fortune which he had gained in a dubious manner, and spurned him in the bargain."

Signar smiled, well pleased. "Since we already know what he is, all we need know is his price."

He rose and began to pace the chamber, frowning. "And so, in this very hour, as her couriers seek to alert her legions, these legions will be met by friendly legions made up of our own Althrustrian stock, willing to treat with them on practical terms." He paused, and his face darkened. "We must keep close guard upon her, lest she despair and take her life when she learns she has failed." He laughed mirthlessly. "I am offended that she has underestimated my intelligence. But, still, I have other plans for her."

Siton approached him, his large yellow teeth gleaming wolfishly. "Lord, why delay the hour? He who strikes first hath half the battle. Declare thyself the conqueror of Atlantis, and put this woman to death. While she lives, she is a rallying point for the Atlanteans still loyal to her line."

Signar frowned and gazed toward the gray sea. "Slay her?" he said thoughtfully. "No, I will wait. And when I have Atlantis in my hand, I will deal with her myself. We must await advice as to how her legions received the proposals of our generals for greater bounty, fewer duties and early retirement. And whether my own fleet at sea circumvents hers. In a few days we shall know."

"Lord," said Siton, grinning with anticipation, "deliver her over to me. I waive all booty save this beautiful firebrand. Promise me, as my share, Salustra."

Ganto frowned. "Nay, lord, have I not served thee well? And before thee thy father? I pray thee thou wilt give her to me." He threw the general a contemptuous look. "Siton is a savage. He would gore her to death in one night."

Before Signar's dark scowl, the debate quickly subsided. "Remember well," he said sternly, "that the lady is born a queen."

He laid his hand on Siton's burly shoulder and shook him slightly. "But, Siton, glower not so. Thou mayest have Tyrhia, that gentle little virgin. She is harmless. She is thine." He turned to the offended Ganto. "And thou, thou mayest have thy pick of a thousand women. Take even the scrawny virgin Brittulia, if thou likest. They say that the meat closest to the bone is the sweetest. But remember, old friend, thou art valuable to me. Do thou be temperate!"

The two men's spirits were soon restored, and the chamber rang with their coarse laughter.

Signar added a word of caution, "This dissolute and luxurious court is well hated by the common people of Atlantis. Limit your depredations to the women at court. The common people must be treated courteously and fairly. There are too many of them to offend."

He dismissed his aides and stood in frowning silence for a while, then went out upon the colonnade for a breath of air. A heavy fog drifted in from the sea, which was now invisible. Only an ominous growl, like an animal at bay, gave evidence of its nearness. The garden below shivered in a cold, dank wind. He started back as he saw two women suddenly emerge in the gardens just beneath him. One was Brittulia, the other was Salustra.

Watching the Empress, Signar suddenly remembered her in his arms, her soft lips under his, her warm, pulsating body writhing wildly against his breast; he could almost hear again the rapid beat of her heart.

As though she had tuned to his thoughts, she turned toward the colonnade and lifted her face. She smiled as she saw him and raised her hand. He bowed mechanically. She resumed her pacing and finally disappeared with Brittulia into the shadow of the trees.

Signar returned to his chamber deeply troubled. His hands clenched and unclenched, as though he were enduring violent pain. "Salustra!" he whispered. And then burst into self-mocking laughter. He was no better than those louts Siton and Ganto.

21

THE SEDUCTION of traitors was a comparatively easy matter. Divona was a clever, crafty man, his debauched face not without charm. He liked to think of himself as a figure of delicate elegance. Salustra had repudiated him and his morality. Therefore, he hated her. Toliti, the austere Senator, hated Salustra because he thought her immoral. He was dyspeptic and had no taste for banquets and debaucheries. He had long considered it the sacred duty of all virtuous men to oppose her. There were other traitors—for one, the grim Jupia, the High Priestess, an elderly virgin secretly envious of a younger, beautiful woman who frankly enjoyed what Jupia had so obviously denied herself.

There was also Gatus, rancorously resenting the suicide, prompted by rejection, of his wife's brother, Lustri. And the Senator Sicilo, dogmatic, pompous, who never forgot that Salustra had baited him in public. There were the Senators Zutlian, Ludian, Consilini and countless others—cowardly, greedy, rapacious, ready to desert a sinking ship without a care for the captain who had brought them this far. On these Salustra wasted little thought. If things went her way they would pay for their disloyalty. Otherwise, they would feel the hard hand of the conqueror. Of that, she was sure.

After forty-eight uneasy hours, Salustra had had no word from her nearby fleet and legions. Out from the capital rolled waves of command; only silence or, at the most, evasive replies returned.

"What has happened, Mahius?" she asked her councillor anxiously.

The old man tried to reassure her and himself. "Thou

must remember, Majesty, that it is not as though we were moving openly, and thus, all things must be shrouded and vague."

Nevertheless, he had a foreboding of treachery. In the restless need to do something, Salustra sent for Creto, the Prefect of the Royal Guard. He arrived swiftly.

"Thou hast doubled the Palace Guard, Creto," she said abruptly. "Treble it." He made a profound obeisance, and the rigidity of her face softened. "Dost thou love me, Creto?" she asked sadly.

"Thou knowest, lady," he replied.

"Thou hast five hundred picked men, Creto, besides the Guard. Are all loyal to me?"

"They would gladly die for thee, Majesty."

Salustra hesitated, glanced at Mahius. "I trust thee, Creto," she said. In a lowered voice, she told the Prefect of her plans for Signar and his men. "No one at court but thee, and Mahius, knows of this."

The Prefect met the grave eyes of Mahius with an anxious frown. "No one knoweth, Majesty, but Mahius?" he said. "What of the Senate? The Senate hath authority to veto thy orders, Majesty, to disperse both the legions and the fleet. What of that?"

"I had no time," said Salustra. "When all is ready, I shall so inform the Senate. They would have quibbled, doubted, delayed, and Signar could not but learn of it."

The Prefect was filled with gloom. "There are no secrets for long in Atlantis. And when they hear, as they may have already, they will react by countermanding thy orders, Majesty. Who knows but what the veto hath already been given?"

Mahius nodded somberly. "So I fear."

Salustra angrily turned to Creto. "If I give the order, wilt thou put these cravens to death?"

He gave a gesture of obedience.

"If thou betrayest me, Creto, my last order to thee will be the sword. Thou wilt do that for me?"

"There is nothing thou couldst ask that I would not do, Majesty!" he cried.

In truth there were no secrets in Atlantis. First the

Senate and then the barbarians had learned of Salustra's dilemma.

Signar soon heard of the constitutional crisis.

"The Senate," chortled Ganto, "is disaffected. Even thou who held no hatred for Salustra are affronted by the constitutional breach. They have not only repudiated her orders but in secret session voted her death to a man."

"Jackals!" exclaimed Signar with contempt. "What care they about the constitution? The lioness is wounded, so they claw over the remains. They leave an evil taste in my mouth! It will be well to annihilate every one of them when our hour arrives."

His aides gazed at each other in consternation. "That wanton hath bewitched him," whispered Siton to Ganto.

"So they approved her death, eh?" mused Signar aloud, pacing the spacious chamber Salustra had made his. "Is that to curry favor with me?"

"Partly, lord," said Siton, "but this is a constitutional monarchy. Salustra's recent commands without the approval of the Senate are judged acts of treason. At thy word they would order her execution."

Signar twisted his lip thoughtfully between his fingers. "Let her own Senate condemn her if they will. Her blood will not be upon me." His brow cleared. "And the legions? What of them? Thou sayest, Ganto, that her legions have withdrawn from the border, and their fleet hath merged into mine?"

"Yes, so sayeth Divona. Meanwhile, our spies are moving among her legions, and their desertion to us is only a matter of hours."

"Yes, the lioness is trapped," reflected Signar, "doomed because she is the living conscience of a decadent people who hate her for the demands she makes on their wasted natures."

He emptied a flagon of wine and then, with a mercurial change of mood, relapsed into gloom.

The envoys, Tellan and Zoni, were now announced. They were eager to proclaim the success of their plotting. "We have Atlantis, lord!" exclaimed Tellan. "Thou canst move with safety whensoever thou desirest."

Signar tried not to show his contempt for Atlantean turncoats. "What of this Creto, who I hear was once her lover?"

"He was her love, 'tis rumored, and loyal to her. But we have bribed the Guard, and they will turn on him."

Zoni unrolled a flap of parchment. "All in her court have been won over except her senile minister, and this Creto, and one other, the insignificant poet Erato."

Signar uttered an oath. "He must die, this Erato. Mahius is a harmless old man. We might be induced to spare him. I would shed as little blood as possible. I need the good will of Atlantis to rule it."

"And the Empress," said Tellan, "thou wilt deliver her to the Senate?"

Signar rose abruptly and was about to speak when the curtain moved and a guard entered with a warning gesture. "The Empress!" he announced.

She stood against the crimson curtain like a moon goddess, her smiling eyes moving impishly over the surprised conclave. "I am not intruding, my lord?" she said softly.

"Thy radiance, like the sun's, is more welcome for being so long absent," he said gallantly.

She glanced significantly at the others. Signar made an abrupt gesture of dismissal. For long moments the two regarded each other in silence. Then she moved closer with a step full of grace. She laid her hand lightly upon his arm. "The cares of empire are ever with us, is it not so, my lord? There are times when I wish I were the veriest slave girl."

"Thou are a great Empress," said Signar, moved in spite of himself.

"Greatness!" she murmured. "What is it? A passing salute on the lips of a dying people! That which they acclaim today they will rend tomorrow. Fame is as evanescent as the fog. It drifts in, unbidden, and is dissipated by the strange suns of new events."

He knew she had not come to discuss philosophy, but he could well afford to sit back and philosophize with her. "What dost thou consider true fame, Salustra?" he asked in earnest.

She toyed thoughtfully with her necklace. "War, conquest, what are they? Conquerors write their names in blood, and the red river shifts, and the name is no more. But the poet and the sculptor and their breathren glow with increasing brightness above the ever changing tide of human events."

"As thou dost say," Signar rejoined, "death swallows us all, and we are all molten metal again, ready to be poured into new shapes. Today, I am myself. What shall I be tomorrow? Will it matter to me whether I was poet or king, peasant or slave? If I were singer of songs, or a hewer of marble, and am born again, will I recognize that which I have created in the past? Thou dost see, even enduring fame is worthless."

She had not realized before that this facile mind had seriously contemplated the prospect of reincarnation. He was not the barbarian she had thought. She found herself tilting wits with him and enjoying it, though she still resented his excessive ardor at the dinner table as an act of pure intoxication.

"By his efforts," she said, "the artist builds a house of beauty in which we forget for a time the ugliness of life and its terrible futility. We can wander through its columns and inhale the sweet scent of the fragrant flowers that dead hands have placed there for our refreshment. This is what the poet, the composer and the artist leave of fame behind them."

He shrugged, his face glum. "Ah, well, there is little in life even for the fortunate. Drinking what is offered, we find it does not quench our thirst."

"We are truly fools," said Salustra, laughing at her own folly. "Yet we must confess that we would not be other than what we are. Is it not so?"

Signar smiled. "Philosophy is a splendid exercise for the fattening mind," he said. "But it is a passing stimulant and leaves the spirit unsatisfied."

They regarded each other in friendly fashion, notwithstanding that each understood that the other was bent on an opposing course.

"I did thee an injustice, Sire," said the Empress. "I

thought thee a total barbarian, without subtlety or sophistication. But I find thee a wise man, or, rather, I consider thee wise because thy philosophy doth coincide with mine." Her laughter was genuinely gay.

Signar took her hand and kissed it. "I value thy good opinion more than the fairest face."

A faint flush rose to Salustra's pale cheek. "I came, my lord, to ask thee if thou wouldst like to accompany me through places of interest in Lamora. We have many wonders here which may not as yet have gained fame in Althrustri: the Temple of Sati, the solar centers, the Temple Beautiful, the College of Total Knowledge."

"Ah, the Temple Beautiful, the rejuvenation center." He smiled. "Why dost thou not try its wonders on old Mahius?"

She laughed. "He had one such experience and wants no more."

As Signar pressed her hand, an electric current seemed to pass between them. Their eyes held, and Salustra's pulse quickened. He again bent and kissed her hand and then his lips traveled to hers and clung for a long moment.

Salustra quivered ecstatically. He must die! she told herself fiercely.

She must die! thought Signar glumly.

22

TYRHIA HAD just emerged from her bath and was a healthy rose hue under the gently massaging hands of her slaves. Brittulia held up several robes for her approval and Tyrhia was so absorbed in a choice that she did not even look up as the Empress entered.

"Lazy maid!" said the Empress. "The sun hath reached its zenith, and thou art but rising."

Tyrhia shrugged without answering. She cried out as the slave girl accidentally pulled one of her curls, and slapped the girl sharply. Salustra frowned, with a glance at Brittulia, who raised her eyebrows.

The Empress approached Brittulia and laid a kindly hand on her shoulder. Brittulia winced as though contaminated. Understanding, Salustra withdrew her hand. "How dost thou like the Palace, Brittulia?" she asked.

"It is as I expected, Majesty," she answered quietly.

Salustra regarded her thoughtfully. "And dost thou wish to be relieved of thy position?"

Salustra's face was pale and strained. She appeared drained. Pity is generally alien to the pure in body. But Brittulia for once was moved to compassion.

She caught the Empress' hand impulsively and kissed it. "I am at thy command, Majesty," she said, to her own amazement.

"Nay, it would please me if thou wouldst stay, but I put no command upon thee." She turned to her sister. "Tyrhia, I am taking thy betrothed about the city. It is my wish that thou shouldst accompany us."

As Tyrhia remained sullenly silent, Salustra recalled the girl's mother, the treacherous and pretty Lahia, and it seemed to her that the second wife of Lazar stood before her again. She wondered, as she noted the girl's expression, why the resemblance had not struck her before.

"I would rather remain here," the girl pouted.

Salustra laughed mockingly. "What! Is not Signar agreeable to thee, little maid?"

"I am afraid of him!" cried Tyrhja. "His eye is unpleasant. Were I a slave girl, he could notice me no different. He is an animal." She stamped her foot.

"Thou wilt have an animal for a mate then," Salustra said dryly.

She decided that her sister would only be an impediment in her desire to impress Signar with the solid substance that was still Atlantis. "Ah, well, Tyrhia, if thou dost not care to come with us thou mayest remain here."

Alone with Brittulia, Tyrhia began to weep with fury. When Brittulia attempted to console her, she pushed the older woman aside and resumed her toilet. When this was completed at last, she went into the gardens, accompanied by Brittulia and two slave girls. All the while, she maintained her sullen silence, walking slightly ahead of Brittulia, whom she was beginning to resent as an unwelcome encumbrance.

Suddenly Tyrhia paused, with a low cry. At a distance, before a sparkling fountain, Erato was sitting on a marble bench, pondering the dancing waters with an air of complete desolation. Tyrhia's young breast rose and fell with a new emotion. She turned abruptly to Brittulia.

"Return thou with the slaves, Brittulia," she said in a tense voice.

Brittulia hesitated. "I would rather remain with thee, lady. Thy sister might not like it."

Tyrhia stamped her foot. "What! Darest thou disobey me, Brittulia?"

Brittulia lifted her hands in a gesture of surrender. She called the slaves and reluctantly returned to the Palace.

Tyrhia waited until they were well out of sight. Then, with a soft step, she approached the poet. He started to his feet as his eye fell upon her and bowed perfunctorily.

Tyrhia, smiling warmly, came close to him and laid her

hand upon his arm. "Thou dost appear dejected, Erato," she said softly.

"I am no longer, lady," he answered with abstracted courtesy.

Tyrhia seated herself on the bench and motioned him to sit beside her. She saw that his face was pale and his eyes heavy, as though he had slept little. "What! Can it be that thou art in love, Erato?" she asked, not realizing the truth.

He smiled indulgently as one might smile at a lovable child. "Who knows, lady?" He studied her face, trying to find a trace of Salustra. Yes, in the movement of the head, in the curve of the throat, there was a suggestion of his beloved. He was heartsick enough to take solace in this resemblance, and his expression lightened.

"I, too, am in love," said Tyrhia softly.

"Thou hast a mighty lover, lady," he said gravely. "There is no greater figure than Signar."

Tyrhia cried out pettishly, "I loathe him! He makes me think of a ravenous wolf, with his wicked eyes and avaricious mouth!"

Erato glanced about nervously.

"I would rather die than marry him," continued Tyrhia warmly. "I would rather marry a slave than him. I shiver when he touches me."

Because he loved Salustra, Erato was conscious of a sympathy for this lovely child. He took her hand and fondly kissed it.

Obsessed with her own passion, she was now convinced that Erato returned her feeling. "Why cannot Salustra marry him?" she murmured. "It is she that he desires. Do I not see it? He devours her with his eyes.'"

Erato's face darkened, and he dropped her hand, without Tyrhia for a moment suspecting the reason.

She laid her golden head upon his shoulder. "Erato, dost thou love me?" she whispered.

So warm and appealing was she that he impulsively put his arms about her, as he would have put his arms about a child. "I love thee," she cried, her soft lips inviting his.

Erato's arms fell from the girl, and a dull flush came to

his cheek. "What art thou saying, girl?" he said in a shaken voice.

Tyrhia's eyes widened. "I said, I love thee, Erato. Is that a revelation to thee? Didst thou not know it?"

Erato continued to gaze at her in a mystified manner. And then after a long moment, he smiled. "Sweet little maid," he said gently, "thou dost not know the meaning of love. How canst thou love me?"

Her eyes flashed. "Fool!" she said with the imperiousness of Salustra. "I know not why I love thee. I only know that I do."

Erato was easily touched. Deciding to deal gently with her, he put his arm about her and drew her to him. He was amused by the manner in which her arms stole about his neck, and the way the light beamed in her eyes. "And how could I help but love thee, Tyrhia?" he murmured, kissing the shining crown of her head, as he might have kissed a young and very dear sister. "Thou art as sweet and clean as the sunshine, and as radiant."

She clung to him passionately, sobbing a little in joy. He gently kissed away her tears, sympathetic, but still amused at what he considered a passing inclination.

"And Salustra hath arranged all!" she cried furiously. "And I am to marry the barbarian. But thou wilt rescue me, wilt thou not, Erato?"

"And how can I do that, dear one? To where should I take thee? Dimtri? Alas, the lions of Atlantis would devour my little country in one mouthful. But canst thou not persuade the Empress to relieve thee of an odious union?"

Tyrhia's small face hardened, and at that moment Erato saw a clear resemblance to the sister he loved. "She is fire and ice," said the girl bitterly. "She would only laugh me into silence." She turned to Erato imploringly. "But is there no place to which we might flee and be in peace?"

Still humoring her, Erato shook his head. "I fear not, sweet Tyrhia. Both Salustra and Signar would be upon us. Thy only hope is to ask the Empress for a reprieve."

"She will not free me! I know it. But hark, here cometh

that frozen Brittulia." She surveyed the approaching woman in sulky silence.

Erato rose to depart, seeing that Brittulia was regarding him with displeasure. Tyrhia ardently pressed his hand and whispered in his ear.

What a child! he thought. And yet she is very comely, and not so much younger than I.

23

"VICE IS merely an excess of good," said Salustra to Signar, as they began their tour of the Temple of Sati. "Man is intemperate; he carried good to excess, making it evil, and then mistakes good for evil, and attempts to crush the original good in the name of righteousness. Behold, Signar, the temple of righteousness, or distorted good."

"We have naught in Althrustri to compare with this," said Signar, looking about the vast hall, with its walls and ceilings of solid gold crusted with rubies and pearls.

"My father lavished the ransom of an empire on this temple," said Salustra. "He knew that worship springs involuntarily in the human soul, and he gave the setting a magnificent materiality the worshippers would appreciate."

They spoke in undertones, but the echoes reverberated over their voices. As they moved to the altar, they stood in a pool of yellow light that fell from the eternal flame. Salustra lifted her eyes, and her face grew somber. In that instant she remembered the inseparable gulf between them.

"Thou art weary, Majesty?" he asked, with a show of concern.

"Nay, I am never weary," she replied, toying with her necklace. She attempted to disengage her hand, but he carried it to his lips.

"The great Sati was never so fair as thee, Salustra," he said softly.

"I have misunderstood Althrustri. Apparently, pretty speeches are not unknown there."

"We speak the truth between friends," he said with sudden gravity. "Perhaps that is a virtue unknown in Atlantis?"

"Truth should be used with discretion," she said. "But it is not unknown in Atlantis." Anger touched her face like a flame. "And Atlantis is not as low as her enemies would believe."

A heavy silence fell between them.

I love her! thought Signar. And so she must not die!

Thought Salustra, I love him! But he must die, or else . . .

She turned calmly and motioned with a shapely hand. "Here, my lord, is our famous College of Total Knowledge. Here, in this temple dedicated to speculation, the philosophers wage war on the vague battleground of the intellect. Here Talius, the sickly exponent of virility, hatred, strength and courage, preaches his doctrine that *equality* is the watchword of the democrat and that man should cultivate his inherent ruthlessness. Here Morti, the gay cynic, declares that of one thing only can we be sure: that we know nothing. Here Yonis declares that the ultimate happiness of man depends on natural simplicity and a return to nature, and that man is inherently good and merely acquires evil; Zetan expounds his theory of the great pantheism, that God and the universe and man are one, all moving together toward some yet unknown goal. Here Lodiso evolves his dreams of some ideal state, wherein all individuals will be coordinating wheels, turning smoothly together for the common good. We have them all, these parasitic spinners of fantastic dreams, these shadows dreaming of shadows in their shadowy chambers."

"Thou hast little respect for philosophy, I see," said Signar, smiling.

Salustra shrugged. "Thought is the death knell of action. However, I admire Talius, though I disagree that man is enervated by excessive virtue. I can laugh with Morti, who laughs at everything, including himself and me. At times, when I am depressed, I enjoy Zetan. He almost makes me believe that my soul is immortal; he props up my languishing ego with pillars of spiritual strength. I love to argue with Lodiso and crush the fragile fantasy of his ideal state with the hammer of fact. Yonis infuriates me with his enthusiastic simplicity. He tries to convince me that man is born good, when I know that he is born neither good nor evil."

She gave him a look of friendly inquiry. "Thou hast few philosophers in Althrustri?" she said.

"True," rejoined the Emperor. "We set them to work."

Salustra laughed. "As thought kills actions, so action kills thought." They entered a tremendous chamber, where, on a raised dais, the philosopher Zetan was eagerly expounding his doctrine of infinite oneness. The pupils, dozens of youths and maidens in white robes, rose as the Empress entered.

"When I was very young, my father brought me to these philosophers. My father had a low opinion of feminine intelligence, but he would say that I had the active brain of a man in the body of a woman. For some reason, he considered that the highest flattery!"

"I prefer action," said Signar, "as the best cure for melancholy."

"This is Zetan, my lord," said Salustra smilingly. "His doctrine is a triumph of hope over evidence." She pointed to a tall, dark man with a wen on his nose.

Zetan was mildly affronted. "Nay," he retorted quickly. "It is a triumph of knowledge over materialism, Majesty."

Signar glanced carelessly at the youths and maidens. All had sensitive, expressive faces, and the magic of unfulfilled dreams in their eyes.

"All philosophers claim to hold the precious jewel of truth in their hands," he said. "Look sharp. You will find that the radiant gem is but a piece of glass, after all."

Zetan's smile was gently dissenting. "It is not ours to conjecture whether the goal is worth the effort, or to decide the issue," he said. "However, whatever we so desire, we must flow toward the goal. God is in us, and we are in God. He is closer than our hearts, and as far from us as the farthest-flung star. We are neither here nor there; we are one with Him in His Creation. Time and space are mere illusions, mere phenomena. For there is only one God, and naught else. God and matter are one entity, not yet perfect. It is God's effort toward ultimate perfection that causes such vast upheavals in nature, and in the affairs of men. He tries an experiment with us. We are imperfect and so it fails; and so he erases it, and us with it."

"And when perfection is reached, what then?" asked Signar, smiling. "How unutterably dull! Imperfection, continual experiment, failure. These all add zest to life. The uncertainty is the joy in the chase. When passionless perfection is reached, this God Himself must expire in sheer boredom."

Zetan's eyes were tremendous, full of a liquid brilliance and ennobling thought. There was nothing of the zealot in his face, only benignness and an amused indulgence. Signar, though disagreeing, found himself offering his hand to the philosopher.

"Jupia, my High Priestess, loathes Zetan," said Salustra in an aside. "He is stealing her votaries from her. She preaches darkness and superstition, intolerance, hatred and fear. He preaches light and knowledge, tolerance, love and courage." She shook her head at Zetan banteringly. "I am afraid that thou art doomed, Zetan. The hosts of darkness are always in the majority."

They next visited Talius, the exponent of triumphant courage, cruelty, ruthlessness, strength and virility. He, too, was an unprepossessing and feeble man. His voice was gentle like a woman's, yet the words cut like steel.

"We admire in others what we lack in ourselves," observed Signar in a whisper to the Empress.

"He confuses virility with cruelty," she replied in a low voice.

Signar found in Talius one great virtue, an almost instant loathing of mediocrity.

"We are producing no great men in this age, Sire," said the philosopher wearily. "We have submerged individualism beneath a doughy mediocrity. We have leveled the mountains of thought, and a vast barren plain stretches about us. Greatness flourishes only in a reign of individualism; collectivism forces the great to sink to the level of the mass. We have preached for generations: the greatest good for the greatest number. The greatest number are beasts, yet we have compelled the great to grovel with the beasts and mediocrity has become our national anthem. We call the mediocre great, and the great, madmen. We have killed beauty and radiant originality, and are well pleased. If we but realized our offense, there would be hope. But instead we consider that we are virtuous, and that we have accomplished a worthy end."

Signar laughed. "Theoretically, I agree with thee, Talius, but I would not wish such doctrines to be taught in Althrustri. It would make it very hard for us kings, priests and statesmen, exploiters of our fellowmen!"

"A dangerous man!" he said to Salustra as they walked away. "I wonder that thou hast allowed him to preach his revolutionary doctrine right in the shadow of thy Palace."

Salustra shrugged. "Causes grow by persecution. I have disarmed him and made him harmless by giving him freedom of speech and a place in my College of Total Knowledge."

"Still, much that he said was true," said Signar. "Yon philosopher is too close to the truth for my comfort. For were all men individually great, there would be no mass conformity, and that would dispose of us."

"And are we so necessary, we self-perpetuating Emperors?" said Salustra.

In the next classroom, the gay cynic, Morti, was lecturing his class, a smiling group of amiable, cultivated young men with somewhat dissipated faces.

"We print the foolish mouthings of absurd men," he said to the class, "and, gazing on the printed word, call it God. We think by compulsory education to free the average man from the darkness of illiteracy and ignorance. We think to free him from his cunning exploiters, so he would be able to think for himself. But we have discovered the fallacy. He cannot think. We have only given him the ability to read the writings of fools such as himself. And a multiplication of fools is no better than one fool. Just as zero times zero adds nothing to zero. The exploiters once could only reach the illiterate directly, a slow and tedious task. Now, thanks to education and the printed word, they are able to seduce the millions, where once they were only able to seduce hundreds."

The young men, taking copious notes with great avidity, smiled in approbation of their teacher's words. Morti began to talk of happiness. "Pleasure should be the one aim of life. No matter how presumably virtuous an act, it is a vice if it inflicts pain on either the doer or the receiver. An act is virtuous only if it gives pleasure. We have a false god among our false gods, and his dark name is Duty. Our teachers, particularly our religious teachers, have taught us that *duty,* and not *pleasure,* should be our watchword. They seem to think that duty can be virtuous only when it is unpleasant. They are rather vague as to what constitutes duty; they speak of duty to the state, duty to one's family, duty to the gods, duty to business. But they fail to speak of duty to oneself. And that is the only virtue. They seem to think duty is synonymous with self-castigation and deprivation. They have confused vice with virtue. Love is a pleasure; if one should deny himself love because of a previous matrimonial error, he is called virtuous by the masses, whereas I call him vicious. He has deprived himself of a great joy, and not only himself but another. If he longs for a gay night of wine and song, to relieve the monotony of an intolerable existence, he is considered virtuous only if he deprives himself of the pleasure in the name of duty. He, too, is vicious for, by depriving himself of the pleasure, he becomes irritable and unkind and inflicts these shortcomings upon his hapless family and friends.

"The priest deprives himself of joy and is determined that others so deprive themselves. The greedy statesman desires duty to be taught to the masses, in order that he may the more readily exploit them. He is like that wolf who taught the sheep to be submissive that he might the more easily devour them. The pedant spends his life amidst skeletons and cannot understand the warmth of life. The emasculated man has vinegar in his veins, instead of blood; therefore he regards pleasure as unvirtuous. These men have controlled education, and so seduced the average man that they have drowned his reason in a sea of hollow platitudes."

"Thou dost speak of the drowning of the average man's reason," said a pupil respectfully. "Talius says that the average man hath no reason."

Morti considered the question judiciously. His eyes began to dance with the light of verbal battle. "I am almost in agreement with Talius," he said at last. "The average man's organs of thought are still very rudimentary. He cannot think; he is like a drowning man in a vast ocean, and he seizes at straws. We must give him a raft. So far, the raft given to him has been composed of lies and hypocrisies and pious fallacies. But he must have a raft, and that raft (for he cannot think straight) must be composed of rules or platitudes. When thought fails his feeble brain, he may always rely upon a platitude. But as long as we must give him a raft, why not a raft of comparative truth, instead of lies? Instead of saying to him: 'My country—whatsoever she doeth I shall regard as right and just,' say, 'My country—I shall love and respect her only so long as she is worthy of my love and respect.' Instead of saying: 'Be contented,' say, 'Be thou discontented, for it is by discontent only that the soul grows.' Instead of saying: 'Chastity is sexual continence,' say: 'True chastity is of the spirit, and the thoughts of the self-repressed are foul and evil.' Instead of: 'Charity is divine and virtuous,' say: 'Charity killeth the soul of him who receives, and debauches the one who giveth.' Instead of: 'Industry is desirable,' say, 'Industry is desirable only when its object is beauty or when the worker is happy in his work.' Instead of: 'The rich are not happy,' say, 'Poverty is always a source of complete misery and only the rich may truly express themselves and be happy.' "

The faces of the students were fired by Morti's eloquence.

"This man is dangerous," whispered Signar to Salustra. "Should his platitudes be accepted universally, it would undermine the society that makes gods of us."

But Signar was too sure of himself to feel threatened. "Thy philosophy doth attract me most inordinately, great Morti," said he with a smile. "But tell me, like most philosophers, thou dost cherish the ideal of the truly happy man. Who, in thy opinion, is the happiest of men?"

Morti smiled sadly. "The truly happy man?" he repeated slowly. "Only a true cynic can enjoy life utterly. He has no regrets, no anticipations, no disappointments. He lives easily, for nothing can disturb him. Hatred, love, wind and sun, adversity and prosperity, health and illness —all pass with time, and nothing is worth desire, regret or sorrow."

"In other words, he is without passion, virility, joy and ambition," said Signar with a curling lip.

Morti shrugged. "This life is so transient it is not worth the struggle against its manifold ugliness. Better to acquiesce to fate."

Signar's shrewd gaze traveled from the restless eye to the mobile mouth. "Thou art not the true cynic, Morti," he decided at last, stifling a yawn. "Thou are too impressed by thy own words."

They moved on to a neighboring building, a low, round, pearl-like structure surrounded by square marble columns.

"And this, my lord," said Salustra, "is my school of arts and sciences. My father established it during the early years of his reign. It has been my pride and pleasure to be its patron."

The school stood upon an eminence, commanding a sweeping view of the city on a clear day. The imperial visitors were conducted into the cool interior of the school to the laboratories, where scientists were delving into the different uses of changing matter.

"Here are the priests of a true religion," said the Empress. "It postulates no dogmatic faith, but rather seeks truth by experiment and proof. By examining the works, who knows but what we may eventually come upon the Worker?"

Signar, alert to the practical advantages of such research, entered into a discussion with one of the scientists.

"We have grown out of the atomic theory," said the scientist. "For we have discovered that the atom is not a beginning, but is, in fact, a minute but exact solar system in itself. Everything revolves around a common nucleus, and we discover that the nucleus is but a revolving system in itself. The deeper we delve the more we are convinced that there is no definite beginning, but all things ebb and flow into each other."

With instruments, he demonstrated the vibration of molecules for the Emperor. "As we know, there is no limit to the energy of these molecules. It is a question of harnessing them without blowing up the world."

At this the Empress gave Signar a piercing look, which he affected not to notice.

"But behind all this apparent, impersonal mechanism, there must be a vital force," said Signar.

The scientist looked thoughtful. "Yes, we see its influence, but we have not yet ascertained its character." His thin face lighted with enthusiasm. "We may yet discover what the Creator is, and how He works! This quest constitutes our religion, and the universe is our church."

They went into another laboratory, where men were gravely poring over delicate lenses and moving transparent slides under them. "Here, Sire," said Salustra, "are our true soldiers, our true generals. One of these gentlemen has been instrumental in eliminating a certain disease that ravaged whole cities. He discovered the organism which caused the disease, and he concocted a specific for it. Hundreds of thousands of lives would have been destroyed had it not been for his discovery. And what have a grateful people offered him? I urged my people to make this hero a substantial award. They gathered a grudging sum and tendered him a gold medal. I remember the day! A modest crowd had come together for the ceremony, and my hero, nervous yet pleased, listened self-consciously to the speeches of praise. After that he rose and, in a trembling voice, expressed his thanks and announced that he would devote his life to further beneficial discoveries. In the very midst of his modest speech, a fanfare of trumpets sounded at a distance, and it was discovered excitedly that a certain noted pugilist was arriving in Lamora. In a twinkling of an eye, the crowd about my hero dissolved, and with one accord, they hastened to greet the boxer. The scientist concluded his speech hastily, for there was now only a handful listening to him! Such is the fate of those who serve humanity!"

Signar laughed. "One hath only to have a strong enough back, and one is crowned with flowers."

Their next visit was to the department of biology. "All my school is anathema to the priesthood of Atlantis," she said. "But this department provokes the greater part of the holy thunder. Here, my beloved clients have dared to assert that man did not spring fully endowed from the eternal gods by a special act of creation. They have dared, in their heroic impudence, to declare that man evolved gradually, painfully, tortuously, from lower species, and that he is but a twig on the great tree of life. By so asserting, according to my holy ones, they have attacked the sacredness of human origin and lowered the dignity of man. I will give the holy ones credit; they like drama. It is much more dramatic to have man leap magnificently from the loins of the gods than it is to have him creep painfully and laboriously and blindly up the stony slope of evolution toward the light of perfection. Thus it is demonstrated again that religion is another expression of man's astounding and insolent ego."

They talked at length to a famous biologist, a thin-faced man with eager eyes. "We have abandoned the theory of suddenly acquired characteristics," he said. "Thy guess that only intrinsic characteristics are inherited hath been proved correct. This will assist thee in thy hope to eliminate the biologically unfit from propagation."

Salustra glanced at Signar with a humorous twinkle. "Blasphemy!" she exclaimed. "My dear Morinus, we must be careful. Thou dost know that the priesthood have asserted that we must put no restriction upon births whatsoever, no matter how inferior the potenial progenitors. Those who pay the taxes must continue to suffer for the tax-eaters."

Signar found himself thoroughly enjoying himself. "Art thou assured, beyond doubt, of man's evolution from the ape?" he inquired of Morinus.

"Much as I desire to refrain from insulting the ape, I must confess that I am so assured."

The tour continued up a broad flight of marble steps to the great observatory upon the roof. Here, astronomers with cumbersome instruments were absorbed in penetrating the thick atmosphere so they could continue to observe celestial movements. They surged about Salustra with enthusiasm and conducted her to a huge heavenly map, which lay upon a table. "Just before this curtain of mist fell, we had discovered a new planet, Majesty!" exclaimed the royal astronomer. "Thou dost remember I reported to thee that the known planets showed a certain irregularity in their orbits, heretofore unaccounted for. When they should have appeared in a certain position, it was discovered that they lagged alarmingly. So we have labored over the hypothesis that there was a planet yet unknown, near the sun, which was exercising influence over the other planets. And now we have discovered it, the tenth planet, which we shall name Salustra."

Salustra gave Signar an amused smile. "Is it not true fame!" she cried. "I shall have my history written in the heavens."

She turned to the astronomer with a solemn expression. "What thinkst thou of this cursed fog?" she asked.

The astronomer pursed his lips and looked wise. "It could very well be caused by the action of sun spots."

"Everything is sun spots," she said, "and when will the sun be felt instead of its spots?"

"Only a matter of time, Majesty."

"We will all be spots by then," she said with a grimace.

She showed Signar an odd invention upon the roof of the department of physics. To his surprise, he found it guarded with soldiery. In a glass chamber, cold and un-adorned, was an immense crystal disk, which rotated horizontally upon a golden axis. It was fully twelve feet in diameter and rotated so rapidly that the eye could not follow its motion. Though of a clear and translucent crystal, it threw off sparks of radiant light; he saw that its surface was ribbed with flashing crimson and gold, blue and green. So rapidly did the thin ribbons of color appear and depart that it was impossible to catch more than a suggestion of them. As the disk rotated, it gave off a low humming and murmuring sound. It was a fascinating object, with its miniature rivers of radiant colors eternally flashing and disappearing upon its shining surface.

Beside it, watchful and alert, sat a young man at a small table. He watched the flashes of radiance with an air of resignation. "The messages go out," he said, "but there is no response. It is as if they were consumed by the atmosphere."

"This, my lord," explained Salustra to the intrigued Emperor, "is a very recent invention. In every large city throughtout Atlantis is a similar apparatus. By a method of which I am but vaguely informed, verbal messages can normally leave Lamora and be instantly transformed into print and pictures at other receiving stations." She shook her head. "But with this infernal mist nothing works."

So this is why couriers were sent to her legions and her fleet, thought Signar. "We have nothing like this in Althrustri, lady," he said. "All our means of sending messages are still barbaric."

As they moved along, Salustra's enthusiasm seemed to increase. "My father spoke often of the inevitable decay of civilizations. I still hope to reverse the traditional process of struggle, growth, prosperity, luxury, then decline."

They stepped out onto a colonnade overlooking the city. The school of arts and sciences offered a majestic view, through gaps in the mist. But Signar had no eyes for the city. He was fascinated with the downy hair on the nape of Salustra's neck, and the merging of her throat into the marble whiteness of her shoulders.

Apparently unmindful of his gaze, the Empress stretched a languid arm toward the city below. "Look at them, my lord. In the helter-skelter of the streets, one thinks himself important. But looking down, one can't help wondering why all this feverish scurrying about."

Signar had long ago decided such talk was fruitless, but he indulgently fell into her mood. "We look for God in the vast ecliptic of the wheeling planets, and we find only atoms of tortured life floating in boundless space," he said in a burst of eloquence. "We pursue life down to the smallest-celled creature and up to the most stupendous suns, all in a passionate search for the why and the whither, and we discover we have but opened one more door in the vast corridor of mysteries. Before the great riddle of life our philosophers are chattering simians, our scientists crying babes, our priests senile mumblers."

As before, Salutra was impressed by his unexpected depth. "Morti says that life is an individual idea. Each man looks upon a universe that no other man looks upon. It is as though a group stood about a statue at different perspective. How absurd, says Morti, that each should argue that only the angle toward him is the real statue!"

Signar frowned thoughtfully. "If one pursues Morti's philosophy to its end, there is no real, solid, objective universe. It is merely the individual idea. Following it still further, one might state that the universe does not exist, that it is pure illusion, and life but fantasy."

"Morti would say subjective. He would say that just as the man's existence is subjective, so his death is subjective. Each man looking upon a dead man may have his own distinct idea of what death consists of; one might even deny the man was dead. So, too, it is shown that death is subjective."

Signar laughed contemptuously. "Let them leave the body in the sun three days, and they will find how subjective death is."

Salustra's eyes gleamed with pleasure. "How long have I waited for a man with whom I might talk and find a reflection of my own thoughts."

She spoke impulsively, as though thinking aloud. Not

until the words had passed her lips did she realize what she had said. She flushed self-consciously.

A smile quivered on Signar's lips. "Thank you, lady," he said with a bow. "You do me too much honor."

24

THROUGH the cypress trees, Jupia's A-shaped house gleamed like a naked skull. The glass doors swung open at their approach and showed a bleak interior. Here there were no flowers, no statues of marble or gold. Only a silence so profound that it seemed alive.

They were met at the door by two eunuchs, robed in black.

"They are deaf and dumb," said the Empress. "Jupia has no desire that her private conversations reach the ears of the outer world."

To the watchful Signar, it seemed that the slightest whisper of a smile flitted across a least one eunuch's face at the Empress' words.

Along a narrow path they followed two more eunuchs who seemed to emerge from the dimness. The footsteps echoed through the silence as the steps of intruders in a tomb.

The eunuchs held aside a heavy curtain, and Salustra commanded her courtiers to wait and entered the chamber beyond, attended only by an uneasy Signar. In the center of a bare floor, gleaming with pale lights, sat a large black throne; almost swallowed up in its immensity was the cadaverous figure of the High Priestess. Beside her stood a crystal globe of shimmering crimson, which glowed with inner fires, like a ruby, and cast rainbowed rays into the chamber.

As the royal pair entered, the High Priestess rose, touched her breast with one emaciated hand, and inclined her head.

"We are late, Jupia," said Salustra carelessly, advancing into the chamber with her slow and languid step.

"Yes," said Jupia gratingly. "But the honor of this visit compensates for any wait."

Jupia's eyes lingered for a moment on Signar, then moved back to Salustra.

The Empress, with a glance at Signar, said in a sardonic voice, "I have spoken to my lord of thy matchless ability in soothsaying, and he hath expressed a desire to have thee read the future for him."

Signar had expressed no such desire but was amused nevertheless.

Jupia noted his surprise, and a dull color touched her cheeks. "The future," she said solemnly, "is no mystery to one who knows the past and the present. The future does not spring, unique, unformed, new, out of the sterile air; it is a continuation, a weaving together from the past of diverse strands."

"Yet there may come a new order, a new world, a new dispensation," said the Empress. "And these may have nothing whatsoever to do with the past. The gods may evolve a new system, a new galaxy of stars, which has nothing in common with the present or the past. What then?"

An expression almost of fear passed over Jupia's features. She glanced at the crystal at her side. "Who knows?" she murmured. "I have seen strange things in my crystal of late, I have seen the world dissolve in mist and water, and be no more." She reached out a gaunt hand and drew the crystal closer to her, and became rapt in concentration, her eyes burning into the glittering globe.

Salustra glanced at Signar again, her eyes reflecting her amusement.

Jupia glanced up at this moment and her brows drew together angrily. Wanton! she thought.

Signar, irked by Jupia's manner, stood up abruptly. As he did so, his shadow fell across the crystal globe.

A sharp exclamation burst from Jupia. She bent over the crystal, and something in her expression stilled the jest on Salustra's lips. "Sire," murmured the High Priestess in a shaken voice, "look thou within, and see what thou wilt see!"

As Signar bent forward, Salustra smilingly rose, approached the crystal and gazed down with the Emperor into the globe. For a moment nothing was visible, and then a dark chasm appeared to open up and from deep within its depths emerged a hand with a jeweled ring. As they peered, wide-eyed, they saw that the hand held a goblet of red wine in which lay coiled a writhing snake. The shadowy image remained but a moment, and then was gone, not, however, before the ring on the small hand became plainly visible. That ring was the royal Signet of Lazar, which the Empress wore constantly.

"Thou hast enemies, my lord," said the Priestess in a somber voice. "Beware of poison."

Signar examined the crystal with frank disbelief, smiling at Salustra, who managed to conceal her anger. Crone! she thought. She guesses my thought, and by some trickery contrived the image. No doubt, she prepared this in advance. She laid her hand carelessly upon the crystal. "And now, Jupia," she said in a rasping voice, "tell me what thou dost see for me."

In silence Jupia pointed to the crystal, and Salustra and Signar bent over it. For a moment the image was indistinct, and then they saw, in miniature, a woman's bared breast, transfixed by a quivering sword.

Salustra recoiled with a sharp cry, and as she did so, the light faded, and the globe was benign and pale again.

Signar, still unbelieving, nevertheless felt a sudden chill. "Absurd," he exclaimed. "Who would harm the Empress?"

Jupia said nothing, but smiled darkly. She glanced at Signar as though sharing a secret with him.

Salustra looked at Signar to judge his reaction. "To die by the sword is easy, my lord," Salustra said, making an effort to be casual. "It is a swift death."

She approached the globe again and stared at it intently. In that one flashing moment she had recognized the sword as Signar's. She laid her hand again on the smooth surface of the crystal, and whether by design or accident, she stumbled, pushing the globe from its base. It fell with a crash, and after bouncing on the marble floor shivered into a hundred fragments.

With a loud shriek, Jupia leapt to her feet, and Signar fell back, startled. He glanced at Salustra. She was swaying a little, and he sprang to her side, catching her in his arms.

The enraged Priestess made a move as though she would smite Salustra. But meeting Signar's eyes, she quickly dropped her hand and forced a smile. "It is nothing, Majesty," she said, unctuously. "I am sorry the crystal is gone. It is very ancient. But it was an accident, I am certain."

Salustra glanced at the fragments and shivered slightly. "Accept my apologies, Jupia," she said coldly. She unfastened a gleaming pendant from her breast and tossed it at Jupia's feet. "Buy thyself another crystal, Jupia, and see to it that it is not as imaginative as this one. Such flights of imagination may prove disastrous, and not only to the observer."

Jupia stood expressionless, like a statue. She made no move to pick up the jewel.

At the door they looked back. The High Priestess stood now with one hand lifted, as though invoking a curse.

25

THE VISIT with Jupia had cast a pall over the royal pair.

By talking, Salustra sought to dispel this dark mood. "That old harridan is a sorceress. She put into the crystal that which lay in her mind. It is a form of thought transference that will be commonplace one day, when man has outgrown the man-made machines that can now do as much, such as the disk I but recently showed thee."

Signar, normally unimpressionable, found it difficult to erase Jupia's prophecies from his mind. "I like not that wretched witch's thought of a sword in thy breast," he said. "It is far too lovely to be a depository for cold steel."

"And what dost thou think of thy own poisoning?"

He shrugged indifferently. "What is my destiny I could not give away if I would."

"Is it not possible that destiny can be given an encouraging thrust?"

"Only if that is the gods' intention."

"I am not such a fatalist as thou," she said with a frown. "Otherwise there would be no point to launching any thought into purposeful action."

"That may be," he said thoughtfully, "but how many things turn out, lady, as one visualized when he commits that thought into action?"

She looked at him with a start. Did he know how close Jupia might have been to reality?

His demeanor immediately reassured her. For he now said with a half-jest, "Thou didst promise me a glimpse of the Temple Beautiful and its rejuvenation chamber.

Hath this tilt with the old harpy altered thy intention or is it still my destiny?"

She found her mood lightening. "Normally, Jupia is the custodian of the chamber. But I shall be the only law in this case, as seems my lot recently."

He gave her a look of inquiry.

"The chamber works somewhat like a bank vault. Jupia turns the dial opening the door to one particular point, Mahius twists and turns the knob to the second point, and then the Empress makes the third and conclusive move." She laughed. "But Lazar, my father, was not one to trust his welfare to minions, and so his scientists secretly installed an alternative entry system which he alone controlled."

She touched the jeweled clasp about her neck. "And with this necklace, itself a stimulator, he passed this secret on with the burdens of his empire."

It was Signar's turn to laugh. "Is all this in thy head?"

She nodded. "With many other bits of information."

"And wouldst thou use this chamber for thyself?"

They were moving toward a relatively small building, at the base of Mount Atla, which overlooked both the College of Total Knowledge and, farther on, the Palace itself.

"I have no fear of growing old," she said. "It is not my destiny."

His voice was still light. "Perhaps we shall grow old together."

In the same vein she replied, "Or perhaps die together, if Jupia has her way."

Their entourage discreetly kept some distance behind them. They paused finally before a cavernous door of solid marble.

"This door is twelve feet thick and immovable," she said, "unless one knows the combination."

He noticed a series of knobs in the rock. "And these?" he asked.

"For Jupia and Mahius to tinker with."

She put her face within six inches of the door, which

resembled more a wall, and spoke sharply in a tongue completely foreign to him.

Suddenly the wall commenced to groan, and the ground under their feet began to tremble. Before Signar's startled eyes, a chink was beginning to form at the top of the door, gradually getting larger as the marble wall continued its slow descent into a receiving slot.

In a minute or so, the top of the door was even with the ground, and they were free to make their passage through the doorway.

He looked at her in amazement. "Though I stood at thy side, I did not see how thou managed it."

She put her hand to her lips. "Certain words, now archaic, uttered at a certain decibel level, set up a vibratory wave which tunes precisely into the frequency under which the door opens and closes. There is no magic to it, merely a fundamental understanding of the power of the sound wave when properly synchronized. Over this, fortunately, the mist has no influence."

"Atlantis," he murmured, "has much to show its neighbor from the north."

"And thou hast much to show us."

They left the entourage some distance outside the cavern as they moved into a large corridor, the door almost instantly closing behind them.

There was a look of puzzlement on his face. "Would it not be possible to break through this door with powerful explosives, which thou hast no lack of, or with thy solar rays?"

She nodded appreciatively at his question. "My father considered all this. While one sound wave establishes access to the chamber, any vibration of a sufficiently violent nature to cut through marble would at the same time bring the mountain down on the chamber." She smiled mischievously. "And with the chamber destroyed, nobody could be rejuvenated, not the mightiest conqueror, not even the mighty Signar."

His head inclined slowly. "Would I had known the

great line Lazar. From him I could have learned much, just as," he added with a bow, "I am learning now from the lion's cub."

They proceeded for approximately a hundred yards down a long, dark corridor when she suddenly turned off, and they found themselves in a dimly lit room, rosy with a glow that seemed to permeate its every corner.

He looked around curiously. The room was no more than twenty feet square and led into a series of smaller rooms, in which there could barely be seen through an open door, sleeping quarters and bathroom facilities.

"The initiate remains in this chamber for twenty-four hours," Salustra explained, "exposing himself to the crystalline rays which penetrate into each and every cell of the body, from the brain to the little toe, regenerating the body through its revitalizing action on the tiniest molecules that make up each cell."

He looked about the room curiously. "And from where," he asked, "does this red ray emanate, when none of thy energy systems presently give off light or power?"

She sat down in a comfortable chair, with soft cushions piled up to her neck. "Twice," she said, "my father took this seat. It would not have prolonged his life any further to have sat more, as the cells can only regenerate twice. Beyond the age of two hundred there is not enough collagenous or fibrous material in the connective tissues to provide a basis for cell renewal."

He repeated his question. "The source of these wondrous rays, lady?"

She looked at him in surprise. "Is it not obvious? Look about at the walls, the ceiling, the floor itself. It is all a giant ruby crystallized from mountains of stone when the first atom-splitter was detonated in ancient times. This vitreous substance that was formed by the great heat absorbed in time all the beneficial nuclear rays set off when the destructive force was unleashed. It is now a constant source of radiating, life-renewing rays."

He was engrossed with this whole process beyond anything he had yet heard. "How was it known that these rays had this effect?" he asked.

"Merely by chance," she said, "like nearly every other invention of note." She paused a moment. "When my ancestors touched off the first atom-splitter in their fight against the dinosaurs, there was a wide swath of destruction in every direction, in some instances unexpectedly destroying populated areas. Eventually people slowly started returning to the familiar places and rebuilding their homes. These people, it was noted after a while, stayed younger-looking and lived longer than people elsewhere in the land."

"And how widespread was this?" he asked.

"Only in one area, where a combination of factors counteracted the harmful radiation remaining from the explosion and transformed it into something compensatingly good, as nature often does when left alone by man."

Signar had never been so fascinated.

"And that area? Where was it located?"

She smiled. "You are surrounded by it, Sire. Out of this furnace of vaporized destruction came the giant red crystal that you stand on and see. And on this memorable site was erected the original capital of Atlantis. And this—" she pointed around the room "—is the keystone of all that remains of the early city."

His eyes followed hers. "What happened then to the first capital?"

She shrugged. "Time takes care of everything. You have seen our volcano, the hungry Mount Atla, which spews forth angrily every so often. It has razed three Lamoras in its time."

"Then why keep building on the same site?"

She laughed. "We are a stubborn people, Sire."

He overlooked the challenge in her voice, and his eyes roved curiously around the chamber. "I assume we are being rejuvenated, lady, as we stand here conversing."

"In a slight sense, but it actually takes at least twelve hours for the cells to react, and twenty-four hours for the full-scale treatment to become effective."

As he looked around the room at the empty benches, chairs and lounges, he was vaguely aware that something was lacking. "I see no attendant, no slaves of any description."

She was amused by his practical observations. "Nobody can safely absorb more than thirty or thirty-six hours of this radiation over an extended period. Any longer, and the cells overreact beyond the desired point and become subject to a cancerlike growth, bringing to the victim a horrible death."

He pointedly examined a small timepiece carried like a pendant around his neck. "We have already been in this chamber for fifteen minutes, lady."

She half smiled. "Doth thy eye feel any keener or thy step any springier?"

"You jest," he said, "and yet I already feel invigorated."

"It is the power of suggestion," she said. "For no change in the tone of the body, no loss of wrinkles or superfluous skin, is noted for weeks after the chamber treatment. The rays work slowly but surely."

Signar stared at the huge wall of radiant red crystal.

She followed his gaze. "Wouldst thou care to spend the next twenty hours in this chamber, Sire? Thou couldst be my guest."

"Thou honorest me too much, lady."

"It is indeed an honor. For thou wouldst be only the third personage in some seventy years to know this honor, my father and my minister Mahius being the exclusive recipients of this great reward. Jupia hates me because I will not give my consent for her rejuvenation, though she has applied many times." She spoke contemptuously. "Her ugliness is such that I fear indeed that her face might crack the crystal."

Signar, in his interest, ignored the dry witticism. "Why

dost thou give it so sparingly when the energy is freely flowing, and nearly all would aspire to shedding the ugly marks of age?"

Salustra nodded slowly. "My father said that nothing is appreciated unless attained with the greatest difficulty. We offer it to only those that the priests, represented by Jupia, the Assembly, represented by Mahius, and the Empress, representing the people, consider indispensable to Atlantis' welfare." Her lips curled slightly. "I can never agree with the others."

He was still driven by curiosity. "Why would not Jupia be a likely candidate?"

The Empress snorted. "Again, I consider her anything but indispensable. Indeed, Lamora would be far better for her absence. She is the strongest single influence in promulgating the old superstition which mulcts my people of their brains, will and money."

His face reflected his bewilderment. "Then why offer this prize to me, whom thou must regard as intruder at best?"

"From thy veins, my lord, shall flow the issue of the great Lazar. As the father of a new dynasty, thou surely deservest all that Atlantis can offer."

He gave her a searching look "Thou must be jesting, lady, to reward a feat of propagation with rejuvenation. 'Tis a strange irony, that."

She moved toward the cavernous door by which they had entered. "What sayest thou, Signar?"

He looked at her steadfastly. "Dost think I need rejuvenation?"

Her eyes twinkled. "In no way, Sire. But in fifteen, twenty, twenty-five years, even thy loins may weary."

"Even then," he said, "I would not want it. My bones, flesh, my very eyes, ears, nose, taste may become more sensitive, my reproductive organs those of a team of bulls, but what of my mind, my memories of wrongs rendered and received, my thoughts of remorse and joy? Even happiness comes as a burden when one remembers all the chapter and verse connected with it."

"But think what thou couldst do in time with the

weight of seventy years behind thee and a new, powerful hand to lend strength to what thy mind has learned?"

His voice became grave. "I tell this to none but thee. But with the decisions I must tend to, and the adversaries I must look to, affairs sometimes grow heavy for my weary head. Thou dost know how weighty a crown can be, lady."

She restrained an impulse to reach out and touch the craggy face that suddenly seemed lined with care.

They had paused now at the door, and she repeated the command which had earlier appeared so much gibberish to him. As before, the section of marble wall slid down into a slot, and they stepped out into the open air.

Almost in unison they inhaled deeply. But even with the next breath she shuddered, her mind still dwelling on Jupia's prophecies. "I would like," she said, "to give Jupia more than she wants of the chamber. Her fishlike eye would see no more tragedies in that misbegotten crystal of hers."

He shook his head with a smile. "It is my hope that thou lovest as fiercely as thou hatest."

She sighed. "One of my most earnest hopes has been that I might strike the fetters of religion from the limbs of Atlantis. I dreamt that I might build a state founded on man's natural instincts, thus making him happy. And what, I pray, is more worthy of a ruler than to make his people happy? But at every turn, I have been opposed by the priesthood, the pious, the cunning, the righteous, the perverted. Once the people were compelled to mark the three great religious holidays. One of the first things I did was to rescind this obligation of the people, while making enemies of their spiritual captors."

They had paused in the shadow of the Palace porticoes.

Signar regarded the Empress with a new compassion. "Thou art concerned with Atlantis' soul. When a nation concerns itself with its soul, it is already decaying. Just as a young ardent man identifies only with the vital present, so I believe that a young, ardent nation identifies only with the vital present. Only the old and feeble worry about the soul."

Salustra smiled. "Atlantis may be old," she said, "but she is not feeble, as her enemies may learn."

Signar's face became a blank mask as he calmly changed the subject. "Thou hast not forgotten, Salustra, that I am giving a quiet entertainment for thee on board my flagship, *Postia,* this evening?"

"Nay, how could I forget?" answered the Empress with equal blandness.

They parted with a smile and an embrace awkwardly given and awkwardly received, and Salustra retired to her apartment. Upon entering her chamber, she promptly sent for Mahius.

The minister found her pacing agitatedly up and down the colonnade. "How soon may we strike?" she demanded without preamble.

The old man hesitated. "Thou art determined upon this man's death, Majesty?"

"Yes, he must die."

"Is there no other way?" asked the minister sadly. "I do not like treachery."

"There is no other way!" cried the Empress. "If I could spare him, I would not!"

Mahius stared at her in unfeigned surprise. "And why not?"

She did not answer. For a long time the old man peered into her face, and then, very slowly, understanding touched his face like a shadow. He fell to his knees and pressed her robe to his cheek. "Poor lady," he cried.

26

FROM THE sea came a murmur like the sigh of a woman unloved, a restless despairing murmur. Otherwise, an ominous silence filled the air.

As she breathed deeply of the night air, frowning at a new, trenchant odor, the cool wind lifted Salustra's hair and flung it to the breeze. She felt free and untrammeled, as she had only infrequently as a child. And then, like a stab, came the thought of Signar and the knowledge that both could not survive.

In a chamber beyond, slave girls were singing moodily. She half listened to the melancholy lyrics:

> Thou dost ask me why I weep, my maid.
> Now hark, while I tell thee why.
> I weep for a corpse that is barely laid,
> And the light in a vanished eye.
> For lips I loved and no longer love:
> For these do I groan and sigh.

Vile poetry! thought Salustra. Neverthless, the singular aptness of the song sent a shiver down her spine.

Deep in thought, she started as she felt a touch on her shoulder. She turned quickly and saw a familiar face.

Silently Erato knelt and kissed her hands.

She studied him with dispassionate eyes. He rose to his feet and after a moment of hesitation kissed her lips, recoiling at an unresponsiveness that was totally unexpected.

"What aileth thee, Salustra?" he whispered.

She smiled ironically. "Can an Empress not feel out of

sorts at times, or is such an indulgence accorded only the lowly?"

He touched her cold cheek with uncertain fingers. "No darkness is so great that dawn will not come again," he said with loving gentleness.

"Doth this pass for poetry?" she asked sardonically.

He looked at her in bewilderment. "Thou art weary, Salustra. I tell thee again, there are many years of happiness for thee in the future."

"Perhaps in death. For in death is the great and unknowing peace." Her arms fell to her sides and her head dropped. "I am tired," she said dully. "I would that I might die this hour."

Erato smiled. "Thou art depressed, dear one," he said tenderly. "Tomorrow thy mood will change."

"Tomorrow I will still be myself. It is strange," she added as though speaking to herself, "that the trap one sets for another so often traps oneself. That I, always unloving, should be at last unloved."

Erato was understandably bewildered. "Nay, I do love thee, Salustra!" he cried. He caught her in his arms and kissed her rapturously. She closed her eyes for a sweet moment, imagining him to be another. Suddenly, with an anguished cry, she thrust him from her.

He recoiled as though shot. "Thou dost not love me, Salustra," he said with a sob.

Salustra watched him half sadly, a twisted smile upon her lips. "Wilt thou do me a great favor tonight?" she asked in her usual voice.

"Thou hast but to ask, Salustra." He had quickly caught hold of himself.

"Then do not attend the festivities on Signar's flagship."

His look turned to one of surprise.

"It is my wish, Erato."

He bowed. "So be it."

Still shaken, he left a few moments thereafter, for the first time without kissing her.

Erato returned to his house, filled with the gravest misgivings. His step was slow and heavy, his heart profoundly depressed. He threw himself upon a couch that looked out on the sea.

Tossing restlessly, Erato thought bitterly. He had discounted stories of the Empress' capriciousness, thinking with a lover's egotism that he had been the one finally to touch that fickle heart. And now she was already wearying of him. He sat up in an agony of insane jealousy. "Salustra!" he cried in anguish. He beat his clenched fists upon his forehead in a frenzy of hate and resentment. One moment he convinced himself that he hated her; the next he was overcome by his consuming passion. His despair and suffering mounted. He shivered at the memory of that passion. What fool had said that the male was the predator of the species? He, Erato, had spiritually been a pure and crystalline stream emptying into a murky pool. The women he had known before the Empress were all shadowy and indistinguishably impersonal gratifications of a physical desire. His inner spirit had remained untouched until Salustra had reached out and taken his love. In the frenzy of rejection he now felt contaminated by her insincerity.

"I can never write again!" he cried despairingly. "I am unclean!"

Without his noticing, the curtains of the chamber parted softly and a slave girl entered. He looked at her with a jaundiced eye. "A lady wishes to see thee, my Lord," she murmured respectfully.

Erato leapt to his feet. His despair vanished as did his hate. He trembled now in anticipatory relief and delight. But his joy vanished as quickly as it had come. A veiled slight figure of a girl stood hesitantly in the center of the chamber. Erato regarded her in apathetic silence, almost blaming her for his disappointment. As she came toward him, she lifted her veil, revealing a pale, tear-stained face.

As he remained silent, she fell upon his breast and smothered his lips with kisses. With a gesture almost of repugnance, he thrust her from him.

She drew back, wounded, her childish lips quivering. Her veil slipped from her face, her yellow hair falling in damp rings about her cheeks. "Erato?" she murmured, "dost thou not love me a little?"

He laid his hand on her shoulder. "What art thou doing here?" he demanded. "Thy sister will punish thee for this folly. Art thou alone?"

"Nay. I have my slaves with me. The gods only know how I was able to elude that frozen-faced Brittulia."

As she looked at him timidly, hoping for some crumb of affection, Erato's soft heart melted. He put his arm around her and kissed her forehead lightly. "Why didst thou come, little one?"

The girl clung to him, her eyes shining. "Because I love thee, Erato, and because I have found a way for us to be free."

As the girl pressed his hand first to her cheek, then to her lips, Erato felt faintly annoyed at his own blindness. He withdrew his hand and, seeing himself, indicated that she assume a place beside him, a vastly older brother about to chide a silly little sister.

The girl curled up beside him on the couch, her head on his shoulder, her eyes fixed adoringly on his face. Under her radiant gaze, his stern resolution faltered. He could no more hurt her, he decided, than he could slap a child in the face.

"Thou art reckless, Tyrhia," he said firmly. "If thy visit is discovered, the Empress will be angered, and thy betrothed as well."

"What do I care?" she cried defiantly. She sat upright, eyes blazing, her childlike features sharpening with the passion of the moment. "I have a way for us to rid ourselves of her, Erato—forever."

He fixed intent eyes upon the girl, and a coldness passed over him. "Little fool!" he cried. "What art thou about?"

She stared at him, startled. "The Senator Divona . . ." she began.

"Dost thou trifle with those who would ruin the Empress?" he interrupted wrathfully. "Tell me what he said to thee."

She began to tremble, her teeth chattering. "Nothing else," she faltered, beginning to weep again.

Erato fell into dark thought. The Empress must know, but how to protect this ridiculous child?

And then, as a winding road suddenly opens up, disclosing unexpected vistas beyond, so did Erato suddenly see the bend in the road that took him inescapably to Signar.

He glanced about wildly, then clapped his hands. Slaves immediately appeared. He ordered his sword and cloak, and when they were brought to him, he would have rushed from the chamber had not Tyrhia clutched his arm.

"Where art thou going?" she asked tremulously.

He fought off an impulse to seize her little throat and strangle her. Instead, he forced a smile. "I will first take thee home, child," he said more calmly. "And now promise thou wilt never speak again to that traitor Divona."

The girl sobbed with relief. "Yes, I promise thee. We can find another way."

27

SIGNAR'S FLAGSHIP, *Postia,* was alive with the signs of a gala evening. Lights glittered from every pole. Music drifted out over the water, above the gay laughter of the milling guests.

Salustra had never looked more beautiful or alluring. All eyes turned to her with mingled envy and admiration as she came aboard with the inevitable Creto. She was met by an attentive Signar and ceremoniously conducted below decks to a throne beside his own. She settled herself comfortably, her eyes picking out familiar faces. The present guests included the Senators Contani, Divona, Tilus, Patios, Vilio, Contalio, Sicilo and Toliti, with their gaily attired wives and mistresses. Of the philosophers, Zetan, Morti and Talius were the only ones represented. Among the industrial giants she noticed Ratulio, the great steel-maker; Hanlio, manufacturer of fine silks and linens; Ducius, the builder; graybeard Seneco, with his newly acquired young wife, defiantly ablaze with gems. Icio, the inventor, was also present. But most of the guests were from Signar's own court.

Salustra gave her host a pleasant smile. "I regret, Sire, that thy betrothed, the Princess Tyrhia, was indisposed."

He shrugged indifferently. "With thee present, Majesty, who would note the absence of other women or even children?"

Salustra kept her eyes half-averted. She seemed hardly a part of the company. Abstracted, she barely touched her lips to the wine.

"Thou art not drinking, Salustra!" exclaimed Signar. "I swear to thee that it is not poisoned."

Salustra started and the color receded from her cheeks.

Her brows came truculently together. For a moment the two rulers held each other's gaze, and then, very deliberately, Salustra lifted the goblet to her lips and drained the contents.

Signar's amusement increased. "Who is sadder," said Signar, "than the sober in a company of drunkards?"

"A wise man in a company of fools!" retorted the Empress warmly.

Signar laughed and clapped his hands. His look took in the assembled revelers. "It is true they are on their way to being drunk, but surely thou art no Brittulia."

Salustra smiled disdainfully. "I am a hater of nothing that contributes to pleasure. But pleasure lies in doing the thing one desires to do. I do not wish to drink, therefore drinking is no pleasure to me."

Signar filled her goblet again. "Sad, that my entertainment is lost upon thee." His face had become flushed with wine. He moved closer to Salustra, his breath on her cheek. "I have an enemy," he whispered.

"Who would hurt thee, Sire?" she asked mockingly.

He leaned toward her, lifted her hand, and inspected the rings on her fingers, closing over the signet. She looked down at the crown of his bent head, and closed her eyes, as if to blot out the reality of her own emotions.

"Nevertheless, I have an enemy," he continued, examining the rings closely. "This enemy is ruthless, insatiable, hating and hated. This enemy is myself. I can pit my strength against others. But there is one I cannot defeat, one that devours my spirit, and darkens my brain, myself. I might lay waste empires, and breathe life into a thousand legions, cause great vessels to move at my slightest whim. But my own bitter thoughts numb my hand, turn my wine to gall and my food to dross."

He released her hand, fixed his eyes upon her, and spoke slowly, as though measuring the effect of his words. "I am lost," he said, "vanquished by an enemy which is my own executioner."

She smiled sardonically. "Thy digestion is disordered, Sire. Allow me to send my physician here tomorrow."

The mood of this remarkable man suddenly changed

and he laughed over the crowd, slapping his knee as he did so. "And what will he prescribe for the relief of my inner demands, Salustra? What will quench my restless yearnings, my alternating hopes and despair?"

She refused to take him seriously. "I am convinced that thou hast been feasting too generously and exercising too parsimoniously, Sire."

He leaned toward her again and began to toy with the jewel at her throat. "I have always before known the gaiety of adventure, the lust of conquest." He held her hand tightly. "What, thou dost not ask why?"

Easily, almost perfunctorily, she replied, "I am convinced that under no circumstances wouldst thou give me the right answer."

He shook his head with undisguised mirth. "I will tell thee later. But now let us go to the banquet I have arranged." He rose and gave his hand to the Empress. Together, they led the way to a still lower level, followed by the laughing guests.

Salustra ate little and drank less. The noise, the heat, the confusion, all wearied her. She rested an elbow on the table and looked around her with a passionate longing for silence. Animals, she thought. Where is there a man who loves a woman except for her flesh?

Feeling neglected, Signar reacted as a jealous man would. He conspicuously ignored the Empress now, transferring his attention to the wife of Morti, at his left. As befitted a philosopher's wife, she was young, stupid and shamelessly lewd. It had been a bitter pill for the Empress when her favorite philosopher had married this ignorant, boorish female.

Signar was not to be outdone in the area of entertainment. With a blare of trumpets, a handsome young man leapt on stage. Save for a garland of poppies about his loins, he was naked. As the music soared, several nude and shapely dancers tripped out in quick succession. These were the Virtues, seven in number, from Chastity and Charity, to Modesty and Truth. They screamed, shrank, veiled themselves and gathered before the divan of Sati. The goddess was sleeping, her lips parted in sweet slumber, her golden hair rippling about her and falling to the floor. The music became wilder, gayer, more sensual, more insidious. All present recognized in the dancing youth the personification of Tatio, Sati's first lover.

The youth circled merrily about the divan, seeking to dart between the ranks of the Virtues, who interposed themselves between him and the object of his desires.

"Love's eternal pursuit of beauty," said Signar, turning back at last to Salustra, who was watching the scene with indifference.

"Nay, say, rather, the eternal pursuit of lust for chastity."

Signar stared at her in assumed surprise. "May I credit my ears!" he exclaimed. "Surely thou, an admitted authority upon the subject of love, art not speaking so? Perhaps it is thou who shouldst consult the physician thou didst recommend to me?"

She looked at the ribaldry beginning to take form about her. Had debauchery ever really pleased her, or had she been merely endeavoring to escape from her own intellectual isolation? She was conscious of a curious malaise. Tatio had moved closer to the Virtues, and then, to a clash of cymbals, he broke through their ranks, flung himself on his knees beside Sati's divan. He caught the sleeping goddess' hands, covered them with kisses; kissed her throat, breast and finally her lips. She awoke, saw beyond him the frightened Virtues and then, with an infinitely lazy smile, entwined her arms about his neck. At this the Virtues, led by Chastity, fled, weeping, into the darkness.

Disgusted, ineffably bored, Salustra turned from Signar and got up abruptly. Before the others could rise with her, every light in the room suddenly went out. Under cover of darkness, she fled, as the Virtues had, up the stairway, holding her amethystine robes closely about her. The upper deck was deserted. It was silent, except for the sea, which was growling ominously. Even the gulls were strangely absent.

She had fled the banquet in a tizzy that a young virgin might well have felt. A bitter laugh escaped her lips. "Am

I a school girl," she asked herself, "to languish for love of a man I must destroy?"

Drinking in the rather fetid night air, she turned to stroll the deck and found herself face to face with Signar.

He was standing in silence, watching her. "Is my poor entertainment so worthless that thou must flee?" he asked. He took her hands as she began to tremble. "Why didst thou break that old crone's crystal?" he whispered.

"I break it!" she exclaimed. "It was an accident, as you saw."

"Have it thy own way." And then before she could move a finger he caught her in his arms, pulled her to him, and with a sweep of his arm, ripped her gown to the waist, and began to rain kisses fiercely on her body.

She struggled furiously, but Signar laughed as he parried her blows, seeming to know that she was resisting only because she was angry.

"For this," she cried, "thou shalt die!"

"Nay, for this I was born!" he exclaimed, pressing his mouth to her exposed breast.

"May the gods strike thee down," she cried. At this, as though her outcry had been a signal, the ocean suddenly gave a great heave and the ship was struck by a mountainous wave. It reared with a sickening lurch on its side. There was the roar of a second crashing wave, and the prow of the ship pointed almost vertically to the sky. Salustra and Signar, desperately clinging to one another, were thrown sprawling to the deck and almost washed overboard. As the ship straightened out with a sigh and a groan, they could dimly hear the crashing of overturned furniture and the cries of panic from guests as they began to pour up the stairways. Signar sprang to his feet and pulled Salustra after him. From the crest of the mountain of water on which the ship was momentarily poised, he could see other peaks, glimmering with a strange and ghastly light. Remarkably, not a breath of air was stirring. The dark sky above was serene, and through the mist the few lights of Lamora twinkled tranquilly on shore.

Salustra and Signar stared in awe at the towering waves that tossed the ship like a feather, drenching them and a

scattering of gibbering ha[lf-crazed] courtiers in a flood of
seawater.

"What in the world is it?" [sai]d Signar, as he put a
protective arm about Salustra.

"An earthquake," she muttere[d as] deck sliding under
her feet.

"We shall be drowned," cried S[ignar] over the howling
of the sea.

But even as he spoke, the great cre[st of the] water suddenly leveled, and the surface was again i[ncred]-
ulously calm and smooth. The ship wa[s...] oment mirac-
ment, swayed slightly, then settled grudg[ed for a mo-]
y to its an-
chor.

All stared in stupefaction at each other [and] the silent
sea.

"A miracle!" cried Signar. He turned to Sa[lust]ra, who
was staring somberly at the ocean, as though list[eni]ng to a
secret voice. Showing an extraordinary resilience, [h]e was
quick to jest and laugh. "When Sati writhes in unw[elc]ome
arms, the very ocean turns with her."

She looked at him, without smiling. "Jest not of Sa[ti,]"
she said. "She jesteth not."

28

THE ⸺ANGE disturbance had not touched Lamora's sh⸺ Nevertheless, marking the unprecedented
waves, th⸺pulace was struck with panic. As usual, the
scientists⸺d a ready answer. Geologists explained the
phenom⸺n casually. "Shifting strata in the ocean bed,"
they ar⸺unced. "Nothing to cause alarm." But the people's f⸺s were not so easily assuaged. Ancient prophecies ⸺ative to Atlantis were darkly dredged up. Had it
not ⸺en prophesied that one day Atlantis would be swal-
low⸺ by the sea, and life would know her name no
m⸺e? And why else, ran the argument, would Atlantis be
d⸺troyed, if not for her sins? Vainly the geologists
⸺reached that nature was entirely indifferent to sin or virtue.

The priests seized upon the opportunity to regain lost
prestige. Had they not warned repeatedly that the gods
would punish the people for their corruption and godless-
ness? This was but a foretaste of what would take place if
the people of Atlantis did not return to Sati. Fear was a
prompt spur. The coffers of the temples resounded with
the rich clank of gold. The altars were buried with floral
offerings and animal sacrifices. The pews were solidly
packed with a fearful tide of humanity as Jupia rejoiced.

Salustra, though spared by a miracle, did not visit the
temples. She thought, by this example, to convince the
people that nothing supernatural had taken place. In-
censed, they felt she was defying the gods, who might
further avenge themselves upon the people because of
their Empress' impiety.

"Baboons!" she cried to herself. Undeterred, she proceeded with her private plans against Signar, while suppressing a growing inclination to abandon the project.

A few days after the rising of the ocean, the Empress, attended only by Creto and his guards, came unannounced to the house of Jupia. So insolent had the High Priestess become since the day of the miracle at sea that she kept Salustra waiting in her antechamber.

The old crone is riding the tide, thought the Empress with a smile. Well, after today, I shall soon be finished with her. The sea can reclaim her.

When finally admitted, she showed no sign of impatience. "Ah, Jupia," she said urbanely, "I regret if my coming hath caused thee inconvenience."

Jupia's face was blank. "The appearance of Sati herself could be no more welcome, Majesty," she replied.

Salustra laughed lightly, seating herself. "I realize that thou art most assiduously employed allaying the tremors of my frightened people."

"They have returned to their gods," replied the Priestess grimly, "heeding the threat of destruction, which is the result of their vices."

Salustra laughed again. "Had it not been for fools who made so much of a wave, none would have known of it in Lamora." She leaned toward Jupia and smiled. "But I am not concerned. I know that my good Jupia will tenderly soothe their qualms." Jupia was silent as Salustra continued to smile. "Thank the gods, Jupia," she went on. "They have been good to thee. The coffers in the temples are full to overflowing."

Salustra studied the Priestess with contemptuous eyes, her fingers playing, as they so often did, with the gem at her throat. "I am here to ask something of thee, something of a private nature. Is this understood?"

The High Priestess inclined her head in silence.

Salustra lowered her voice. "Thou art famous for thy wondrous poisons, Jupia. In fact, so famous art thou that many mysterious deaths have been imputed to thee, of some of which, no doubt, thou art innocent."

Jupia started and her face became the color of chalk.

Salustra stifled a yawn. "But have no fear," she said genially. "There are so many fools in the world that a few less are truly a public benefaction."

Jupia's hands clenched convulsively under her robe.

"Moreover," continued the Empress, "it hath come to my ears that with the crafty Senator Divona thou art fomenting revolt against me and hast been whispering to the people that the gods are dissatisfied with my administration." She paused for an ironic glance. "But I could not credit reports that spoke of such ingratitude. Nay, I said, Jupia is my most loyal friend, devoted to my interests." Salustra's eyes were like the tips of swords.

Jupia watched her silently with a baleful eye.

"I have come to thee for assistance," Slaustra went on equably. "I will not cavil with thee. I desire thy strongest, swiftest, least distinguishable poison. I wish a poison tasteless, odorless, easily administered, that will kill without delay and without pain, making death seem most natural."

Jupia sucked in her breath. "Is this a command, Majesty?"

Salustra's face hardened, "Unless thou wouldst take the potion thyself."

Without another word, Jupia summoned a slave, whispered in his ear, and, folding her arms upon her breast, sank into silence, her gaze bent upon the floor. In a few moments the slave returned with a small golden casket. Jupia opened the casket and drew from it a tiny crystal vial. It was filled with a sparkling red fluid.

She held up the vial for Salustra's inspection. It had the hue of blood and seemed to be alive. It moved, sparkled, frothed, cast little red spears of light into the dimness of the chamber. Salustra leaned forward and stared at the poison without breathing.

"This is absolutely tasteless," said Jupia somberly. "It is to be administered in wine, where its color will not be detected. Hours after drinking the wine, the victim will fall to the floor, dead before he strikes it. It will appear to be a massive heart attack, and in reality that is what it will be."

Salustra stretched out her hand for the vial. "Your gods brew powerful medicine." She paused, and added with a lowered brow. "No word of this on thy life."

Without another glance for her High Priestess, Salustra stalked out of the house and entered her litter.

Salustra had barely left the High Priestess when Jupia dispatched a message to the Senator Divona. He arrived soon thereafter. Without preamble, but without concealing her anger, Jupia told him of the Empress' visit.

"I would have given her a harmless potion," she said bitterly, "but know she will try it upon an animal. Thou dost know for whom the poison is intended?"

"Most certainly," said the Senator. "It is destined for the Emperor. That is quite to be expected. It will be necessary to warn him not to partake of any wine without precaution. Of course, he hath his taster with him on public occasions. Her only opportunity will be to administer it to him in private." Consistent in his treachery, Divona hurried to the Palace, but found Signar ostensibly indisposed. Vainly he protested that he carried information of the gravest import. Cool-eyed aides suggested that the message be given them for delivery to Signar. But wishing full credit for his treachery, Divona drew back. And then he had an inspiring thought. Summoning a slave, he sent him to Tyrhia, requesting an interview. Waiting near her apartments, he spied the poet Erato, who had been hoping for an audience with Salustra.

Erato's eyes fell upon Divona and filled with contempt. He took the Senator by the arm. "What art thou doing here?" he demanded fiercely.

Divona shook off the poet angrily. "That is no concern of thine, boy," he said loftily.

At this point Erato's slave appeared to announce that the Empress had left but an hour before for the Chamber of Law. Erato retreated, crestfallen, as Divona's own slave now returned to conduct him to Tyrhia's apartments.

He found the young Princess in an emotional state. "It is madness for thee to come here, Divona," she said sharply. "So hasten and tell me what thou wilt."

Divona's uneasiness increased. "Why, lady?" he asked. "Who knows of this but thee and myself?"

As she kept silent, he approached her softly. "The hour hath come for thy release. A little courage on thy part will bring thee freedom and power."

Tyrhia continued to regard him darkly.

"The Empress obtained poison but two hours since. She intends it for Signar. He must be warned at once. Think what it will mean to be the one to save him!"

Tyrhia uttered a stifled cry. "Poison! How absurd."

Divona nodded portentously. "Not so, for only with such a poison will the death appear natural. There must be no delay. Thou must go to him at once."

Tyrhia thought of her sister's wrath and trembled. "I am afraid," she whispered. "What if he tells Salustra the source of his information?"

"He will not if thou dost request it."

She pressed her cold hand against her cheeks, and resentment overcame fear. "I will do it," she said at last.

"Thou will tell him from whence thou didst secure this knowledge, lady?" Divona's tone was wheedling in its persuasiveness.

"I will tell him," she said impatiently. She unceremoniously showed Divona out and then hastened to Signar's apartments. The guards saluted her respectfully. After what seemed an incredible length of time, she was taken to the Emperor's chamber.

He indeed appeared indisposed, his eyes shadowed with dark circles, his face unshaven. He received her with an air of abruptness.

"I will remain but a moment, my lord," she said through dry lips. "I have come to warn thee."

He raised his brows without speaking.

"I have received information from the Senator Divona that the Empress this morning obtained poison intended for thee."

Signar hardly moved a muscle. His eyes were all that seemed alive in his face. They burned into the girl's eyes until she found herself quaking inwardly. Finally he moved away from her and contemplated the sea through the white columns. At length he took Tyrhia's hand and studied her curiously. "What made thee bring me this information? It is not love, I know."

Tyrhia was silent a moment, then in a tantrum cried, "Salustra betrothed me to thee, knowing I loved another."

Signar looked amused. "And who is the fortunate youth that thou dost love?"

"He is Erato, cousin to the King of Dimtri."

"Erato!" exclaimed Signar, bursting into a gale of laughter.

Tyrhia looked at him in suppressed anger.

"And doth he love thee, lady?"

"So I believe." Another thought suddenly assailed her. "Thou wilt not tell Salustra, my lord, that I warned thee?"

Signar shook off her hand roughly. "I will see that she doth not harm thee," he said indifferently.

He turned his back to Tyrhia as an aide showed her the door. He stood in silence for a long time, his head bowed in thought, his fingers slowly clenching and unclenching themselves. "There is no love in this land," he finally said between his teeth.

29

SALUSTRA, returning from an extended session in the Chamber of Law, found a message waiting from Signar. "Majesty, thou hast denied me the radiance of thy presence for several days. Can it be because thou art mortally offended? Canst thou not pardon a poor brain stupid with wine?"

Salustra crushed the parchment between her fingers, then rapidly wrote a reply and sent a slave. After the slave had departed, she laid her head upon the table and sighed bitterly.

Opening the message, Signar read eagerly: "Sire, thy actions on thy vessel I can readily forgive. Thy apology I cannot. Wilt thou not join me in my apartment tonight for a private supper after the outdoor theater?"

So it hath come, he thought. Tonight, she poisons me. He felt strangely depressed. "Fool that I am to have imagined that her cheek flushed with love at my appearance, that her hand trembled in mine." As his mind was darkly considering the various courses open to him his generals, headed by the irrepressible Siton, entered. "Salustra's forces everywhere have joined with ours," they triumphantly announced. "The empire is thine, Sire, for the taking."

Instead of becoming elated, he felt his melancholy deepen. I have never loved before, he thought as they handed him an empire. How ironical that I should now love a woman who plots my death and whose empire is virtually given to me.

He had little time for self-indulgence. His lieutenants

were looking expectantly to him for leadership and so he gave orders quickly, curtly, for the military takeover. Then, as his aides departed on their errands, he prepared to join Salustra with his principal advisers. He felt an almost savage desire to know the truth for himself.

She was awaiting him, with Tyrhia, Brittulia and Mahius. She watched as he came through the marble portal with his general and minister. He was, she decided reluctantly, an Emperor not only by birth but by qualification. Despite his barbaric dress and a lavish display of gems, there was an air of nobility in his face and demeanor which distinguished him from other men. To him, watching her covertly, she seemed to be pale and shaken. Nevertheless, she greeted him pleasantly. "Ah, my lord, it is my hope thou wilt enjoy this day. It is the first day of the National Games, which the Empress always attends."

He kissed her hand. "To accompany thee, lady, will be sufficient pleasure." He looked beyond her to Tyrhia. As his eye touched hers the young Princess shrank fearfully behind her sister.

The Lamora amphitheater was just beyond the city proper, near the Great First Road. All avenues to the amphitheater were swarming with horses, carts and pedestrians, all apparently oblivious of the deadly heat and the heavy mist that hovered over the city like a gray blanket.

Already the thousands of seats in the oval arena were jammed with a restless, eager multitude. The whole theater hummed like a vast beehive. Here and there a protective awning of green or scarlet cloth struck the eye with its patch of color. The air was like that from a burning furnace, dry and parching.

The bronze doors at the top of the amphitheater suddenly swung open. As the blare of trumpets announced the arrival of the Empress and her party, an almost mechanical roar came from thousands of throats.

The Empress moved slowly to the imperial box, followed by a retinue of Senators, ladies, Nobles and Jupia, the High Priestess, as was the custom for the opening of the games. Beside Salustra, in royal scarlet and gold, moved Signar and his aides. The Empress responded to the ovation with an uplifted hand and an inclination of head.

"It is obvious that they love thee," said Signar with a smile.

"Nay, they are merely good-natured today." She shrugged indifferently. "They are grateful for the entertainment, to distract them from their fears and boredom."

"True," he said, "the favor of the mob is fickle."

Her whole body suddenly seemed to droop.

"Thou art tired," he said gently.

"I am always tired of late. There seems to be a heaviness in the air, a menace." She frowned, then smiled almost gaily with amusement. "I was called up to judge a most extraordinary case this morning. Thou must know I do not encourage new religions in Atlantis. The gods know, the old religion is bad enough. Moreover, I agree with my father that an old and depraved nation cannot afford new faiths. It seems, though, that a new religion hath appeared in Lamora, sponsored by a group of fierce, dark-eyed men with barbaric manners. I do grant freedom of worship in Atlantis. All I ask is that new religions create no disturbance and seek no converts. But this one band of aliens has been haranguing the people loudly, preaching of some vague wrath to come. They declare that their God, whom they name Jehovah, is weary of the sins of the world and intends to submerge all creation in a vast flood and wipe mankind from the face of the earth. However, so they say, his hand may be stayed by proper repentance. This would be laughable if it were not that my people are thus reminded of the old Atlantean prophecies. Have not their own gods so warned them? So they listen, fearfully, and become converts to this abominable religion."

Signar received all this with surprising seriousness. "And what are the tenets of this new faith?" he asked.

"They acknowledge but one God, which is an improvement. Moreover, they declare this God is a loving but just father, all-seeing, omnipotent, wise, merciful. And strange to relate, this God hath no mistresses. A stern and austere God, is it not? He is concerned, so say these savages, only with the making of all men righteous, preparatory to giving them eternal peace. He is, so they say, angered by the sins of this present generation because of their idolatry and superstition. With this I agree. However, He is also an enemy of joy, feasting and pleasure. This I do not agree with. Indeed, I would like to discuss the matter with Him, and I might well lead Him to repent His obvious obtuseness."

Signar laughed appreciatively. "I am amazed that these men can secure converts to such a spoilsport God."

Salustra shook her head. "These men appeal to fear, to which mankind is ever vulnerable."

"Is this Jehovah young and beautiful?" asked the Emperor.

Salustra half smiled. "I gather that He is old and bearded and ugly. But that may be a prejudice on the part of His servants. Many of them are old and bearded and ugly, and man has a tendency to create His god in his own image."

She frowned and lowered her voice so that only he could hear her. "I would ordinarily tolerate these men, but they are more obnoxious than ever since the disturbance of the sea a few nights ago. They say this was a warning. And the people are listening to them. I have almost a mind to turn Jupia upon them. She will make short work of these dangerous rivals."

Signar's interest mounted. Why he could not say. "And what occurred in court this morning?" he asked.

"Several were arrested and brought to me for judgment. I talked to them. They were not afraid of me, though they expected death. They replied to my questions clearly and with dignity. They told me that they had been sent from some distant place, which they would not name, to warn mankind that their Creator's wrath was about to fall upon them."

She laughed as she thought about it. "I drew them out. I involved them in a discussion as to their Jehovah. 'But we have nothing in this life except a few scattered grains of pleasure,' I said to the leader, a black-bearded man with fierce eyes.

" 'Happiness and pleasure are not one and the same,' he responded. 'Happiness is the deep peace in the heart of him who knoweth God's will. Happiness comes to him who hears the voice of God in the still of the evening and to him who knoweth that the work of his hands is good and that he hath done evil to no man. Pleasure is the lethal drug of the man who hath fled God and of him who knoweth that his hand hath wrought no good thing and that evil and malice are in his heart.' "

Salustra gave the Emperor a candid look. "And dost thou know, Sire, though I smiled, I knew that he spoke the truth? No man seeks pleasure as assiduously as the unhappy man. No man drinks so deeply as he who hath sorrow to numb. No man laughs so loud as he whose heart is breaking. No man seems so gay as he who hath a bad conscience. Even so, I shrink at the austerity of the life which these men advocate."

The Emperor nodded in apparent agreement. "Thy life is too exhilarating for such sterility," he said.

Jupia, sitting in silence behind the royal pair, now leaned forward and gazed at the Empress. "It is strange to hear thee speak of the gods, Majesty."

Salustra glanced at Signar humorously, ignoring her High Priestess. "The gods are very convenient. They should be ministers of art and beauty; otherwise, they should be abolished."

As she spoke the musical prelude suddenly ceased. A giant shadow, like a meteor, had streaked across the sky, darkening the arena for a moment, and thousands of uneasy eyes turned skyward.

"It is too dry for rain," remarked the Empress, trying

by her example to pass off the second ominous phenomenon in a week as of little moment.

Signar bent his head to catch a remark of Ganto.

"How calm is the wanton!" whispered Signar's general. "She thinks herself as secure as yonder mountain. She will have an awakening tomorrow!"

At Signar's frown, Mahius leaned forward and said in an undertone to the Empress, "Majesty, I like not the look of things. See how Signar whispers."

Salustra gazed at the Emperor. His pale eyes were fixed, unseeing, upon the stage.

Actors had begun to appear on the platform below. In the unprecedented heat they were sweltering in their heavy robes. But they were soon distractd by the majestic power of their drama. It was a simple play, which many thought especially timely. It appeared that once there lived in a sinful city one righteous man. The temples of the gods were deserted, this man complained, and men were engrossed in lewd pursuits. The righteous observer of all this corruption, one Ionto, rigorously pursued his abstemious life. He prayed thrice daily to the gods and was often the only worshipper in the temples. He had one daughter, a graceful maid, who loved life and pleasure. Accordingly, she, too, was accursed.

One day as he was praying in the temple, Ionto was visited by one of the gods, who appeared to him in a cloud as a radiant youth. He told the amazed Ionto that the gods had decided to destroy the city for its sins. Ionto begged that the gods stay their hand. The youth, relenting somewhat, directed that Ionto build an altar in the center of the city and there sacrifice his daughter. The gods would then spare the city.

Ionto was overwhelmed with grief. Uncertainly, he returned home to surprise his daughter in the arms of a lover. His mind was made up. But questioning now the virginity of his daughter, he wondered whether the gods would accept so impure a vessel. This wrinkle in the play never failed to delight the audience, as Ionto attempted to explain to his impious daughter, with gestures, what constituted a loss of virginity. In desperation, he concluded finally that all women were fools and that the virginity of their minds could never be violated. So perhaps the gods would grudgingly accept her, at least as being mentally intact.

He built an altar of the most magnificent proportions, much to the enjoyment of the sinful populace. Then, after he had heaped the altar with flowers, he dragged forth his daughter, lifted the screaming girl upon the altar and, to the public stupefaction, sank his sword into her bared breast.

As the girl expired the avenged god appeared again, radiant and pleased. Ionto knelt reverently, but the outraged multitude stared at the god in sullen silence. And then, with a cry of grief, the girl's lover, hitherto in the wings save for his one previous act, leapt upon the stage. He drew his sword and sprang upon the smiling god. He buried his sword in the god's breast. The sound of thunder rent the air. A glistening robe, representing a cloud, fell over the god as he crumpled to the floor. The lover tore the cloud aside, and, lo, the god had disappeared and a loathsome reptile was in his place. Turning on Ionto, the lover slew him and then drove the sword into his own heart.

It was normally a cynical play. Ionto was made to appear a half-mad fanatic, the daughter a little wanton full of the love of life, the god hypocritical, desiring the girl himself, the lover a righteous avenger.

The spectators, who had seen this play many times, always enjoyed it immensely. They always shouted with laughter over the command that Ionto sacrifice his daughter to save the city. They always groaned when the maid was slain. They always glowered as the god appeared, shrieked with approbation when the lover slew the god and when the god assumed his rightful form, that of a reptile. They had always shouted their approval when Ionto was slain by the lover and always wept when the lover slew himself.

But today the humor of the audience had unaccountably changed. They watched the play in uneasy silence, glancing at the darkened sky with fear. When Ionto was told the gods had decided to destroy the city, the people shivered as though touched by a cold wind. When he threw his daughter upon the altar, there was a faint splatter of applause, and after a brief hesitation the rest of the amphitheater took it up until the air rang with their tribute.

"Gods!" muttered Salustra, her fingers playing with the gem at her throat.

Jupia smiled darkly and fixed malevolent eyes upon the Empress. Her priests had worked well!

The play continued. The god appeared; the lover leapt upon the stage and slew the god. The people groaned. Salustra leaned forward from the imperial box and watched tensely. The cloud, simulated by a cloth, fell upon the god; the lover kicked the fabric aside, and the reptile was revealed. The people groaned again, shouting. Through the maze of noise protests were heard against this blasphemy. The Empress sat as if frozen into immobility. Then the lover slew Ionto to a renewed storm of protest and groans, and finally slew himself. At this final act, the people rose and applauded wildly; women sobbed, men shouted. The players themselves were unnerved and hurriedly left the stage. And then, as if at a signal, thousands of faces were turned toward the Empress.

Signar stared in astonishment. It needed no subtlety to recognize that something momentous was taking place. He glanced at Jupia. She alone was serene among those in the royal box.

"The people are displeased," quavered Mahius, but Salustra did not hear him. Her eyes were moving slowly over the standing multitude. She smiled contemptuously.

Signar touched her arm, "Let us go," he whispered. "I like not their air."

As Signar rose the multitude burst into shouts of acclamation. "Let us go," he said again.

"Go?" she repeated softly. "Shall I prove to these jackals that the daughter of Lazar is afraid of such as they?"

Salustra lifted her hand imperiously. At the signal, bronze gates to the arena flew open to the sound of trumpets and the great wrestler Noti, beloved of the Lamorans, appeared with the champion from the Fifth Province. The people resumed their seats in silence and the games began. The naked bodies of the contending athletes gleamed in the yellow light, their huge muscles straining. Enthusiastic roars greeted each dexterous move of Noti. Feverish betting began. When Noti finally overcame his opponent, the amphitheater shook with applause.

Racers followed on foot and on horse, then weight-throwers, jumpers, jugglers, singers, musicians, magicians, comedians, pugilists, lion-tamers. The people began to be bored and grew restless, uneasy, sullen. The heat seemed to increase; the sky was definitely darkening, and thunder, ominous, muttering, clattered through the burning air. Many began to look speculatively at the exits. Even the lion-tamer failed to hold their attention, with the beasts angrily springing at the crackling of the whip.

And then another ominous incident took place.

The pent-up atmosphere of the theater must have communicated itself to the sensitive beasts in their pit. Growling savagely, a big cat unexpectedly reared up and snatched at the tamer's whip. All might still have gone well had not the tamer stumbled and fallen headlong. Instantly, the beasts were upon him. The agonized shrieks of the victim unnerved the multitude, they shouted in incoherent sympathy, which was itself not without its excitement and delight.

Slaves and guards ran into the arena armed with pikes. The spectators scrambled over each other in morbid attempts to see all that was happening. The lions turned upon them, bowling over many with blood-stained claws. Dozens were crushed in the jam and women shrieked and fainted. Blood began to form in little pools.

Signar, considering the violence might be contagious, stood deliberately beside Salustra. In a few moments, however, the lions had all been slain, the dead were gathered up, and the rain began to come down in sheets. In the thundering downpour, the imperial party hastily withdrew, with Signar and his group bringing up the rear.

30

AN OMINOUS stillness hung over Lamora. Over-head, the sky was lost in black brooding cloud. The sea, growling uneasily, roughly lashed the shore. The air was full of sinister expectancy.

Signar, preparing to join Salustra in her apartments, looked out gloomily on this melancholy scene. The air was hot but an icy current blew through it. The Emperor, from his window, noticed that the guard about the Palace had been multiplied. Soldiers carrying flame-throwers paced resolutely before the gates. Creto moved quietly among them. The Emperor smiled and then sighed. He had already given his own orders. Everything was ready, waiting for his word.

Salustra, meanwhile, had given her commands to Creto. "I have none to trust except thee, Creto," she said gravely. "Do thy work well. If I fail, I shall still have use for thee."

"Majesty, my life is thine," responded the young Prefect, kneeling and kissing her feet.

"I am full of presentiments," said the Empress wearily. "Thou didst mark the uncertain temper of the people at the theater today."

"They are afraid," he said slowly. "Jupia's priests have been muttering to the people for some time, and after the disturbance of the sea they renewed their warnings of catastrophe and blamed it on thee."

Salustra nodded grimly. "Thou wilt bring Jupia to me tomorrow. And, Creto, the imperial guards, they are still faithful?"

A shadow touched Creto's face. "They would die for thee, Majesty," he said mechanically.

After dismissing Creto, she arrayed herself as one about to die or become a bride. She bathed, submitted to being rubbed with perfumed oils, garbed herself in a robe of transparent silver. On her arms gleamed jeweled bands; at her throat her father's gem seemed to glitter with increased fire; snuggled in a fold of her robe was the vial of poison.

As Salustra fingered the vial, the curtains stirred and parted, and without a sound Signar entered. For a moment they gazed at each other in silence. Salustra, with a smile, gave the Emperor her hand. "Ah, Sire," she said languidly, "it is an evil night. Hast thou noted how the heavens and sea seem to leap together?"

"Evil is—" he stood looking at her "—as evil does."

"Exactly." She smiled. "Let us dine."

Signar had a sudden desire to delay the inevitable hour. "Nay, not yet, Salustra," he said. She sighed and sat down upon a silken divan and lowered her eyes to the floor. Signar, after a moment's irresolution, seated himself beside her.

For an instant he was moved to tell her he knew of her plans. Then he dismissed the thought, hoping that Salustra herself might abandon her plot. He studied her haggard profile; her eyes had dark shadows beneath them. She looked thin. Hope began to form in his heart. Surely this manifest anguish could have but one meaning.

She turned and faced him, her lips parted as though she would speak, and then, under the gentleness of his regard, a dull crimson crept over her face. She rose quickly and went out upon the colonnade. After a moment he joined her. A howling wind lifted their garments and took their breath away. At one moment the city was in darkness, the next a ghastly vista of black and silver in the sky-splitting lightning. The sea, black, foaming, fanged, crashed upon the land, and behind, overlooking them, Mount Atla was muttering again.

"How violent the night!" cried Signar over the uproar. "And yet how magnificent! It makes one desire to shout with the wind and leap with the sea."

Salustra moved a step beyond him. She looked at the

heavens and then very slowly lifted her arms as if in supplication. The gale blew her hair about her like a streamer and molded her shimmering silver robe to her slim, sensuous figure like a winding sheet.

Signar watched her fascinated. To what wild god was she praying? To what terrible spirit was her own spirit speaking?

When she turned back to him, her face was as impassive as the face of the dead. She stepped back into her chamber as though she walked in a dream. He followed her, his depression increasing. He moved to the table, waiting for her to seat herself, and watched her covertly.

Tyrhia had warned of poisoned wine. But he had determined, as well, to eat and drink nothing that the Empress did not share. She held out a dish of fruit; he picked an orange that was nearest to her. She urged him to partake of the small candied doves, but he took only that bird which touched the one she had taken, and then merely picked at it. She offered him the golden cakes; he was careful to lift one cake from under those at the top. The crystal goblets on the table were already filled with wine. Was his already poisoned?

"Thou art eating but little, Sire," she chided him.

He glanced at her own plate. She had touched nothing. "Neither art thou," he responded. Salustra forced herself to eat, but the food formed a lump in her throat.

Signar looked across the table at his imperial hostess. He watched her white hands moving slowly. Her eyes were half-closed, as though she were suffering unbearable agony.

"What a strange world we live in!" he said, following the train of his own gloomy thoughts. "That which we desire above all things is denied us. That for which others envy us fills us with indifference. Is it some perversity in our nature which makes us covet that which we have not, or has some malevolent god decreed that whatever we desire shall not be given unto us?"

Salustra lifted her eyes to his. "I believe," she joined, "that the gods amuse themselves by tormenting us. They fire us with thirst, then give us stagnant water with which to quench that thirst. They endow the sensitive with majestic desires, with yearnings for beauty, with radiant spirits with which they might enjoy glorious things, and then let these unhappy wretches eat out their hearts in unsatisfied longings."

"Or," said Signar in a low voice, "they give us love which consumes us alternately with joy and anguish, and decree that this love is lavished on those who love us not."

Signar had not as yet touched his wine, nor had Salustra tasted hers. He studied the red liquid in the crystal goblet. Was it only his fancy which made it appear that it had a different hue from that in the Empress' goblet? He looked closer at his wine. Little bubbles rose continually to the surface. Against his will, a conviction that it was poisoned possessed him.

Salustra gave him a lackluster look. "Tell me about Althrustri, my lord," she said softly.

He shrugged carelessly. "My country," he said, "is not like Atlantis. It is a fierece land, the northern sections icebound and under snow and heavily timbered. As thou dost know, only the eastern and southern borders are settled. The rest is virgin, with vast natural resources. But I have visions of great cities where only wilderness now flourishes. My people are strong and adventurous and need only a little encouragement to expand their flair for commerce."

His candor surprised her. "Where dost thou expect to obtain such encouragement?" she asked.

Signar played with the stem of his goblet. "The gods may be kind."

"Thou dost mean thou wilt force the gods to be kind."

Their eyes held each other for a long moment. Then Salustra glanced aside and a shadow fell over her features again.

He laid his fingers over hers. "Who can demand that another be kind?" he said softly.

She withdrew her hand, lifted her goblet, and held it

high in her hand. The wine cast a red glow over her pallid profile. "Let us drink to our friendship, Sire!"

Still gazing upon her, he raised his glass, touched it to his lips, then drew back his head as if to drink, and paused.

"Wait!" she commanded.

He put down the goblet and looked at her with surprise.

"What aileth thee, Salustra?" he asked. "Shall we not drink to our friendship?"

"Let us talk first," she said.

He lifted his goblet again, his eyes dancing with a reckless mirth. "Let us drink to futility!" he cried. He again touched the goblet to his lips, as though to drink.

"Wait!" again cried Salustra, half rising. He stared at her in feigned astonishment, returning the goblet to the table. She sank back into her seat, her face ashen. "A feeble toast!" she said. "Hast thou no better?"

He shrugged. "What better? The gods, in a sportive humor, created us, as a writer of plays creates a drama, for their own amusement."

As he spoke, Signar just barely heard the sound for which he had waited, muffled footsteps behind the crimson curtains.

He lifted his goblet again and regarded the wine critically. "In this," he said lightly, "we have our antidote. Drowned in wine, we can even mock the gods and curse them gaily." Again he touched the brim to his lips, watching the Empress closely.

"Wait, my lord!" she cried a third time, her hand outstretched in command. At that moment, the heavens were divided as though by a colossal sword, and a great peal of thunder and lightning shook the earth. The lightning seemed to find a focus in Salustra, every gem upon her body shining like a star. She seemed oblivious of this new tremor.

"I wish to talk to thee," she said in a strained voice. "Let us not drink yet." She fell back into her seat and covered her face with her hands for a moment, then lifted

her head with a bitter smile. "I have discovered something, Sire. I am a coward. I lack courage and resolution.
In other words, I am a woman."

She looked up wildly, laughing now, her face flushed.
"My lord!" she cried. "Let us drink! But do thou give me
thy wine. See, I have touched my goblet with my lips.
Drink! It is a little custom in Atlantis, for friends to exchange in this manner." She was leaning across the table,
still convulsed with laughter, her goblet extended in her
hand. Grimly he gave her his goblet, and took her own
goblet. She lifted his goblet to the light. Her eyes were
sparking, her teeth gleaming between her laughing lips.
"To thee, my lord!" she cried. "To Atlantis, which I now
betray, and to the infernal gods!"

She put the glass to her lips, drew back her head, and
would have finished it in one gulp had not the Emperor
suddenly reached forward and dashed the cup from her
lips. The wine splattered over her dress. Simultaneously,
the earth shuddered under the clattering crash of thunder,
and the leaden skies turned into a flaming orange ball.

After that last earthshaking crash they sat together in
stunned silence. The Empress looked down at her stained
robe, and mutely shook the drops from her hands.

"Why didst thou desire to die, Salustra?" he asked softly. "And why didst thou spare me?"

She looked at the shattered goblet at her feet and her
head dropped.

"Tell me why thou didst spare me, Salustra," he repeated gently. "And why didst thou intend to die in my
stead?"

Her eyes were closed, as though she hoped to close off
reality for a moment.

His voice was compassionate. "Didst thou wish to die
because thou didst think thou hadst betrayed Atlantis?
Nay, think not so, Salustra. I knew the wine was poisoned
before I came to thee. I would not have swallowed it. So
condemn not thy cowardice."

She lifted her head. "Thou didst know the wine was
poisoned?" she said dully.

"Yes, I was warned."

She pushed aside the damp curls that clung to her forehead. "Who told thee?" she asked.

"Thy sister, Tyrhia," he said in a low voice. "She was told so by another."

"My sweet little Tyrhia," she said whimsically.

"Not so sweet," he said dryly.

"I have violated the great law of hospitality, Sire," she said. "I have sought thy death."

She held out her hand and he looked away. "What!" she exclaimed. "Thou wilt not take my hand? Well, thou art no hypocrite." In a sudden shift of mood, her voice was almost gay now. "But thou dost not ask if I will attempt thy death again, for thou are in my power, thou must remember!"

He laid his hand upon her shoulder. "Nay, it is thou who art in my power, Salustra."

He rose and walked swiftly to the crimson curtains, and flung them aside. In the hall outside stood her own imperial Guard. At their head was a smiling Siton.

Salustra didn't flinch for a moment. With a calm stride she moved toward the soldiers. A few paces from the guards, she halted. Under her piercing scrutiny the soldiers shifted uneasily. "So," she said humorously, "you, too, soldiers of Lazar!"

A murmur rose from the men, but they did not meet her gaze.

Smiling lightly, Salustra touched the foremost soldier on his asbestos breast. "Thou didst fight beside my father, Uslio," she said gently. "Thou wert wounded, fiercely beset. He stood over thy body, bleeding from many wounds, and saved thee, though he well nigh died himself." She paused. "He loved thee as did I."

The soldier's eyes showed his shame.

Salustra turned to another of the mailed giants. "And thou, Lio," she said in that same gentle voice. "My father took thee from slavery whilst thou wert a child. Thou didst wash his feet with grateful tears."

The soldier groaned and turned aside. Siton glanced

uneasily, gripping his sword. Signar shook his head with a frown.

Salustra's smiling eyes moved over the rest of the men, almost tenderly. "My father gave you to me," she said. "All of you swore to serve me to the death." She shrugged. "Poor flesh!" she said sadly. "I do not blame you. You were bought by one stronger than I and I commend your discretion."

She turned to Signar with a mocking gesture. "Take them, my lord. May they serve thee better than they served me. What was it thou didst say of futility?" She moved back to the table, standing there, smiling, as though at some secret jest. "I am to understand that all of Atlantis hath deserted to thee, Signar?"

He inclined his head without speaking. She looked at him with ostensible admiration. "My only shame," she said, "is that I must have appeared a blind and stupid fool in thy eyes."

"Nay!" he exclaimed. "I know thee for what thou art."

"And Creto?" she asked. "What of my poor Prefect?"

"Do with him what thou wilt. I will free him at thy word."

"And Mahius?"

"He, too, is spared. He loved thee. That is sufficient."

"And Erato?" she murmured.

A frown darkened Signar's brow. Then he shrugged. "He is thine, Salustra," he said in a low voice.

"And Tyrhia?"

He smiled grimly. "As thou must know, I was only playing thy game. She is free to love whom she wilt."

"Or hate whom she wilt," said Salustra bleakly. She sighed. "I have no other friends," she added half-aloud.

He inclined his head. "Thou didst give thy all to thy people and they have betrayed thee. I have learnt a timely lesson."

She shrugged. "There is neither right nor wrong; there are only strength and weakness," she said indifferently. "And may I ask, Sire, what is thy intention for Atlantis?"

"It will be annexed to Althrustri," he answered eagerly.

"I intend no reprisals. Atlantis will gain. She will become stronger, more vigorous, imbued with new life and new hope and strength by the infusion of the young blood of Althrustri."

She was silent, gazing at the sky. The orange glow had disappeared, but the thunder grumbled sporadically in the distance.

"Thou hast asked for others, Salustra," said Signar gently. "Thou hast not asked what I intend to do with thee."

"I?" she asked. "Thou wilt, of course, have me executed."

When he made no answer an expression of alarm crossed her features. She laid a trembling hand on his arm. "My lord," she said tremulously, "take everything, but grant me death; let me die quickly, without humiliation."

"I do not wish thee to die, Salustra. I have other uses for thee." His face was stern and unyielding. "Moreover, I require a solemn oath that thou wilt not attempt to take thy life. And I will hold Creto, Mahius and Erato hostages to that vow. If thou dies by thy own hand, these three will follow thee by no easy road. Dost thou understand, Salustra? If thou diest, these who love thee die also."

"My lord, of what use can I be to thee? Art thou mean enough to hold me up to the scorn of a world I have ever despised?"

"I desire not thy humiliation, lady. Thou givest thyself little credit by such a thought. Wouldst thou have treated me so if thou hadst conquered me? Nay, I will not insist upon an answer! But come, thy promise."

"My promise?" she murmured. "Take it. It is thine."

"And now, think not that I am ungenerous. Mahius will spend his days in comfort and seclusion. I shall try to induce that foolish Creto to join me. Erato shall be returned to his cousin, the King of Dimtri. All those for whom thou hast a weakness shall retain their honor and dignity."

She lifted her burning eyes to his, "Sire, thou hast denied me the one thing I desire. But grant me one boon. Give me tomorrow with all my old power. That is all I ask."

He hesitated and looked beyond her. The sky had lightened. A faint rosy light appeared in the gloom. It seemed a good omen.

"Take it. It is thine."

31

THE EMPRESS Salustra's abdication was a simple affair. "It is apparently the will of the people that we abdicate the throne of Atlantis and that the Emperor Signar be crowned in our stead, with the two mighty nations joined into one. We hope that the people will prosper under the new reign and will accord the Emperor their devoted allegiance, striving, with him, to create a new order worthy of Atlantis."

The message bore the Empress' seal.

The fickle public now began to question their own lack of support for Lazar's cub. Women began to weep, men to give vent to noble sentiments. Lazar was emotionally remembered. But it was too late. Salustra, philosophically committed, cared nothing for the changing sentiment in her behalf. "To protest against the rise of Signar," she told Mahius, "is like protesting against the rising of the sun. I have had my day. And now it is his."

But her sun had not quite receded. She prepared to use her one last day of power swiftly.

In the morning, after a restless night, she laid her hand on Creto's bowed head. "Thou lovest me still, Creto? Then do my last will. I bow to the inevitable. But private betrayal calls for private vengeance." She paused, fixing him with piercing eyes. "The one I loved most turned on me. Signar would still have overcome. But it is the desire that I cannot forgive. Dost thou understand, Creto?"

The Prefect looked at her steadily. "Thou dost mean thy sister, the Princess Tyrhia, Majesty?"

She moved her head slightly, noncommittally. "There are others as well. But first, thou knowest that Signar hath accorded me full power for this day." She withdrew a vial from her robe, a vial not quite full of a sparkling red fluid. "Thou wilt take this at once to Jupia, my High Priestess, with my compliments. And thou wilt remain with Jupia until she hath drunk of this vial."

She gave Creto a roll of parchment. "In it Signar decrees that all my commands be obeyed this day."

The Prefect took the vial from her hand, rose, and saluted. "For thee to command is for me to obey," he said quietly.

Salustra flashed her old, languid smile. "And thou wilt return immediately," she said.

When Creto had gone, she fell into a reflective silence. There were none of the accustomed callers, no courtiers, friends, clients, Senators, Nobles. Today the great dim halls yawned emptily, except for the soldiers under orders from Signar to watch the Empress closely.

But she was not to enjoy her unaccustomed solitude for long. The curtains parted, and Signar entered, unexpected and unannounced. At his appearance, Salustra rose, swaying a little from strain and weakness. She was no longer wearing Lazar's pendant, as if she had no further use of it. She caught the arm of her chair, then recovered quickly.

"Nay, Salustra," said Signar. "Thou art still the Empress today, rise not for me." He gave her his hand and assisted her into her seat.

A humorous smile touched her pale lips. "I have been thinking, Sire, that thou must ask my pardon for a breach of hospitality."

"And thou—" he smiled "—for attempting to send me to my ancestors."

She laughed softly, shaking her head. He had the impression that she was not laughing at his remark but at her own thoughts. "Thou dost not ask what are my intentions toward thee, lady," he said, after a moment.

"I am not interested," she said with a shrug.

"But I am," he said firmly. Again silence fell between them. "Are thy commands being obeyed implicitly?" he asked at last.

She inclined her head.

"Believe me, lady," he said, taking her hand, "I feel naught but compassion for thee—"

She snatched her hand from his. "Thou hast everything, my lord?"

He nodded silently. "Thou art satisfied?"

"I am, Salustra."

"Then, my lord, spare me thy pity."

She turned from him and fell once more into a detached silence. Signar sat for a few minutes, then with a shrug of his shoulders retired awkwardly without saying anything more. My presence, he thought bitterly, is like the grave to her, and yet I want only to see her alive and happy—at my side.

She sat thus for an hour, until Creto, his face flushed, stood before her with a nervous glitter in his eye. "It is done, Majesty," he cried. "She resisted the suggestion but I made the alternative seem less pleasant, and so she finally drank, cursing thee with her last foul breath."

She laid her hand on the Prefect's arm and fixed her hypnotic eyes upon his face. "And now," she said, "go thou, Creto, to the Princess Tyrhia's apartments. Thou hast the decree of Signar. Gain admission without delay. And then," dropping her voice to a whisper, "thou wilt bring her to me."

The Prefect trembled and his face turned the color of new parchment.

"Majesty—" his voice faltered "—I implore thee . . ."

Salustra smiled wanly. "It is not what thou thinkest. Go to, Creto."

32

THE SLAYING of Jupia jarred the city to its sanctimonious core.

Ganto and Siton reported the savage humor of the people to the Emperor. Strongly, they counseled that Signar deliver up Salustra to the justice of the city. "Who knows but that the people may refuse to accept thee if thou dost condone this blasphemy?" said Ganto. "Deliver her to her own people and they will love thee for it."

Signar glumly sent his guards for Salustra. She entered calmly. Her quiet glance disdainfully passed over the group standing before the Emperor. He did not rise as she stood before him.

"Thou hast murdered thy religious leader," he said accusingly.

"I murdered the treacherous exploiter of my people," she answered evenly.

"Her death cries out for vengeance," he said.

She smiled. "Kill me then."

Signar stirred in his seat impatiently. "Thou mightest have murdered a thousand others and no hand would have been raised against thee. But the murder of a High Priestess, a representative of the gods, it is indefensible." As she made no answer, he looked at her with increasing sternness. "The people cry for thy death. But I shall declare that Jupia was murdered without thy knowledge by Creto, who wished only to defend thee."

She smiled faintly. "And I shall deny it, Sire."

He rose with an oath. "And I shall declare thee mad, and by the gods, I believe thou art mad!" Still smiling, she bowed her head. His frowning eyes commanded hers. "If I turn thee over to thy people they will inflict the vilest shame upon thee before they allow thee to die in torment. Does the prospect please thee?"

She recoiled the least bit. The soul that could endure death without equanimity could not endure shame.

"Grant me a swift and speedy death now, my lord," she whispered.

He thrust her from him angrily, and at that gesture her old pride came back and her figure stiffened.

"Send for the woman who may watch over her," Signar said aloud to Siton. The general left the chamber and soon returned with a weeping Brittulia. "Take thy mistress to her apartments, woman," said the Emperor, "and see that she does herself no mischief."

Salustra looked at him defiantly. "I still have thy word that my wish shall be command for twenty-four hours, and twelve hours still remain by my timepiece."

Signar flushed. "What new horrors dost thou contemplate?"

"Let me keep Creto yet awhile."

"He must pay for thy misdeed."

Salustra threw back her head. "A king's promise, Sire, is only as good as he."

He scowled darkly, and then his face cleared. "But know that one moment thereafter thou art at my disposal."

Before he could say any more she turned and left the chamber. There was no faltering in her step and her face was serene. She looked every bit a queen, and Signar's eyes followed her in rapt silence.

"See the way the wind blows!" whispered the minister, Ganto, to the general, Siton. "I shall hasten to pay my most humble and royal court to that beautiful vixen."

Siton frowned. "And I, too."

Upon returning to her apartments, Salustra had a surprise awaiting her. Her anteroom was crowded, no Senators, no courtiers were they, nor the Nobles who had formerly fawned upon her. They were the philosophers, Yonis, Talius, Everus, Zetan, Lodiso, Morti, and a group of scientists.

They hastened to greet her and kissed her hands with reverence. "Ah, sirs," she said in a shaken voice, "I little expected that you would remember me."

"How could we forget our noblest friend, our most understanding patron, our kindest benefactress?" cried Zetan. "Thou dost give us little credit, Majesty, for ordinary gratitude."

"Gratitude?" she echoed bitterly. "I have always said: 'Dost thou desire an enemy? Then, assist thy friend!'" Nevertheless, it was evident that she was moved by their loyalty.

"The agonies of today are the jests of tomorrow," said Morti. "Only by indifference and humor can we defeat the gods."

She hesitated, watching them keenly. "Have you heard, sirs, that I put the High Priestess to death?"

"Yes, Majesty," replied Everus quietly.

"And you are not horrified?"

Morti took her hand. "Nay, Majesty. What horrifies us is the treachery that made such an act necessary."

Salustra's eyes dimmed. "I have but one thing further to say to you, sirs. It is dangerous to love me and to be my friend. Attempt to see me no more. The Empress of Atlantis is dead."

After dismissing them she turned to Brittulia, who was again weeping. "Thy work is done, Brittulia," she said. "The virtuous always find consolation for their virtue when the unvirtuous are brought to ruin."

Brittulia knelt and tearfully kissed the hem of Salustra's garments. "Majesty," she said, "grant me one prayer."

"It is granted, Brittulia," she said, laying her hand on the woman's head.

"Then, Majesty, permit me to remain with thee. I came to care for a slip of a girl but learned to care for thee instead. Thou hast more of virtue in thee than any virgin."

The Empress raised Brittulia to her feet and kissed the pale forehead. "Do not shame me with thy virtue," she said. "I have already borne more than the unvirtuous can stand. Find Tyrhia for me."

Brittulia did not wince as usual at the Empress' touch. "Thou still hast enemies, Majesty, the Senator Divona, for one."

She laughed hollowly. "What mischief, pray, can Divona and his ilk do me now? In any event, he is on the good Creto's list, though I am sure his new master would otherwise make short work of him. A traitor is much like a man who cheats on his wife; he can be counted upon to repeat his duplicity with his new partner. The habit remains, only the names change."

33

SIGNAR had proclaimed officially that Salustra was not responsible for Jupia's death. The High Priestess, he explained, had been slain in madness by the young Prefect, Creto, who would pay with his life for the unspeakable crime.

Divona, the Senator, sought the Emperor's protection. The Emperor listened coldly as the Senator referred to past favors.

"Salustra is helpless now," he said. "She cannot harm thee."

Divona shook his head. "She is an evil woman, Sire. Not until she is dead shall I feel safe."

"Then," said Signar, "thou shalt not feel safe for some time." He looked at the Senator cynically, "And was it not thou, Divona, who didst once ask for Salustra as thy reward for thy betrayal of her?"

"I have changed my mind," the Senator stammered. "I would as soon have a hungry tigress in my bed."

Signar regarded him scornfully. "Go whilst thou can," he said.

Divona blanched and slunk out of the room.

There was no place in Lamora he could hide. It did not take Creto long to find him. The cynical Senator, devoted to a life of deviousness, found that the last to respect a traitor is he who employs him.

"Wouldst thou kill me," he said to the simple Creto, "when I can make thee a rich man with everything thou ever dreamt of, great estates, slaves, women to do thy bidding?"

Creto could not forgo a triumphant moment. "How

canst thou help me, traitor, when thou canst not help thyself?"

And with this he plunged his sword deep into the bowels of a man consumed by his own hatred.

The Empress had impatiently awaited Creto's return. One look, as he strode in, was all she needed to know.

"Had this deed been done long ago, Creto, Atlantis might not be helpless today."

The Prefect knelt and kissed the hem of her robe. "What more, Majesty, before I die?"

She shook her head sadly. "I would gladly trade Signar my life for thine."

"Thou hast little room for sentiment, Majesty," the man of action reminded her.

"Thou must still fetch my sister. I have one more duty to perform." She reflected a moment. "Take a guard to Brittulia's house. The little fool may well be hidden there, while Brittulia seeks her in the Palace."

The Prefect hesitated, and a look of misgiving came to his eye.

"What is it, Creto?" she demanded.

"I pray, Majesty, that my last act is an honorable one."

Salustra's face was illuminated by a quick smile. "Fear not, I intend this foolish girl no harm. The vengeance I consider is of another sort."

No sooner had he clanked out of the room that Brittulia arrived with a message from the poèt Erato, pleading for an audience.

"I will see him in the garden in an hour," said the Empress agreeably, much to Britullia's surprise. "Now tell me, what hast thou done with the Princess Tyrhia?"

Brittulia's face was full of contrition. "She has disappeared, Majesty, as from the face of the earth, perhaps fearing that Signar may exercise his claim on her."

"She is indeed a fool," said the Empress. "She reminds me more of Lahia, her mother, each day. Signar knows not, nor cares, whether she is alive, and never intended to marry her. It was but a ploy on his part." She paused a moment. "Now make haste, Brittulia, to thy own home and meet Creto there." With shining eyes, the virgin Brittulia bent and kissed her hand. Salustra gazed at her pityingly. "Go now," she said kindly. "Thou poor thing."

The hour was fast approaching when Salustra would lose her borrowed authority. She sat calmly, reviewing in her mind without regret the recent flow of events. She cared not for astrologers and their predictions but she could not view the gray sky, smell the sickening atmosphere, or contemplate the cessation of electrical energy without considering these as fateful steps toward a more sinister drama yet to be revealed.

"Signar's coming," she told Mahius, who had just entered, "is another spoke in Atlantis' ruin, brought on, as those bearded fanatics have warned, by her own lack of moral purpose. What reason is there for Atlantis to exist? It has seen and done everything noble, everything rotten and degraded, until it has become a sink of iniquity. Its people would rather be fed by a paternalistic government than work, and prefer dissipation to contribution. They are not worth saving, and this the gods must surely know as they shake the earth."

Mahius permitted himself a smile. "Signar's reckless use of the atom-splitter has, I am sure, contributed to the recent behavior of the elements."

She thought for a moment. "We are all instruments of an inscrutable destiny and it suited the gods for Signar to do their work with the aid of Divona and his friends." Her teeth came together. She was the Empress again. "But Divona, like Jupia, will trouble his countrymen no longer."

The old man shrugged indifferently. "Small matter, Majesty, if thy forebodings are correct."

She gave her minister a shrewd glance. "You would like that, old man, wouldn't you?"

He shook his head. "Only for myself, Majesty. Let others who have not tired of life's dreariness grow as weary of this meaningless pastime as I."

"Thou hast served too severely, Mahius."

"Say not so, Majesty. In all my years with thy father and thyself I hold but one grievance."

"And what is that, old man?"

"That thy august father gave me the rejuvenation chamber."

She looked at his bleary eyes and shriveled skin, at the bent figure that could no longer stand erect, and said curiously, "Wouldst not thou like it better, old man, to have the face and form of a Signar or Erato?"

"Nay, Majesty, for when I gaze into a mirror and see that wrinkled prune gaping back, I know that death cannot be far off."

"Hast thou had such a hard life then, old man?"

He shook his head. "No, Majesty, I did enjoy everything I found in season. But once the mind has grappled with a problem, it has no more incentive for going over the same ground, knowing from experience what the outcome must be."

"By thy definition, then, I too am ready for this surcease thou speakest of."

"Not so, Majesty, thou art disenchanted presently by the frailties of others and self-disappointments, but thou art still young and wilt get over these obstacles."

"And so when, old man, do we become too old to live?"

"When we are no longer enthusiastic at the promise of what lurks around the corner. Then, Majesty, we are ready for Drulla."

"I am too old then." She sighed.

"Not so. Thou hast never married, borne a child, known the love of a man of thy own stature—so how canst thou have finished with this experience?"

"There is none to love who loves me," she said wistfully.

He gave her a look of infinite insight, born of two lifetimes of examining the underlying motivations of man. "Majesty, in serving thy father, I discovered one cannot count on what a man says or even what he does; it is by knowing what he wants that we know his nature. And so I ask myself what is it that thou truly wantest."

"And what dost thou see, old man?"

"I see thee yearning for a mate, an equal, but telling thyself it is impossible." He gave her a look of avuncular devotion. "And I tell thee, daughter of Lazar, thou art loved, as thou lovest."

She gave him a look of scorn. "Dost thou speak of the poet Erato, old man?"

He looked at her indulgently. "I have known thee, Majesty, from the cradle, and I know the honest affection locked in thy heart. Let it out. Thou hast naught to lose."

She shook her head as if to free herself of some captive thought. "I would see Tyrhia disposed of before I leave, and then I am ready to meet the great Lazar."

He chuckled. "And why so concerned about this empty-headed daughter of a woman thy father detested?"

She shrugged. "She is my sister, I see it at times in her temper and the tilt of her head."

"Be honest with thyself, Majesty. Thou wouldst not padlock the Emperor's heart to an ignoble creature whose emotions come of her glands."

She saw no need to point out that the mismatch had been abandoned. "And who is it I love that loves me, old man?" she said.

As Mahius was about to answer, Signar was announced. He was alone save for a slave. He looked about vigilantly, noting the Empress' careworn expression and the resignation in the minister's face.

"Salustra, I am told thou hast not touched food for days and thy head hath not known its pillow. What madness is this?"

Her manner suddenly changed. She said with a twinkling eye, "Sire, wouldst fatten me for the kill?"

His eyes became stern. "Speak not nonsense. Thou art not Tyrhia but the Empress Salustra."

She shrugged in her frustration. "Thou must have spies even in my household?"

"Not spies, Majesty, concerned servitors."

"Call them what thou likest. It is the same."

He made an impatient gesture and sent his slave to bring food for Salustra. With his own hands he arranged fruit, cheese, meat, bread and wine upon a table.

"I cannot eat," she said simply.

"Thou canst try," he said. He poured wine into a gilded goblet and extended it to her.

"I swear to thee that it is not poisoned," he said with amusement.

He had an hypnotic effect on her. She took the wine and drank it. A faint color appeared on her cheek. She broke a piece of bread and brought it to her mouth but could not stomach it.

"Come," said Signar sharply. "I gave thee credit for more intelligence." He stood by her until she had partaken of the meat and cheese and fruit and had tasted more wine.

"Why dost thou desire to keep me alive, my lord?" she asked. "I am of no use to thee."

He fixed his eyes upon her. "Why didst thou spare me that night, Salustra?"

"Who knows?" She shrugged. "Perhaps I did not think thee worth the killing. Perhaps I desired thee to live because thou didst amuse me. I cannot tell."

He took her hand smilingly. "Someday, thou wilt tell me thyself. And when thou dost I will tell thee why I desire thee to live."

He turned abruptly to the silent Mahius. "What sayest thou, old man?"

Mahius moved his frail shoulders slightly. "What is there to say, Sire?"

34

THE SKY was still behaving strangely. A pallid yellow light mirrored by the mountains turned the sea a greenish yellow. The air was heavy and humid, making breathing an effort. Once the earth trembled and a crash like thunder came from the sea.

Salustra, moving slowly to the gardens, was bathed in a yellowish light. At the bottom of the marble stairway stood an agitated Erato with outstretched hands.

Siton and two soldiers, who had followed the Empress, watched with interest. They could not hear the conversation but saw the young poet kneel and kiss her hands with adoration. Not waiting for further developments, Siton went immediately to Signar and reported what he had seen.

Signar's face became like a cloud. He buckled on his sword, usually worn only on ceremonial occasions, and without a word hurried to the garden in time to see Salustra's white robes disappear into a glade. He followed closely, as he had once before, and saw Salustra seat herself on a marble bench. Erato, at her feet, alternately kissed her hands and pressed them to his face. Their voices, though low, carried clearly in the breathless quiet.

"Nay, it is the end," Salustra was saying sadly. "What he intends to do with me, I do not know, nor do I care."

"Come with me to Dimtri," pleaded Erato once more. "Let us pray to him for this permission." Again and again in an ecstasy of desire he kissed her hands.

"Thou art kissing the hands dipped in a priest's blood, Erato," she said.

"Were they thrice dipped in such blood they would not forfeit my love," he answered staunchly.

As she remained silent, Erato leaned his cheek against her knee and frowned. "I tried to warn thee of treachery, beloved. But thou wouldst not see me."

"A warning would not have helped me," she replied distantly.

He hesitated, looking at her uncertainly. "Salustra," said he finally, "tell me if it is true, as some say, that Signar loves thee."

Salustra looked at him incredulously. "Gods!" she cried. "What things will these fools say next? Signar hates me. He is preserving me for future humiliations."

Erato studied her with a lover's penetrating eye. "But thou dost love him, Salustra," he said quietly.

She leaned her chin in her hand and said nothing.

Erato sighed. "I suspected it when last I saw thee. And how could he but love thee?"

Salustra shook her head fiercely. "I know not whether I love or hate him; it is confusing."

"Oh gods!" groaned Erato. "If I could but fly with thee to some distant place. Even if we were caught, death would be better than this agony."

She gave him a pitying glance. "Were we caught thou alone wouldst suffer. I forbid thee to speak of it further."

"Thou will not consider it because thou dost love him!" cried the young man bitterly. He took her in his arms and kissed her bare shoulders and throat.

Signar, in the shadow of the trees, bit his lip till it bled.

Salustra gently disengaged herself from Erato's embrace. "Thou art still a poet with a poet's ardor, Erato," she said with some amusement.

"And thou, Salustra, what art thou?"

"Not even an Empress." She shrugged ironically.

In his impotence Erato began to beat his head with his fists. "His next conquest," he cried, "will be of the little helpless kingdoms whose integrity thy father did guarantee. Conquest? Nay! He will merely take them. In Dimtri I shall wait for Signar. I shall face him man to man and we will see who is the better one!"

As he spoke thus a shadow fell upon them. They

looked up, startled, to see a formidable figure looming over them. Signar was smiling but there was a thinly veiled menace in his dark face. "I am here, Erato," he said calmly. "What hast thou to say to me?"

Erato was as pale as death. "What have I to say to thee?" he cried recklessly. "Nothing, except that thou art less than a man, less than a slave, less than the dust beneath Salustra's feet!"

Salustra turned to Signar urgently. "Lord," she said in a low voice, "he is but a mad and foolish youth."

Thinking she thought only of Erato Signar shook her hand from his arm. He turned on the poet, and before the younger man could move he had seized him by the shoulder as a lion might seize a dog.

"Effeminate fool!" he exclaimed scornfully. "I would be all those things you say were I to quarrel with thee!" He struck Erato's cheek sharply with the flat of his hand.

Erato recoiled, stunned, and then a wave of anger, long pent up, swept over him. His sword flashed and glittered in the yellow murk, and Signar swiftly drew his sword.

A stifled cry broke from Salustra as she caught Signar's arm. "My lord, thou didst promise to spare those that I love. It would be cowardly murder, unworthy of you."

Signar, pausing, glanced contemptuously at Erato. "Dost thou love him, Salustra?" he taunted.

"Yes, lord."

"Then take him! It is meet that the daughter of Lazar should have a singer of songs as a lover."

As Signar stood there, proud and disdainful in his regal splendor, the stripling poet, the contemptible Erato, struck him across the face with the flat of his sword. "Butcher like thee I never was!" he cried. "But a man unto himself, which thou art not!" The blood spurted from Signar's cheek and flowed into his eye, partially blinding him. But he attacked fiercely, his sword raining blows like those of a great hammer. Before that battering assault Erato gave ground steadily. But suddenly, as he parried an overhead blow, he made a lucky thrust of his own on Signar's blind side.

Salustra let out a cry, for Erato had struck Signar a near-mortal wound in the breast and the blood was already staining the Emperor's white tunic.

Signar stepped back for a moment, more startled than dismayed. The smile vanished from his face. His jaw hardened and his one clear eye took on a pale gleam. The sight of the Emperor's blood had renewed the poet's dwindling strength. And then, as Signar rallied strongly, the tiring Erato took a direct thrust in the throat and began bleeding profusely. A torrent of blood seemed to spurt from the great vein, and Salustra with a sickening feeling sank upon the marble seat and watched with a sense of impending doom.

The yellow air had become more brassy, more stifling. The swords of the men glittered with a golden light, their feet trampled the blood-stained grass, their breath came in agonized gasps. Once the ground under them trembled and a mighty roar from the sea disturbed the air. But these things they did not feel or hear.

Signar was bleeding from several small wounds on his arms and a thin red rivulet was running from his cheek. Erato was growing rapidly weaker. He had only that one wound in his throat, but it was fast draining his strength away. He stumbled, fell backward; Signar's sword flew up, caught Erato's weapon, tore it loose from his hand and sent it spinning into the air. Salustra rose, and as she did so, Signar in the fury of fighting prepared to drive his sword into the breast of the defenseless man.

But a slim wraith of a figure, appearing as out of nowhere, suddenly threw her body between the two men, falling on her knees before the Emperor.

"If thou hast any love for the house of Lazar spare this man, whom I love more than life."

Signar's sword paused, then dropped to his side.

In a voice weak from his own loss of blood, Signar managed to say with a faint smile, "I am pleased that this house is capable of love, though it be wasted on a poet."

Tyrhia had just arrived with Creto and Brittulia in response to Salustra's summons, and now with a cry of anguished relief she threw her arms around the half-swooning Erato. Tenderly she kissed the blood from his lips.

Erato smiled faintly, his eyes closed, and then very slowly his body crumpled and he fell face forward upon the bloody lawn.

Tyrhia knelt beside him and drew him into her arms. With his head pillowed upon her breast, and his blood staining her white garments, she looked up at Signar, who stood in silence, the bloody sword still poised in his hand.

At this moment the Palace Guard, alarmed by Tyrhia's outcry, came flying. Signar pointed to the Princess and the man in her arms. "If he lives," he said weakly, "spare him. As for myself . . ."

He staggered and would have fallen if Siton had not caught him in his arms. They carried the two men back to the Palace, to Salustra's own apartments.

The imperial physician, Cino, examined the Emperor first and shook his head gravely. "A thread closer to the heart and death would have resulted immediately," he said. "As it is, recovery is uncertain."

Moving then to the unconscious Erato, he could only shrug helplessly. "It is with the gods."

In a frenzy of grief, the Princess Tyrhia advanced on her sister. "It is thy fault," she cried. "Signar slew him for love of thee."

Salustra sat as if in a dream. "He is not dead yet," she whispered. "Have hope."

She beckoned to the weeping Brittulia. "Tell this foolish maid that it was my wish to bring Erato and herself together, and for that reason I summoned them to my garden."

Tyrhia clinging to the poet, as if by her own will she would keep him alive, would not be consoled. "If he dies, my sister, it is thy doing."

Salustra looked at the clock on the wall. The twenty-four hours of authority given her by the Emperor had terminated. With a leaden heart she turned to Mahius, present as always in time of need.

"I want reports on the hour on his condition."

"Whose condition, Majesty?"

"Signar's." She stared blankly ahead.

A curtain of gloom settled over the Palace. Beyond the Palace moat, a mighty crowd gathered, silent, sullen, looking fearfully to the sky. The yellow haze of day had faded but the night sky was a smoldering orange flame. An unearthly light lay upon the uneasy sea, the restless water billowing like a moving flame. Even the shadowy mountains were slashed at intervals as though rivers of fire were running down them.

Salustra had no sleep that night. With her sister she sat by the dying poet's couch, marveling at the serenity of the chalklike features, and yet her mind, perversely, was on another man.

Meanwhile, the bright hue of the sky deepened and the sea became turbulent beyond measure. Geologists, astronomers and oceanographers whispered fearfully together and watched the instruments that registered the tremblings of the ocean floor.

A hurricane wind sprang from the sea, and with it the heavens seemed to open. A solid mass of water fell upon the earth and the sea became a howling demon.

At the height of this tempest Erato's eyes opened and lighted on Tyrhia, whom in his stupor he mistook for Salustra. Tyrhia bent over him and kissed his cold, damp brow. His hand moved feebly and she took it in her own. Death was upon him and he struggled against it that he might speak once more to the woman he loved. His last whisper rattled in his throat.

"I love thee, but not as a poet." He sighed and smiled drowsily. "If the gods will, I will soon be a philosopher." With that, he died.

A saddened Salustra looked at her sister. "It is of thee he spoke," she said.

35

THE RAIN continued with unabated fury, as though the floor of the heavens had opened, for twenty-four hours. Few dared venture beyond their threshold, and all business was suspended. Through the wide, deserted streets and canals of Lamora rushed the waters, swirling about the ancient statues and pillars and carrying everything before them. The earth crumbled, foundations of buildings were undermined and they shook precariously. Through the torrential uproar, above the screaming of the wind, beyond the roaring of the swelling waves, could be heard the dull thud of pillars and walls crashing before the flood. The mountains seemed to dissolve into black rivers, which descended upon the stricken city. Earth and heaven and sea were one churning vortex that seemed to gobble up anything that was floatable. Occasionally, the earth rumbled ominously as if in protest against all this indignity.

For days the storm raged, seeming to gain momentum. The inhabitants of the section bordering the shore retreated as the water began to rise through the lower streets, floating away their houses. Upon the broiling surface floated refuse of all description. The sewers spewed their contents into the streets and here and there a dead body swirled by. The orange of the sky had faded and a purple glow seemed to have fallen like a mantle over the face of the earth. But there was no end to the ominous rumbling, which seemed to come from the earth and sea and sky simultaneously. At times it seemed that invisible chariots were rolling overhead; again, as though a great army were rushing in from the sea on giant horses. It was as if the very core of the earth were crumbling and a precariously thin shell floating on top was about to splinter into some bottomless abyss beneath the raging sea.

The scientists were understandably filled with astonishment, even as they recalled the recent prophecies of destruction. "If you were not to think me mad, sirs," said one sage to his colleagues, "I would declare that the sea was rushing in under the land into vast subterranean caverns, the walls of these great caverns are being battered, and this unprecedented pressure is causing this steady rumble."

"In that event," said another, "it is only a matter of time until the solid bedrock of the earth crumbles and the crust collapses."

Meanwhile, the public agitation grew, as delayed reports began to come in from other provinces. Widespread death, destruction and desolation were reported. Thousands were losing their lives, and untold throngs were rushing eastward toward higher land before the surging waters. The inhabitants of whole cities were on the move. But where could they go? The entire earth seemed to be dissolving into water. By word of mouth rumors swept through the inundated world. Some said that Althrustri was still safe, protected by its own frosty climate. Others turned hopefully to the west. Mass migrations from Atlantis' central and southern provinces began to the north and west despite the continuous downpour.

And then, after seven days, the storm seemed to subside. The wind dropped, the sky lightened, the rain ceased abruptly. And in a sky of azure blue the sun shone with pale radiance upon a half-drowned world. The air was cold and the sea rolled in great waves, crashing with the clap of thunder upon the battered shore.

Despite the persistence of the subterranean rumbling, men began to breathe more easily. All over Atlantis millions made their way to the temples, there to pray for their deliverance. They stood, in many instances, knee-deep in stinking water, shivering, cold, but grateful that the gods had apparently spared the world. Millions were homeless. Nobody knew how many dead there were.

The priests began to whisper among the people. This calamity had not fallen upon the land as impersonally as the impious scientists insisted. Shifting strata indeed! Tidal waves—folly! Seaquakes—absurdity! The gods were enraged. Why did they assault the earth? Because the people of Atlantis allowed an evil and blasphemous woman to flourish in their midst.

The priests did not forget their archenemy now that the earth seemed secure again. Throughout the shivering capital the fearful and resentful began to mutter, egged on by their religious mentors.

"Hear the angry warnings of the gods," said the priests of the continuing subterranean rumbles. "They have temporarily abated their wrath. They are giving the people of Atlantis one final chance to redeem themselves. And they will be pacified only by the death of this bloody murderess."

The priests realized that a majority, unorganized, is helpless against an organized minority. They summoned the people to the temples and in impassioned voice demanded the trial of Salustra by the Senate on murder charges.

At first, the people fell into uneasy silence, disconcerted by the thought of responsible action. The priests were quick to sense the indecision of the people, and with their customary craft they seized upon a new celestial phenomenon as a retaliatory gesture of the gods.

The sun, now clearly seen, had assumed a reddish tint and was surrounded by a circle of scarlet which seemed to flame and flicker. The people, fearing another deluge or worse, surged through the streets to the Senate Chamber and there demanded of the Senate that it bring Salustra to justice at once.

With the wounded Signar still in coma, the Senate Guard, supported by the Senate, were ordered to arrest and detain the Empress. Led by an exultant Gatus, avenging his ill-starred brother-in-law, Lustri, they made their way to the imperial Palace, followed by a shouting multitude. They were like ravenous wolves ready to pounce on their prey once they were assured no risk of retaliation. And in their abdicated monarch, indifferent to her own welfare, the craven mob had their perfect quarry.

36

FOR SEVERAL days Signar had lain close to death. His chamber was heavily guarded, and slaves moved about on velvet feet. The physician Cino was in constant attendance.

Siton and Ganto had remained with the Emperor, sitting by his couch through the nerve-racking days of the great storm. The crafty minister and the burly general, fanatically devoted to their Emperor, had kept their vigil without more than occasional catnaps. Once, during a lucid interval, Signar opened his eyes, fixed them on Ganto, and said faintly, "Protect Salustra as thou wouldst me."

Signar then lapsed into unconsciousness.

"It is strange, the power this murderess hath over him," whispered Siton as he watched his slumbering master.

Ganto looked up admonishingly and touched his lips. "We may yet be bending a knee to her. So govern thyself accordingly."

As Signar slowly regained his strength, Salustra's life force appeared to be waning. She neither ate nor slept but spent the days in almost catatonic silence, mindless of both the elements and the demands for a Senate trial. It seemed to the grieving Brittulia and Mahius that Salustra had died and that her body, propelled by some mysterious inner power, maintained an independent life. Her eye did not brighten with recognition when it fell upon them, nor did she hear their voices. She sat for hours in her ivory chair, her unwinking eyes fixed on some vague spot in space.

Once Siton softly entered and approached the Empress.

She frowned, as though trying to distinguish his words. Then her eyes stared off once again.

"They say that Signar is recovering," whispered Mahius to the visiting Siton.

Before the general could answer Salustra looked up alertly. "Signar," she murmured. "Hath he died yet?"

They assured her that he still lived. But she did not seem to hear.

Confident that Signar would not recover, the Senate Guard made its way into the Palace as the mob swarmed in the gardens. Overhead, the skies were darkening again and anxious eyes turned heavenward. Trees stood limp, still dripping water; vegetation had disappeared. One disaster seemed to lead into another, and the mob, egged on by its leaders, had happily found a scapegoat. Halfway to Salustra's apartments, Signar's elite Guard, headed by Siton, routinely halted the Senate force. A parley ensued. Siton listened to the Senate's declaration of arrest. He pretended to deliberate with Ganto, but used this only as a delaying tactic, saying in an aside, "We must save her. Otherwise, we would never dare face the Emperor again."

Gatus stepped forward boldy. "My lords," he said, "the power of the Atlantis Senate supersedes that of the sovereign. This is a legal arrest and I would suggest that none detain us." He made a significant gesture toward the angry mob below.

Still stalling for time, Siton and Ganto stood aside before a superior force, allowing the Senate Guard to continue on their mission as if it were no great concern of theirs.

Gatus entered Salustra's chamber first. Alarmed at the noise, Brittulia and Mahius had risen and were standing protectively before the Empress. Gatus held a roll of parchment in his hand. "We have come for Salustra," he said, stepping farther into the chamber.

"On what charges?" demanded the minister.

"On the charges of murder and treason."

Mahius would have spoken again but at that moment the Empress rose. She looked first at Gatus and then at the soldiers behind him. Her dull eyes glittered. Salustra was herself again. The mention of treason had been enough to wake her.

"Thou hast come to arrest me?" she asked calmly.

Gatus made a deep obeisance.

"Let me see the warrant," she said. Almost automatically he surrendered it. As she read a faint smile touched her lips. With the utmost composure she tore the parchment and let the fragments drift to her feet. "On those spurious charges," she said calmly, "I will gladly be executed." She gathered her robes about her. "I am ready."

Stepping forward, Mahius interceded in his mistress' behalf, "Thou hast not the seal of the Emperor to the warrant," he said. "I demand that thou dost obtain such a seal."

Thinking of Signar as a dying man, Gatus smiled scornfully. "The power of the Senate supersedes the power of the throne. Besides," he said, gesturing toward the garden, "the people demanded her imminent trial and execution."

He motioned to the soldiers. They came forward to seize Salustra, but Brittulia flung herself before her mistress, her own bosom shielding the Empress. At a nod from Gatus a soldier drew his sword and buried it in Brittulia's breast. She slumped to the floor in a pool of blood, moaning only, "I die because I sinned in my heart. May the gods forgive me." Stung out of his lethargy, Mahius seized the sword in his hands and attempted feebly to wrest it from the soldier. Another guard, excited by the struggle, drove his sword into the old man's side and he, too, crumpled at Salustra's feet.

All this had happened so swiftly that Salustra had had no opportunity to move. Her white robes were splattered with the blood of those who had loved her, and before she could utter a word of protest the soldiers had seized her.

When Salustra was brought before the Palace a mighty roar rose from the bloodthirsty multitude. Clenched hands were raised and voices shouted oaths and imprecations. The soldiers had difficulty keeping back the mob surging against their lines.

Salustra stood in silence. Her tall figure, in its blood-stained robes, seemed to shine with a snowy luster; her unbound hair fell over her shoulders. Her face was turned with majestic indifference upon those who had only recently acclaimed her.

Her eyes looked beyond the multitude to a sea again grown turbulent. The horizon was obscured by a gray shadow that was steadily approaching. The mountains, like squat mounds, seemed to tremble in rhythm with a continuing underground rumble.

Salustra saw a strange thing: All of Signar's fleet had been lost in the storm except his flagship, *Postia*. It still struggled with its anchor and rode heavily on the great waves. In the distance, her keen eyes detected small human figures, a hundred or more of them, hastening toward the vessel with an air of furtiveness. She saw these things as a mirror might, reflecting them without understanding.

The earth and sky darkened steadily, but only she was aware of it. The people were testing the strength of the soldiers, and their cries shook the air. In their excitement they did not notice a tremor which, though faint, seemed to come from the bowels of the earth.

The guards formed a circle about her and began a solemn procession to the Senate Chamber. Salustra's face held a faintly sardonic smile, which seemed to have fixed itself permanently on her pale lips. Her head was slightly bent, as though she communed with herself.

The Senate was already assembled. The day had so steadily darkened that generator lamps had been lit and they shone fitfully. As the bronze doors flew open, the Guard promptly closed them in the face of the surging throng. Other than Senators, only priests and a few Nobles were admitted. As Salustra stepped through the door the Senate involuntarily rose with its customary salute. But seeing Salustra's satirical smile, they sat down again, utterly disconcerted.

The guards led her to a high and narrow platform facing the Assembly, and there she stood motionless, like a statue.

Gatus, the prosecutor, stood before the Senate body with a roll of parchment in his hands. His eyes fixed themselves for a moment on that quiet figure standing with such aloof dignity before her accusers. Then he began to read:

"We, the People, through our Senate do accuse thee, the deposed Empress of Atlantis, of infamous crimes, among them treason against us, by reason of commands to the military recently issued independent of the Senate. We further accuse thee of the murder of the noble Senator Divona and of the High Priestess Jupia, murders foul in the extreme, and which call to the gods for vengeance. And of a similar foul attempt on the life of the Emperor Signar.

"We further accuse thee of continual insults to the gods, which, though not punishable under the laws of Atlantis, still affront the piety of the people."

Gatus fixed his crafty eyes upon the silent Empress. "To these accusations thou hast the privilege of replying." Under her even glance his eyes dropped.

The habits of a lifetime were ingrained in one bred to rule with justice.

"Where are my accusers, Gatus," she asked in a clear, resonant voice.

Gatus raised his hand, and Mento, the black-robed priest, a familiar of Jupia, rose with his pallid face twisted with hatred. He pointed a trembling finger at Salustra. "Blasphemer!" he cried, his dark eyes flashing fanatically. "Thy crimes have scandalized the gods too long! Thou dost demand proof and witnesses! Whatsoever proof may be offered, thou dost stand convicted in the blood which flows about thee like the sea. Thou hast endeavored from the very hour thou didst ascend to the throne of Atlantis to cast odium on the gods! For thy lack of reverence it is a wonder that these walls do not fall upon thee and crush thee!"

The Empress interrupted with a laugh. "My lords, I have been accused of many things. Again I ask: Where are my accusers? You say I violated the law that the sovereign may not take military action without Senate consent. I did take such a step but for the sole purpose of rescuing Atlantis from Althrustri. Had I convened the Senate there would have been panic, delay, disorganization. Signar would have known of the matter immediately, as he did—" she sighed "—in any case. Therefore, I took the responsibility myself for the sake of Atlantis. My only regret is that I failed."

Her voice trailed off into silence; she bowed her head, as if to withdraw again within herself. The Senators whispered together, glancing uncomfortably the while at their Empress.

Gatus, after this whispered consultation, rose and faced Salustra again. "And thou dost deny these things of which thou art accused?" he demanded.

"Where are the witnesses?" she repeated. There was both pride and scorn in her manner. "Well I know, sirs, that this trial is merely an excuse to offer me as a sop to a confused, frightened people. And because you lack courage to express your own grievances you seek virtuous reasons for your conduct." She raised her hand imperiously and spoke in a ringing voice, with her eyes veiled as if describing a vision.

"There hath been a savior prophesied for many ages. It hath been said that he will be the living truth. Let him beware! Whatever message he hath to give an evil generation will be drenched in his own blood. He will be betrayed, his memory defamed, dust will be cast upon his footsteps. His very existence will be doubted by the generations that come after him. Mankind will so confuse the clear beauty of his words that his countless followers will be persecuted to their deaths.

"He will carry a torch into the universal darkness. He will succor the exploited, the sick, the ignorant and the sad. He will attempt in his misguided love to release man from the chains of oppression. He will open the doors of intellectual freedom and point man to the shining dawn of enlightenment. For this he will suffer a cruel death.

"Such has been, is, and shall be the fate of all those who attempt to free the people from their oppressors. All who have pierced the veil of pompous lies, pious hypocrisies, priestly tyranny and enslavement by the powerful have been murdered and forgotten. But the passion that flames in the saviors of the world can never be quenched; they pass on the light with their dying hands."

She seemed to gather strength as she went on. "I have attempted to free my people from their exploiters, from their cunning priesthood, from the preceptors of unquestioning obedience. I have opened to them the doors of science that they might be freed from superstition. I hoped to free them from the shackles of a man-made religion. And for this crime, of course, I am condemned and cursed.

"All these things of which you accuse me are nothing to you. I might have slain a thousand more and all would have been decorous silence had I been reverent to the gods and subservient to the priests."

So cutting had been her words that the Senate had listened, impressed, despite themselves.

As Gatus paused uncertainly, his colleague, Toliti, regarded Salustra with a judicial eye. "What thou hast to say, Majesty, may be true. But for us to oppose the gods now would mean utter chaos and ruin."

As he spoke there was a tremendous crash of thunder, which shook the walls of the chamber. The massive bronze doors burst open and revealed a wild-eyed multitude. They were caught in a new cloudburst, which made it seem again as if earth and heaven were dissolving into one turbulent sea of water.

The priest Mento, frothing while Salustra spoke, now leaped to his feet and gestured to the panic-stricken throngs surging into the chamber. "This woman hath been blaspheming the gods again, oh people of Atlantis! And in wrath at your tolerance they have again afflicted the earth!"

An animal roar broke from thousand of throats. And with one accord the human tide rolled toward the platform on which Salustra stood with a smile of cool disdain. A moment more and she would have been hauled from the platform and trampled underfoot. But at that instant, slashing their way forward, came a strong force of the elite Guard of the Emperor Signar. Signar's commander, Siton, reached her first. Ho sprang up beside her, caught her in his burly arms and gave a defiant cry that rang out clearly over the noise and turmoil of the mob.

37

ALMOST in a swoon from fatigue and strain, Salustra was half-conscious of being borne through a welter of humanity in a pelting downpour. She felt herself tossed in a small boat and heard the swirl of angry water about her. She peered through a wall of water and that instant saw the gleaming side of a huge ship, its superstructure all encased by a glistening dome. She became aware of being lifted up the side of that ship, and then complete darkness blissfully enveloped her.

This is death, she thought, and before oblivion came she seemed to hear a voice saying, as though from a great distance:

"The fountains of the great deep were all broken up, and the windows of heaven were opened, and the rain was upon the earth forty days and forty nights. The water increased greatly upon the earth, and the highest hills under heaven were covered. Fifteen cubits upward did the waters prevail and the mountains were covered."

And then the voice faded, and she knew no more.

Salustra's first impression was of warm light upon her face. She was lying on a soft couch, and a silken breeze blew across her face. As she rose to the surface of consciousness, she heard voices, faint, far-off, murmuring. These voices seemed to approach, to be at her bedside. A hand touched her forehead, caressingly, pulling back a lock of hair. She sighed, moved her head a little, and prepared to sleep again.

"She is awakening!" a woman's voice said eagerly.

"It is true," responded a man's deeper tones. They leaned over her, as she tried to blot out the reality of another person, whoever it was. She tried to slip back into the darkness. But a beam of sunlight pressed her lids open and she was looking up into the faces of a young woman she had never seen before and the familiar Siton. The couch on which she lay was swaying gently. As her eyes opened still wider, she saw that the sunlight came through a narrow window, and that beyond, through a small circular opening, was the gliding surface of a tranquil sea.

Siton bent over her, smiling, his white teeth flashing against his dark beard. "Thou hast slept long with thy fever, Majesty," he said. "Forty days have passed."

"Forty days," echoed Salustra. Her voice was weak and her tongue felt thick and clumsy. At the sound of her voice the horror of her last recall flashed over her face.

Siton took her hand soothingly. "It hath passed," he said. "And many things have happened while thou hast slept. But thou must sleep more and when thou dost awaken, refreshed, we will tell thee all."

Salustra looked about her, dazed. "I am on a ship," she said feebly. "Are we in the harbor?"

Siton turned his head, and the bright sunlight revealed his pallor.

Slowly Slaustra's memory returned. "The Princess Tyrhia," she cried, "where is she? And Signar?" she cried again, almost frantically.

Siton could only shrug expressively at the first question. Tyrhia was among the millions missing or dead. He had more reassuring news about the Emperor. "Safe and well, Majesty," he said gently. "And when thy strength hath returned, he will come and tell thee all that has happened."

A faint color swept over the Empress' face. She would have spoken again but the young woman laid her hand over her eyes and sleep quickly came.

Salustra was eventually awakened by the cold night air flowing over her. Through the open windows she could see the arching dome of the sky and then the endless expanse of ocean. She got up shakily and stumbled weakly to a window and looked out. She could see nothing but water. A sense of utter doom oppressed her. What terrible catastrophe had befallen the world? Where was Atlantis, where Lamora? What had happened in the forty days that she had lain in a stupor at sea?

She looked about curiously at the silk-walled chamber dimly lit with golden lamps, the hallmark of Signar's flagship. Her first thought was: That barbarian hath abducted me and is carrying me off to Althrustri. But even as this thought occurred to her some inner instinct told her this was not the truth. She who had not feared death was overcome by uncertainty. She let out a cry. A door opened and two maidens entered with Siton. They found the Empress sitting dazed upon her couch. "In the name of the gods tell me what hath happened!" she cried.

The women attempted to sooth her. She brushed them aside with her old imperiousness, her eyes fixed on the soldier. "What hath happened?" she repeated.

Siton filled a goblet with wine. "Drink, Majesty," he commanded, "and then I will tell thee."

She drank automatically, her eyes fixed upon him over the brim of the goblet. And then in a low voice, as though the very telling horrified him, he began to fill in the gap for her. "We saw thee arrested, Majesty. We were in a quandary. Our lord lay ill, but we knew that we must save thee.

"The people were aroused, demanding thy death. And we were still but a handful. Who knew but what our lord might be done to death? He was barely conscious when we went to him. 'Lord,' we said, 'a great flood is about to descend upon the city again. The people are wild, unrestrained. Let us flee to thy ship before the waters inundate all.'

"Though still weak, he laughed at us, not knowing of your danger, for the physician Cino insisted we not upset him. He had been given drugs to quiet his pain. We decided upon a bold move. When he fell into a drugged sleep we carried him through the deserted streets to the harbor. We summoned all our people and commanded that they hasten to the flagship. We carried quantities of goods and wines to the vessel. We did not take water, for the very heavens were pouring down. Our plan was to rescue thee and put out from Lamora. When all was ready, I took the Guard of Five Hundred to the Senate chamber and cut through the cowardly crowd to carry thee off."

As he fell silent, Salustra laid her hand upon his arm and shook him slightly for him to continue.

"When we had carried thee to the ship through torrents," he resumed, "we put out to sea in a veritable wall of water. For a time we despaired, for the storm was great and the vessel rolled first on one side and then on the other, without our being able to see more than a few feet ahead. And then, after we had been knocked about for hours, a calm suddenly prevailed and we saw we had moved but a few miles from the coast. The waves were frightening, like toppling mountains. A great noise rent the air, which came from neither the earth nor the heavens nor the sea. And then, awesomely, we were borne aloft on a wave higher than any other. We looked toward the shore in dread; we would surely be broken upon it in a few moments. We were hurled forward at a fearful speed. The mountains seemed to leap toward us and we could discern, very clearly, the spires of the city. No rain was falling but the air was heavy with a noxious sulfurous miasma issuing from Mount Atla, which threatened to suffocate us.

"The ship was groaning, yet our vessel seemed to skim like a bird over the waters. The city loomed closer, we could even discern the waterlogged streets. And then, just when it seemed that the ship must crash upon Atla itself, a fearful thing happened. The land seemed to heave, to breathe deeply, and then, without a sound, without a warning, it sank gently beneath the waters! Where Lamora stood there was a vast maelstrom, and we were hurled forward as though in pursuit of the devil. Had there been a sound, a cry, the fleeing of multitudes, it would have been less appalling, but the city collapsed like a canoe breaking against the shoals. Our speed was incredible, as though we possessed wings; our flight was the flight of birds, always in pursuit of the sinking land. Daily, millions perished without a sound, without a gesture, without an opportunity to offer a prayer to the gods.

Some few, cast adrift in the sea, we were able to pick up and resuscitate. But then the heavens opened again and because of the wall of water, we could see no more. Profound darkness spread upon the face of the ocean and we had a terrible feeling of being alone."

Salustra had fallen back upon her couch and was staring up at the ceiling. "Atlantis!" she whispered. "What of it?"

Siton did not answer directly. "For many days, lady, we tossed perilously in darkness and rain. But though the rain continued, the wind and darkness finally began to abate and a gray light pervaded the universe. How our vessel survived is a miracle from the gods. The ship sprang innumerable leaks, repaired under most terrible stress, and many times came close to capsizing. An icy coldness began to spread, increasing our misery. Fortunately our provisions were intact and our subterranean chambers still dry.

"Our lord was assured that thou wouldst recover. Once informed of thy safety, he seemed satisfied, though he felt with us that the world had surely come to an end. Through all this, with thy fever, thou didst sleep the sleep of death.

"After forty days and forty nights of rain, the sun shone forth on a universe of water. Land had entirely disappeared. Where our sextants indicated that Atlantis and Althrustri should be, there was apparently only a watery waste; even the frozen tundra of the north had been gouged by a huge glacier.

"Temporarily, we were still filled with despair. Had all life and land disappeared? On the morning of the forty-second day, we saw, to our great joy, a vessel like our own wallowing in the sea like a wounded porpoise. We came upon it and saw that its decks were crammed to capacity with half-drowned wretches. We discovered that they, too, had provisions and were most recently from Lamora. They were part of a company of strange aliens that had lived in Lamora and preached of a single God they named Jehovah and of his retribution. They were calm and confident. They told us that they had known of the coming destruction for many years and that on the appointed day, which was revealed to them in a vision, they had gathered their few converts about them, in pairs and sevens, and had taken them to a vessel they had already prepared with all the animals and the bird-life they could gather.

"They assured us, these men, that God had not forgotten them. They seemed astonished, however, that their God had also spared us. Nevertheless, they felt their God would lead us to some safe harbor. Some few came aboard with us to instruct us in the worship of their fearsome God. We did not like Him, He was too angry.

"We saw no other life, except once, when the moon came out like a pale shadow in the purplish heaven. We saw then an oddly shaped vessel on the horizon, more like a swiftly moving cloud than a ship. We started in pursuit, attempting to hail it, but we could come no closer.

"Our alien cargo was thrilled by the distant vessel. 'Hail, beloved of God!' they cried, kneeling upon our decks and extending solemn hands to the speeding craft. They told us that we would not overtake it, and they spoke the truth. It disappeared as miraculously as it had appeared."

He ceased speaking. Salustra bent her gaze upon the floor. A half-amused smile was upon her lips. "It seems," she said softly, "that there is a God!" She again fixed her gaze upon Siton. "In what direction are we sailing?"

"We are sailing east, as these disciples of God have suggested."

The Empress rose abruptly. As she swayed with weakness, Siton put his arms around her. "Take me to Signar," she commanded.

The iron determination of Lazar, and the energizing jewel that she clasped once more about her throat, now came to her assistance. With Siton's aid, she mounted the stairs to an upper deck. Rugs had been thrown over the flooring and on these rugs and deep cushions lay a hundred men, women and children. Had this been a pleasure ship, bound for some flower-decked shore, the people could not have been more carefree and happy. It seemed almost incredible that this was a ship bearing the remnants of a destroyed people to an unknown port.

For a long moment Salustra looked upon this handful of all who remained of her country, and tears welled in her eyes. She advanced with faltering step, and at her appearance a murmur broke from those on the deck, and with one accord they rose and made profound obeisance. They crowded about her, the women in scanty garments, the children wide-eyed, the men half naked. These people had lost everything and quietly mourned the loss of many loved ones. But their eyes shone with a bright courage and resolution. They had turned already from the dark past, as they listened to the bearded strangers, and were looking toward the radiant yet still uncertain future. Salustra could not help but marvel at the bottomless spring of human hope.

Then, as though at a signal, she raised her head and looked beyond them. Some distance away, Signar, pale, gaunt, still weak, sat in a great chair, his knees covered with scarlet robes. He was watching her with a faint smile. As she glanced at him he slowly extended his hand.

With a faltering step she approached him. As she reached his side she sank to her knees beside him, her head resting upon the arm of his chair. He put his hand under her chin, turned her strained face to the light, and gazed down into her eyes with mingled humor and sadness.

"The gods must love us, Salustra," he said softly. "Of all Althrustri and Atlantis, they have spared only us and a faithful handful."

His hand fell upon his knee again and he looked beyond her.

The warm air blew about them, the sun gleamed from every wave. The great ship's course reversed the path of the sun. But the thoughts of Signar and Salustra were too melancholy for speech. They sat in brooding silence for a while, acutely aware of one another even as they listened to the murmur of the women and children nearby.

Signar finally rested his hand on Salustra's head. "These few, Salustra," he said sadly, "are our empire."

"Nay, lord," she replied in a trembling voice. "They are thy empire. I long only for peace, to know more of this God the strangers talk about."

She shuddered at the vision of a bloodthirsty people. "Thy people treated thee ill, Salustra," said Signar gently, following her thoughts.

"Had they torn me limb from limb, I would still mourn them, for I loved them as my children."

"All that thou hast loved are dead, Salustra—Tyrhia, Erato, Creto, Mahius, yes, even poor, misbegotten Brittulia." He gently touched her cheek with his finger. "I asked thee a question once," he whispered. "Why didst thou spare me that night?"

She turned her face slowly to him. There was no longer any reason for dissembling. "Because I love thee, Sire," she answered softly.

That night, Signar and Salustra lay clasped in each other's arms, their first untroubled sleep since their meeting. The light glimmered upon them, twinkled on their sleeping faces, picked sparks from the crimson and golden cushions upon which they lay, and gilded the robes that covered them. Signar's head lay upon Salustra's breast; her arms were about him, her lips pressed to his head, her tawny hair streaming over them both.

It was a new dawn that greeted them. Salustra awoke sweetly, gently, and at her movement Signar stirred. Their eyes met and then their lips. No words passed between them, but Salustra crept into her lover's arms as though they were the only shelter she needed.

Later they went upon the deck. They were filled with calm. Two doves brought on ship by the strangers had been released and were now overdue. The passengers scanned the sky hopefully. The sun stood directly overhead, bathing the ocean in a golden light as a loud cry burst from a sailor on the watch. "Land," he cried ecstatically, "land ahead!"

Immediately the vessel resounded with a confusion of shouts and prayers. The entire company crowded to the rail and saw on the horizon a long, gray stretch of land. Men, women and children, Atlanteans and Althrustrians together, fell upon their knees, sobbing with joy. Over the water came that indescribably pungent smell of earth. Mountains, like blue-and-white mist, began to be penciled in light against the shining sky; the rippling fronds of great forests rose like a green wall from the shore. The odor of millions of exotic flowers drifted over the ocean to eager nostrils. A great calm, a great and virgin silence, a mighty peace lay over this new world.

Men and women embraced each other. Some continued to kneel, offering thanks to their one God. These were the black-bearded prophets of doom, and their prayers were said in an alien tongue to their jealous Jehovah.

Signar and Salustra stood side by side, their arms about each other, their faces full of mingled emotions. "A new empire, beloved," said Signar at last.

Salustra turned her eyes upon him. "Nay, a new world, my lord," she said, "in which to live again and dispel old lies, abandon old sorrows and ways and start a brave new generation of man." Her eyes shone like the sun. "For this we have been brought from the other side of the flood."

Postscript—1974

MY FRIEND, Jess Stearn, has written several outstanding books on psychic matters and reincarnation, notably the famous *The Sleeping Prophet* and his latest, *A Prophet in His Own Country*. I believe that Jess was just about the first to introduce to the public books concerning these matters. So, to amuse him, I sent him a very old manuscript on Atlantis, the mythical land, which I had written as a young child, before I had even reached puberty.

I cannot remember, at this late date, just when the idea of writing a book on Atlantis occurred to me, but after long reflection I do remember being "haunted" by it for all the short years of my life before I got down to typing it out. It seems to me, now, that I "knew" about Atlantis from infancy, and took it for granted, though I did not recall this until just recently.

I knew, months ago, that Jess was going to do something about my childhood novel on Atlantis, but I forgot it completely in the stress of my existence and my constant despair. So I have no explanation of suddenly "experiencing" my life on Atlantis after all these years, when I dreamed that I was the Empress Salustra in this book. This dream happened a few weeks ago, and then in the weeks following I had two other "experiences" as the Empress Salustra of Atlantis. They were not "repeats" of what is in this book, but were entirely new and vivid and appallingly fresh, as if they had happened only this week.

In the first dream I saw the white colonnade of the palace in which I had "lived," but it was not as a remembrance but as an event which had just occurred. I walked through the gardens, seeing the caged birds behind their golden bars, the peacocks stalking the grass, the pit in which squirmed captured reptiles of a breed unknown to this present world, and animals also unknown to us moderns. I saw the liquid golden sea below the palace; I saw the tumbling and rising forest of white stone of my capital city which lay below and above my palace, climbing the great volcanic mountains which surrounded this area. I could even smell the scent of strange flowers and see huge trees with amethyst and blue blossoms the size of our present sunflowers. They were as familiar to me as my present house and its gardens. There were fountains of gilded marble, singing, and red gravel paths winding through beds of shrubs I do not know, all blooming and scented, and endless statues.

I was conscious of a profound emotional distress as I left the colonnade to walk in the garden, hoping for a little surcease. I did not wonder at it. I knew what it was: the suffering of "disprized love," as Hamlet had mentioned. I knew I was secretly in love with the Emperor Signar of Althrustri, the cold nation to the north of Atlantis, but he was my enemy and he was preparing to seize my beloved country. I did not know which was causing me the more anguish—the love I felt for a man I knew I should hate and have quietly murdered, or my love for Atlantis, my nation, my empire. I knew I must have him killed—yet his nation was now far more powerful than mine. I finally concluded that it would be best for me to die, rather than Signar, for then I would never know what fate had come to Atlantis. I knew, in my dream, that he had accepted my young sister as his bride, and that, too, agonized me, though it was I who had suggested it. So, to escape all this suffering, I had decided that death was my only refuge. This episode, or dream, is not in the book, or at least not exactly.

I awoke, feeling the turbulent sorrow and yearning for Signar, and the emotion was so intense that I began to weep and I could not get oriented to the present for at least ten minutes or so. I felt that somewhere Atlantis still existed, and so did Signar, and I had the most terrible urge to look for them both, and to tell Signar that I loved him—though I was convinced that he detested me. When I finally realized that it had been only a dream I was both relieved and desolated. I know now who Signar "was," but that is my own secret. But it was only a dream. . . .

However, I could not free myself from the "reality" of the dream, its intense and imminent vividness, its immediacy. I could hear echoes of Signar's voice in every room of my house. I tried to work, but it was impossible. (Incidentally, my young sister, in the book, appeared to be a lady I know and who is my present friend.)

Then a week or so later I had another dream of Atlantis and myself and Signar, which also does not appear in the book. I dreamed I had given a feast for Signar and my sister on an immense gilded raft moored in the harbor, and the floor was paved with rugs of intense hues and there were gemmed tubs of exotic small trees set about, and tables covered with cloth of silver, and musicians, and above the harbor was my palace glittering white in the sun, and the vast forest of climbing white stone of my capital city. The raft was thronged with men I knew well, and a few intimately, gaily dressed and with garlands on their heads, and the water was sprinkled with blossoms and had a curious odor which vaguely disturbed me, for it was unusual. It was sulfuric. The volcanic mountain immediately above my city wore a pennant of fluttering scarlet smoke, and it made me dimly anxious. But above all was my torment over Signar, who was sitting on a divan with my sister and boldly caressing her, and I could not endure it. My imperial pennants swayed and snapped in an unseasonably hot breeze, and I could actually feel the perspiration on my forehead, and a sense of foreboding.

Then Signar rose and approached me, smiling in the mocking manner to which I had lately become accustomed, and he saluted me facetiously, and I wanted to murder him and to embrace him. I hurriedly said to him, "I feel that I shall never again see this aspect of my beloved city."

He looked over his shoulder at the city and the mountains and the sky and the palace and said, "That is absurd." His face became even more mocking and he pretended concern. "Or are you sick?"

I replied, "Yes, I am sick of an old sickness and I fear I will die of it." Again, my anguish almost overwhelmed me, and I awoke gasping with it, and again I was haunted by it for several days.

The third dream occurred very recently. But I was no longer in Atlantis. I knew Atlantis had gone forever, and with it my few intimates and my sister and all its millions of people, whom I had loved in spite of their corruption and treachery. For it had been my own, and I had been its empress.

The dream was of a strange land, hot, tropical, with lavender mountains and enormous fronded forests which stretched into infinity, and I knew it was a new land and had no inhabitants except for the few of us who had survived the demolition of Atlantis. The sea was a strange sea I had never seen before, and there was a vast silence everywhere except for the raucous shrieking of birds alien to my experience, great colored birds with huge, hooked beaks and very small monkeys, and catlike animals of a large size, and cattle—if they were cattle—with twisted horns and shaggy coats. The odors of this land were overpoweringly unique to me, some aromatic, some unpleasant, some strenuously sweet with a hot sweetness, and insects filled the green and shining air, insects for which I had no name.

But though I sorrowed and wept for Atlantis I also experienced a joy almost too intense for bearing, for Signar was with me, and I knew he loved me as I loved him. Our attendants had built us huts of gray curling bark, and I was no empress any longer, nor was Signar an emperor. We had labored with our people to establish ourselves in this green, hot land with the curiously hued mountains, and our clothing was primitive and our hands as calloused and worn as those of our people. But we were joyful and at peace. I dreamed I was pounding some nameless grain in a wooden bowl, kneeling, and Signar came to me, touched me gently on my head and said, "This is our empire," and he bent to kiss me and I knew such delight that I closed my eyes—and woke up.

This, too, does not appear in this book.

I cannot imagine from where these strange dreams emerged, or what their significance is—if there is any significance at all. The only thing I know with certainty is that the dreams were more vivid than my present reality, more poignant, more agonizing and more joyful. They haunt me, coloring my whole existence, and I feel deprived and filled with an ancient longing.

Is this evidence of reincarnation? I know no more about it than the reader. Nor do I know why I wrote of Atlantis when I was only twelve years old, and knew it intimately.

Perhaps Hamlet was right: "There are more things in heaven and earth, Horatio, than are dreamt of in your philosophy."

Fawcett Books by Taylor Caldwell

The Arm and the Darkness	C2627	$1.95
The Final Hour	C2579	$1.95
Maggie—Her Marriage	P2420	$1.25
Grandmother and the Priests	C2664	$1.95
The Late Clara Beame	P2496	$1.25
A Pillar of Iron	C2418	$1.95
Wicked Angel	Q2740	$1.50
No One Hears But Him	Q2507	$1.50
Dialogues with the Devil	Q2768	$1.50
Testimony of Two Men	C2416	$1.95
Great Lion of God	C2445	$1.95
On Growing Up Tough	P2305	$1.25
Captains and the Kings	C2415	$1.95
To Look and Pass	X3491	$1.75
Glory and the Lightning	C2562	$1.95

FAWCETT

Wherever Paperbacks Are Sold

If your bookdealer is sold out, send cover price plus 35¢ each for postage and handling to Mail Order Department, Fawcett Publications, Inc., P.O. Box 1014, Greenwich, Connecticut 06830. Please order by number and title. Catalog available on request.